THE
PARENTS

BOOKS BY CLAIRE SEEBER

24 Hours
The Stepmother
The Street Party

THE
PARENTS

CLAIRE SEEBER

Bookouture

Published by Bookouture in 2021

An imprint of Storyfire Ltd.
Carmelite House
50 Victoria Embankment
London EC4Y 0DZ

www.bookouture.com

ISBN: 978-1-80019-631-5
eBook ISBN: 978-1-80019-630-8

This book is a work of fiction. Names, characters, businesses,
organizations, places and events other than those clearly in the
public domain, are either the product of the author's imagination
or are used fictitiously. Any resemblance to actual persons, living or
dead, events or locales is entirely coincidental.

*In memory of my beloved stepfather David,
who usually found the football too stressful to watch!*

*And for every parent who's ever shivered on a weekend touchline,
or helped a youth team burn the energy on the pitch
and not with their fists. Brava!*

Everyone is a moon, and has a dark side which he never shows to anybody.

– Mark Twain

THE CLUB

LIST OF UNDER-14 PLAYERS AND THEIR FAMILIES

Ethan Taylor – *full back (defender)*
Mum, Patti, owns local salon Beauty Bound. Dad Sam, unemployed builder. Sister Luna, university student

Harry Ross – *centre midfield*
Mum, Alex, graphic designer. Dad, Fraser, deceased. Sister Iris, schoolgirl and skateboard freak

Davey Forth – *centre forward*
Dad, Neil, team manager and mechanic. Mum, Linda, teaching assistant. Sister, Angel, disabled, schoolgirl

Josh Calliste – *centre back*
Mum, Hazel, owns the Black Cat Café. Dad, Ray, deceased. Sister Cyn, chef

Maxi Bauer – *striker/centre forward*
Dad, Riker, parish councillor and architect. Mum, Liz, barrister. Brothers, Thomas and Frederick – schoolboys

Hunter Fullerton – *midfielder/winger*
Dad, Dez, professional footballer. Mum, Nancy, model. Brother Logan (schoolboy) and sister Chloe (three)

Ocean Lees – *goalie*
Mum, Meadow, psychic and shop owner, crystal ball reader.
Dad – who knows… the Great Gandalf?

Mikhail Dubiki – *centre back*
Mum, Halinka, croupier. Dad, in Poland

Declan O' Connell – *winger/midfielder*
Dad, Big Feen, pig farmer. Mum, Kezia, dog breeder. Many, many siblings

Kyran Desmond – *centre midfield*
Dad, Trevor, garden designer. Mum, Maria – local councillor and housewife

Tony Burton Jnr – *full back*
Dad, Tony, painter and decorator. Mum, whereabouts unknown

Various substitutes

PROLOGUE

Sunday 1 November

The thing was, people agreed later, it was almost impossible to see the movement, the camera footage was so dark and grainy.

But once you knew it was there, once you knew what you were meant to focus on, it was impossible to stop looking.

It was the object bobbing in the black water, of course, that drew the eye first. An old wooden pallet? Or actually, maybe a big sports bag, which would make sense, given the setting.

No, it was definitely an old Puffa jacket, arms spread, made puffier and swollen from the weight of the water it had taken on.

Only… if you stared hard enough, you could definitely see, there in the left-hand corner, just at the edge of frame, a figure, moving into the trees. Yes, definitely a figure.

And then, slinking from the shadows of the dense woodland behind, a huge animal – a dog, presumably, fur glinting in the moonlight, almond eyes flashing white on the grainy film. Although… no, it couldn't be a wolf… *Could it?*

The animal glanced at the water briefly, and then up, as if it knew exactly where the camera was.

Then it too disappeared into the trees.

In the club shop, hearing about the CCTV footage, Mrs Jessop passed little Sheila the box of salt and vinegar with a typically wry comment about someone leaving the scene of the crime, and Sheila, pausing in her replenishment of Mars bars, nodded calmly, exactly as she always did when the elderly lady said something wise.

It was only later that Mrs Jessop, having learnt the truth, felt a small pang of conscience.

'Once I knew what the object in the water was, you know' – she slid the cuttlefish through the bars to Hopping Stan – 'it felt… wrong.' The budgie cocked his head as if he *completely* understood.

In Mrs Jessop's world, being agreed with made all things right and harmonious – but it didn't make the truth any more palatable.

Ingrained indelibly on the footage, the object in the water floated into the flare of moonlight, meaning the pale thing attached to the main bulk eventually became clear.

It was a hand, extended as if it was mid-stroke: a hand that would not move again of its own accord.

And the object? It was a body.

Which wasn't a huge surprise, Mrs Jessop murmured darkly the following day, waiting for the police to arrive. 'It was only a matter of time,' she said, indicating that Sheila should flip the kettle switch.

No, none of it was much of a surprise really, given recent events at the club. That one of those nasty parents from Saturday's drunken debacle should end up face down, floating in the lake, dead as the proverbial doornail… although whoever said a doornail was dead? It made very little sense.

'I'm sure I saw those nice girls, the Welsh one, Patti, and her American friend,' Mrs Jessop passed the mugs, 'here late on Saturday.'

'The American?' Sheila plopped the teabags in. 'I don't think so. And Patti took her drunken husband home. Plus, everyone was in costume, weren't they? Hard to tell who was who, among all the werewolves and witches.'

Given the history of Tenderton village, where all things to do with evil enchantment had become a huge draw during the past few decades, putting it firmly on the necromancy tourist map, it seemed almost apt that witchcraft might have been involved.

Mrs Jessop passed Sheila the milk. 'I'm sure the police know who was here, and who was not. Not our business, is it, dear. Unless it gets' – she paused, a snap of something discernible in her faded eyes – 'out of hand.'

PART 1

September

1

Patti

Wednesday a.m.: New moon in Virgo

Patti Taylor was an even-tempered woman by nature, but even she was riled by the events of that Wednesday morning.

Truth be told, Patti wasn't having the best of months anyway, let alone weeks or days. Only to be expected really, given that the moon was in Virgo – always a disaster for her. Plus, she'd begun to really rather hate Wednesdays: a sort of nothing day that just had to be got through, without the fuel of a fresh Monday, or the delicious excitement of a Thursday or – even better – a Saturday.

Although Patti couldn't actually remember when anything exciting had last happened to her on a Saturday – or any day really – other than a takeaway from Pizza Pizazz, or the *Strictly* final.

Her last proper excitement had probably been a Take That concert with Linda and Hazel a few years back. They'd treated themselves to a triple room in Brighton's Premier Inn and then, in a desperate bid to relive their twenties, one too many Sex on the Beaches in a bar under the pier, before unwisely choosing to… well, get a little bit too close to the real thing…

Patti drew that memory to a swift and necessary close.

And of course, she sighed to herself, nothing *ever* happened in Tenderton.

Other than last night's huge row at the Tenderton Tigers, of course: her son Ethan's Sunday League football club. It had been brewing for a while now, the tension mounting between a few of the dads, but Patti had still been deeply shocked by the vitriol unleashed.

Somehow it seemed worse because everyone – *all* the club parents – had been so chuffed about the new signing: Hunter Fullerton, son of Dez Fullerton, former Premiership and Wolves striker: the first real celebrity they'd had in Tenderton, like, ever. And with lineage like that, it stood to reason that Hunter would be a brilliant player, and an asset to the Tigers – didn't it?

But actually, for Patti, the real problems had already started the previous spring, with Ethan only ever getting half a game. Neil, the under-14s manager, had said he got too moody on the pitch, and that had wound her husband Sam up no end—

A voice cut through her thoughts. Not even a voice, in fact: more of a bellow. Good Lord! Who on earth was *that* loud at this time of day?

Clacking round the corner into Church Street, salon keys in hand, Patti reached the source of the ruckus.

She might have known! Neil Forth, her current nemesis and the aforementioned manager of the under-14s, was trying to physically hoist a car away from the driveway of his small commercial garage, thumping it so loudly she felt the vibrations through her whole body.

From the safety of the far pavement, Patti gazed at the man she'd recently begun to find the most annoying in the world. Apart from her errant father, and Sam of course – but then that went without saying, didn't it? Dear Sam: once her Adonis, whisking her away from everything she knew in her home town of Cardiff, promising if not undying romance, then at least salvation.

Sadly, not living up to any of that promise in middle age.

Sweaty and ever hairier as the years passed, his belly pushing out rather than in, with a tendency to nod off over *Match of the Day*, mouth unattractively slack. And, good Lord, the snoring!

Patti sighed again as, across the road, Neil swore even louder.

His temper reminded her of Sam and Neil sharing such strong words on Sunday that Patti had had to avoid his wife Linda, her oldest local friend, at Monday night's Cub Scout AGM.

Although that was nothing on the blazing row Neil had had with the referee at the final cup game last season. Patti inhaled sharply at the memory. Monumental, that row had been, really set the tongues wagging, after Neil had mocked the ref's foreign accent when questioning a free kick.

'That was a bit much.' Mild-mannered Tony Burton had led Neil away to take a moment. 'Don't want to get a rep for that sort of thing, mate.'

Usually known for his benevolence, Neil was clearly affected by the stress of being in the local A League, the other parents agreed from afar.

And, of course, Patti knew that both he and Linda were currently distracted by their young daughter Angel's worsening health.

Plus, Patti wasn't one for grudges.

Her breezy 'Morning, Neil!' was met with a loud grunt. 'In your way, is it, the poor car?'

Another grunt as the stocky mechanic rammed his shoulder once more into the old Land Rover, which didn't move. Patti didn't recognise the car: perhaps it had been abandoned. Now that *would* count for high drama in their neat little village.

'I generally find a key works better than a shove, Neil.' She awarded him her biggest twinkle, fully aware it was likely to fan the flames of his fury. He was like that, Neil, these days.

With a half nod, he continued his shunting attempt, his overalls at half-mast at the waist.

'Should you even be doing that, with your back?' Truth be told, though, Patti didn't care about his back, and she was about to hurry on when her eye was caught by something in the upstairs window of Primrose Cottage. A young lad, watching the unfolding scene with something like horror on his face.

But surely Primrose Cottage was empty, since Mrs Grable had fallen on the stairs last winter and been carted off in an ambulance, never to return.

Patti thought absently of the old rumour about the cottage being haunted by one of Tenderton's long-dead witches. But it was meant to be a benign spirit, according to legend, and Mrs Grable had always said she found the presence comforting…

Don't be so bloody stupid, Patricia Taylor! Patti heard her mam snort, and she checked the window again. No one.

'It's blocking the bloody entrance to the garage.' Neil straightened, red-faced, hoisting his overalls back up. *Thank God*, thought Patti, averting her eyes before she saw something she could never forget. 'None of my customers will be able to get in or out.'

In and out. Patti had a horrible vision of Neil and Linda in bed together. Although surely they didn't actually do it anymore? She and Sam had definitely gone off the boil the past year or two; not that surprising, given the longevity of their marriage. But still.

'Whose car is it?' Patti glanced back at the cottage, but the boy hadn't reappeared. Perhaps there hadn't even been a boy. Sam kept saying she should get an eye test, though her vanity had so far precluded it.

'That woman in there.' Neil jabbed a stubby finger at Primrose Cottage. 'Who flatly refuses to come out and move the bloody thing.'

'Oh? I thought it was still empty?'

The window where the boy had been was definitely empty, just stiff yellow curtains standing to attention behind the mullioned windows. But of course, Patti thought with a shiver, the troubled spirit would have ensured no one came to view the place when Primrose Cottage went on the rental market last Christmas.

'No. I saw her.'

'Are you sure, Neil?' Patti used her best patronising voice, long learnt from Sam. 'Mrs Grable moved to her sister's ages ago.'

Hang on a tick! That was a definite flicker of curtain in the cottage's front room.

'Right!' Neil banged open the gate. 'That's it!'

Squinting down at her moon cycle watch – a birthday present from her eldest, Luna, who shared her fervent love of all things astrological (*Geddit, Mum!* the tag had read) – Patti gave a third deep sigh.

Her first appointment was at 8.15 a.m., an early, especially for Dez Fullerton's gorgeous wife Nancy – and Patti really didn't want to keep her waiting, given that it was a new booking. The lovely Nancy usually got all her beauty done up in London on her modelling shoots, and truth be known, Patti had a bit of a crush on her. Almost as big a crush as she had on Dez himself.

She'd planned to open early, get the best rose and honey candles wafting, the whitest robe warmed, ensure her new mood music was playing gently throughout the salon.

Except now Neil was marching up the cottage path.

Patti had long believed Neil to be a bit of a bully. A little like his wife Linda – her dear friend, of course, but who had also become rather passive-aggressive lately.

With a final huff, she followed him to the gate.

2

Alex

With my third coffee in hand since 6 a.m., I was trying my utmost to keep out of sight of the street – not easy in a house this size – and cursing myself.

If I hadn't parked so badly last night after collecting Harry from Heathrow, leaving the old Land Rover too near the MOT garage's drive, my new neighbours still wouldn't have known about us.

After all, I'd been here for almost a week already, since my brother Gray dropped me off in the dead of night, and no one had noticed the cottage was inhabited.

Which was *exactly* how I had wanted it to be.

Later, of course, I might ask myself if I was disconcerted not to have been spotted during that entire time. Images of my decomposing body at the foot of the stairs, or burnt and electrocuted by my hairdryer, lying in the 1970s avocado bath, sprang to mind.

But I'd been happy enough to unpack the few cases and boxes of belongings I'd brought with me from America, pottering around, sorting things out for the children's arrival.

Well. *Happy* might be an exaggeration.

I'd missed the children desperately, and yet I was relieved to have had these few days to gather myself, and to begin to make plans about…

About the rest of my life. Our lives.

Because everything was on me now.

Since Gray had left, I'd found that thought so overwhelming that, most nights, I'd pulled the hairy blanket off the small settee and dragged myself upstairs wrapped in it to sit in the dark window of the empty back bedroom.

The street was chocolate-box pretty. At one end, a small olde-worlde pub – the Witch's Head – bedecked with jewel-bright window boxes and crowned with an alarming sign, featuring a warty-nosed crone in a bonnet. Opposite that, the old Georgian vicarage. (What did the Church of England have to say about witchcraft? Nothing good, I suspected.)

The rest of the road, apart from the garage, consisted of rows of neat little red-brick houses, much like the one I found myself in, the postage-stamp front gardens decorated with a variety of garden gnomes and stone squirrels, some more hideous than others. The only anomaly was that in the front window of every house except mine hung heavy silver, glass or gold baubles. Someone had forgotten to tell the locals that Christmas was over, it seemed.

Luckily for me, Primrose Cottage was detached from the rest of the row by a narrow side return to the small garden. Somehow that made it feel slightly less claustrophobic; assuring me no one was listening through an adjoining wall.

The far end of the street, opposite a tranquil duck pond, was punctuated by a handsome old house, Tenderton Manor, white-shuttered and red-bricked, honeysuckle and ivy tumbling over the walls that kept it solitary.

All in all, the whole village was beyond pretty – and none of it fitted my mood.

And yet, there was a darker undercurrent. On our way into the village that first night, we'd passed a contraption in the middle of the village green, a long plank with a crude wooden chair attached, surrounded by iron railings and a placard I couldn't read from the car.

'Bit inaccessible for kids,' I'd murmured, wondering where the rest of the playground was, to go along with that old see-saw.

'It's an ancient ducking stool.' My brother had slowed so I could see it. 'For naughty housewives. Drowned if you were innocent, hanged if you survived the dunking. Not sure which fate was worse.'

'God, how awful.' I felt the throb of misogynistic tradition right there in my gullet. 'Did it happen much?'

'Tenderton's famous for its seventeenth-century witch-hunts. More dead witches than you could shake a stick at makes a great tourist attraction apparently. Wait till you see the iron boots round by the church hall.'

'Boots?'

'Yep. They heated them up and shoved them on the supposed witch till she confessed her sins.'

'Dear God.' The village's appeal would have been fast dimming – if I'd had any choice of where to go.

'Yep, they're certainly proud of their history,' Gray pulled up outside the little house his new wife Stacey was now in charge of for her elderly aunt. 'Not entirely sure why. All feels a bit *Wicker Man* to me.'

It was only much later that Gray admitted the village's 'ancient witchcraft as tourism' shtick was one reason his wife had eschewed moving in, although deepest Kent had never featured in my brother's plans.

At least they'd had options – which was more than I did.

But I mustn't be ungrateful. Without Stacey's generous loan, we'd be homeless, or still staying with my mother-in-law – and frankly, like either the witch's dunking or the gallows, I wasn't sure which fate was worse.

Thankfully, there was some calm to be had here too, I'd come to realise in the oncoming days.

The upstairs back room, with its view onto a landscape of woodland and hop fields, gave me far more comfort than the chocolate-box vista at the front.

Unseen by anyone, I'd gaze down towards the river, just visible through the tall beech trees. Staring at the silvery ribbon in the Kent country night, I'd dream about where exactly the water led, and whether I could go there too.

It was something I'd been wondering since the tragedy in America; since I'd returned to my homeland for the first time, without my husband.

Since I'd returned a widow – and an impoverished one at that.

Now, entirely due to my own stupidity, we'd been discovered.

I'd finally lost my focus last night at Heathrow after my son Harry's flight was delayed. Sitting in Costa Coffee by the arrivals gate, I'd watched tanned girls trot through with shiny carry-ons, or couples clasped in unwieldy embraces whilst gazing blankly over their partner's head. It was, by and large, nothing like *Love Actually* would have us believe.

But then a tearful reunion distracted me – a big family squealing into each other's arms, smiling and sobbing – and I almost missed my boy arriving.

Almost, but not quite…

Beyond delighted to see him, I could have picked Harry up and swung him round and round, holding on for ever. But that wasn't on when you were thirteen, I realised sadly; plus, he was getting taller and heavier, so I settled for a hug and a chaste peck on his pale freckled cheek.

Reaching Tenderton after midnight in the dark, both bug-eyed with exhaustion, keen to get him to bed quickly, I'd parked haphazardly.

Once, I must have known they didn't do proper street lights out in the sticks, but it was as if I'd forgotten England in the past ten years; used to the bright lights of the lands I'd followed Fraser to, most recently those of America.

And this morning it was time to pay the fiddler, as a thickset, balding guy in blue overalls clomped up my path looking like he wanted to kill someone. Me, most probably…

Behind him, a small, neat woman with a tumble of brown curls followed as far as the gate, dwarfed in a fluffy pink coat. His wife? She certainly looked irritated enough to be a spouse.

'I know you're in there.' The man banged on my front door. 'You need to move your car – NOW!'

Panicking, I plopped myself down cross-legged in a corner of the empty room, out of sight. For some reason, my hands shook on my cup.

'Open the door!'

I clutched it harder.

What the hell was wrong with me? Unable to open the door to a man who – perfectly reasonably – just wanted me to move my car; a car inherited from my brother that I was still struggling to drive.

This was not the time to give in to tears. No way, Jose.

Bang bang bang went the door. 'I know you're in there.'

Footsteps in the hallway.

'Hal…' I scrabbled to my feet. 'Wait!'

'All right, mate?'

Too late. My son had opened the front door. Harry and his effervescent verve for life.

'Is your mum here?'

I froze.

'Or your dad?'

'My dad?' Harry sounded uncertain, and I felt that new but already familiar dive in my stomach. I could picture him, ball under arm, freckled face smiling; tentative but friendly.

'Either of them'll do.' The man was snappy, and my hackles were rising protectively. 'Can you hurry up about it?'

'Oh, sorry, sure.' My ever-affable boy. 'I guess my mum is in.'

I was already moving towards the door.

It was hard to be angry with Harry for long. Still, right now, in this very moment, I found I was fuming – with whom, I wasn't exactly sure, but I suspected it was my late husband Fraser.

I didn't think I was ever going to be able to forgive him for dying the way he had.

3

Patti

Given how hot under the collar (literally) Patti felt by the time she reached the door of Beauty Bound, it was fortunate that gorgeous Nancy Fullerton was fifteen minutes late for her facial. Especially as Patti realised, letting herself into the freezing salon, that no one – i.e. herself – had switched the heating on to its timer.

Good Lord, how much she irritated herself these days with this new, apparently middle-aged brain fog.

And although Nancy's lateness would have repercussions – the girls fiddling with the diary all day to play catch-up – it did at least mean that Patti hadn't kept the nearest person to a star in Tenderton waiting on the doorstep.

Turning on the fan heater, putting the lights on 'sunrise' setting in Room 1, Patti wasn't sure how she felt about what had just happened in Church Street.

The tow-haired kid who'd answered Neil's irate knock had seemed sweet: all melty eyes in a triangular pixie face, and skinny as a rake.

His mother? Attractive too, fair and tall-ish – though not as tall or slim as the gorgeous Nancy. Nice-looking enough, but far less sweet than her son, given how reticent she'd been.

In fact, the woman had pretty much refused to talk at all, shoving bare feet (definitely no nail polish) into old trainers to shoot past them, muttering that she'd move the Land Rover, which left Neil expostulating at no one.

Or rather, at Patti instead.

'Give it a rest, mate,' she'd snapped eventually, relinquishing the idea of giving a warm Taylor welcome to this new arrival. A new arrival now crunching her way through her gears in the most painful way.

While they'd waited, the boy had come back out with a football, which he'd kicked a little forlornly around the tiny front garden, until Neil had calmed down and said, 'Not bad, mate. Enjoy the game?'

For all his pugnacious nature with adults, Neil was great with his team. He enjoyed their company and wanted to help them shine, talent or none. He'd never had favourites; he was fair to them all. Or at least he *had* been, until last season.

'Sure.' The boy looked up. 'But I'm not that good at the rules.'

'Why's that then?' Neil looked at the lad like he was from outer space. *How could you not know the rules to the best game in the world?* Patti could literally hear him thinking.

'They didn't really play soccer in my last school.' The boy shrugged beneath his sandy mop.

'Soccer? All schools play football these days, don't they?'

'Not in America.' He attempted a wobbly keepy-uppy.

America? Now he'd said that, Patti heard the gentle twang to his accent.

'Only one rule you need to know, isn't that right, Neil?' She had winked at the boy. 'The offside rule.'

'Tell you what, son.' Neil had apparently turned back into an ordinary human being. 'If you fancy a game, come along to the club on Saturday at ten, OK?'

'The club?'

Patti was reminded of the time two summers ago when Neil had driven past a traveller boy kicking a deflated ball in the field by the flyover and immediately pulled over to invite him to join the team. 'Got such a strong left foot, has Declan,' he had marvelled. 'Real talent.'

Declan's family had refused at first. They were wary of the locals, and with good reason. It pained Patti to remember how some parents had been a bit sniffy; the mutterings about the travellers, the 'pikeys', not being welcome.

But Declan had ignored it all, quickly proving himself to be one of the team's strongest players, with a great sense of humour. Against the odds, perhaps, he was now revered by the other boys.

'Our football club,' Neil said now. 'The Tenderton Tigers.'

'Thanks, but he won't be coming to any club.' The gate banged, and the boy's mother stomped back up the path. She definitely had an English accent, which made her American son all the more curious to Patti. 'I've moved the car. Sorry to inconvenience you.'

'Right, well, watch where you park next time, OK?' Neil retorted. *Couldn't resist it, could he?* It was certainly true that she'd moved it: the Land Rover was now parked even more badly, down by the Witch's Head. 'That was out of order.'

'Sorry,' the woman repeated, apparently not interested in a row. 'C'mon on, Harry.'

Behind Neil's back, Patti winked at the boy, and he grinned sheepishly, trotting after his mother, who stood at the front door, waiting for her son to duck under her arm.

'Excuse me.' Patti stepped forward. 'I just wanted to say—'

But before she could finish her sentence, the woman had shut the door, very definitively, in her face.

And Patti, feeling wounded, thought: *Well, serves her right then if the place is haunted.*

4

Alex

Up this close to a stranger, albeit a friendly-looking one, I'd just flat-out panicked. Being sad, tired and perpetually scared about our future wasn't an excuse to behave like a moody teenager myself right now, but I'd done exactly that. I'd failed to stay adult.

Still, I hardly slept at the moment: tossing and turning until the early hours, head buzzing with incessant worry. Exhaustion didn't help my mood. But it was stupid not to endear myself to my new neighbours, especially in a village this size.

'Harry! Breakfast.' I found a bowl with *Lion King* characters on it, which gave me momentary pause, memories of a Disneyland trip rushing in; a trip where we'd laughed so much I couldn't breathe sometimes.

Shaking my head to banish them, I dug the cereal out of a cupboard, sincerely hoping the neighbourhood mice hadn't also discovered it. At night I heard them scurrying in the rafters as I lay sleepless, the old cottage creaking and sighing in a way that might have spooked some – but that comforted me. Real life had a way of being far scarier than horror films or ghost stories, I'd realised in the past year.

I poured the cereal and added milk from the tiny fridge, finding the ordinary actions soothing. Swallowing the lump in my throat,

I returned the box to the cupboard, where it hit something at the back. What *was* that?

Kneeling, I fished out a set of thick glass baubles, like the ones in the neighbouring windows. Close up, I could see they were full of tangled bright thread, and they caught the light as I held them up.

Very pretty – but I had no idea what they were for.

Laying them on the tray, I refilled my coffee cup and carefully carried everything into the small sitting room, where Harry sat, Marvel comic in hand, already well thumbed.

He'd brought it from the States, the last copy in a subscription to a rare eighties series Fraser had got him for his twelfth birthday – the last birthday we'd shared as a family. A subscription I knew I couldn't afford to renew.

'Here you go, kiddo.' Side by side, my son and I sat on the spongy sofa, almost the only piece of furniture in the house apart from the beds and drawers upstairs. I must sort some more comfortable stuff out, and soon. Make things more homely.

'What do you reckon these are?' I held the glass baubles up to show him.

'Dunno, Mum.' He tucked into his cereal. 'Christmas decorations?'

To my horror, my eyes filled with the tears that had threatened all morning. Last Christmas, our first as just the three of us, shell-shocked, as if someone had hit the mute button, had been truly terrible. Iris hadn't come out of her room all day. These anniversaries were almost the most painful thing about losing Fraser – and they just kept on coming.

Standing, I moved to the big window, though I needn't have worried Harry would notice my damp eyes. He was far too enthralled by both food and a Black Widow story.

Tenderton was what travel programmes or estate agents might call 'quaint'. Like Miss Marple Land, or… what *was* that

British police show Fraser used to watch on satellite all the time, interspersed with hours of ice hockey beamed in from Sweden?

In the last year of his life, he'd started to stay up later and later, watching TV into the early hours, troubled by work problems he wouldn't share; that eluded me. At first, I'd thought it was me he was avoiding, and that had hurt.

It wasn't until he spoke more about the stress, just before he died, that I began to understand it was nothing I'd done personally that kept him up at night.

I was clutching the window ledge desperately hard now, I realised; so hard my fingertips hurt, the name of that drama he loved escaping me, though he'd watched it so often. It featured a cosy English village where dastardly deeds were carried out by posh or eccentric people. That was how Fraser wanted to remember the UK: not the gritty naturalism of other crime dramas or bad documentaries about benefit cheats, showing the poverty of so many British cities, but the fictional version where a little murder didn't really hurt, and everything was tied up neatly at the end of an episode by capable policemen.

A postman in shorts (shorts! despite the weather!) crossed the road towards the pub, big bag of mail on shoulder, whistling.

Midsomer Murders! That was the name of Fraser's great favourite. And oh God, this village, Tenderton, was just a little *too* quaint for me right now.

As if my gloomy thoughts had conjured it up, a shiny white sports car slid into view to disrupt the peace, the slick little vehicle cruising down the main street, music gently slicing through the quiet.

As with the postman's outfit, I shivered with cold just looking at it.

The British chill was something else I'd forgotten; the way it sneaked into your very bones, wrapping round them like Dickensian fog.

'So can I go Saturday?' Harry's voice chimed into my thoughts. 'That guy said he ran a soccer club.' He slurped the milk from the bowl. 'I guess I might be quite good at it.'

'We'll see, Hal. Checking out your new school later is our priority, OK? And on Saturday, I thought we could get some new things for your room.' With what money, I wasn't sure. My bank balance was dangerously low, and the life insurance claim didn't look like it was any nearer being resolved. 'Make it more cosy.'

But hey, credit cards worked anywhere – didn't they?

Still, an increasingly familiar fear gathered around me like ice.

''K.' Harry shrugged, a milky crescent on his smooth top lip. 'But I'd really like to do the soccer.'

'Football, honey – they call it football here. And yes, of course.' Carefully I picked up the baubles from the tray and hung them over the window catch, where they caught the early-morning light, refracting in brilliant prisms on the ceiling. 'But one thing at a time maybe?'

A man had just swung himself out of the sports car and was jogging past that little garage towards the corner of the high street. Tall and slim, wearing an expensive-looking tracksuit, he turned and, to my horror, looked right at me – and winked!

I pulled away from the window like I'd been scalded.

'Ah, baby.' Blushing hotly, I plonked myself back down beside Harry and kissed the top of his head. He smelt warm and safe, like the hay barn on my grandparents' farm. 'We're going to be OK here, aren't we?'

'Course, Ma.' He managed to smile up at me. Little braveheart. 'Specially when Iris gets here.'

'It'll be great, won't it? Just the three of us.' Carving out a new future together.

I wished I actually believed it though.

Then I thought of all the emails I'd sent in the past few months, and I wondered with a tiny soaring of hope in my heart whether today might be the day I got a response from the person I longed to hear from…

5

Patti

After all the anticipation, the delectable footballer's wife Nancy Fullerton looked less than collected walking into the beauty salon that morning.

Far less Best Bottom of UK 2019, in fact, and much more tired mum of three. Though it still had to be said, with her long platinum hair swept into a messy ponytail and her endless legs in skinny jeans and old UGGs, she also managed to look effortlessly cool. Which Patti, for all her love of other womankind, found just a *tiny* bit annoying.

'Sorry. Had to wait for Dez to take the kids to school.' Nancy smiled and Patti immediately smelt a fib.

Nose like a bloodhound, her dad used to say, and she had once considered signing up for the police force. Being a detective would have suited her well, but she'd fallen pregnant with Luna instead.

Plus, having heard Dez disagreeing with Neil at last night's training about team formation for Sunday's match, Patti really wasn't sure she could see Dez as the domesticated type.

It had been clear from the moment the Fullertons joined the Tigers that Dez was fiercely ambitious for both sons. His elder boy, Hunter, had been scouted by the Crystal Palace youth academy but was currently injured – though not too injured to play for the Tigers. It was obvious that Sunday League was considered merely a pastime, and yet one Dez wanted a big part of, for some reason that wasn't entirely clear to Patti.

There were also loud mutterings that he had the Tigers' managership in his sights. He was the only dad in the Tigers with any real football expertise, so he did have the potential to be a sort of secret weapon.

Or worse, he might actually be the best man for the job.

None of which probably helped Neil's mood.

'Won't be a sec, sugar!' Patti gave Nancy an *OK!* magazine and sent her junior – the girl who did everything from sweeping the floor to painting Patti's own nails occasionally – to make what they called 'frothy coffee' – really just powdery stuff out of a tin.

Whacking the fan heater up in Room 1, Patti could feel her stress levels building. Honestly, what was with her this morning?

She was more rattled than she cared to admit about the aloof woman at Primrose Cottage. Patti prided herself on always being friendly and likeable. Unused to being completely blanked, it just added to an increasingly common feeling of being useless: dried up, unwanted…

Nancy stuck her head round the door. 'Ready for me?'

'Oh, yes!' Surreptitiously Patti kicked the heater under the bed. 'It's so lovely to have you here. Pop your stuff down.'

'Ta.' Nancy dropped her magazine and bag on the chair to slip off her UGGs, revealing mismatched socks, and Patti felt a pulse of relief at the imperfection.

But seconds later, leaning over to check Nancy's pores, Patti saw that her new client's lashes were damp, her mascara smudged under her eyes, and that triumph felt sullied. The woman had obviously been crying.

What on earth could the lovely Nancy have to be upset about? Her massive house being hard to clean? Not getting an invite to Victoria Beckham's Fashion Week front row?

Or something much worse?

'Everything all right, Nancy?' Quietly Patti switched her magnifying lamp on.

'Never better.' Nancy's turquoise eyes snapped open. Sparkly with unshed tears they might be, shadows beneath them, but she was giving nothing away. 'And please, call me Nance. All my mates do.'

Warmth spread across Patti's tummy. 'It's such a nice name, Nancy.' She slipped a velour hairband on to hold back the woman's fringe. 'Always reminds me of *Oliver Twist*.'

'Oliver Twist? Is that the posh fish place in Canterbury?' Nancy shut her eyes against the lamp's glare. 'Haven't got my head round the area at all yet.'

'Oh.' *Surely* she was joking? 'No, I meant the Charles Dickens story? There's that famous film with all the jolly songs...' Patti trailed off as she remembered what happened to Nancy: murdered by her jealous lover, the bully Bill Sikes. Had he strangled her or bludgeoned her with a cosh?

As Patti stepped back from the bed, from nowhere came a horrible flash and a hazy image: a body, floating face down, arms outstretched, in a pool of water...

Heart racing, she glanced down at the magazine spread, and, dry-mouthed, almost laughed with relief. Nancy had been looking at pictures of that sexy morning-TV presenter lounging by a Mediterranean swimming pool.

Stupid to think she'd seen a body, though Patti had always known she was blessed with second sight, just like her great-aunt Gwen. They were very similar, Mam had always said, with an uppity sniff.

'Going anywhere nice for half-term?' she asked firmly, her mother absolutely the last person she wanted to think of.

'Dubai, maybe? Not sure yet. Depends on Dez's business meetings.' A phone chimed prettily. 'Sorry.' Nancy retrieved it. 'Might be the new nanny.'

A nanny. How nice. Patti unscrewed a pot. 'So, first I'll apply the special cleanser…'

Silence.

'Next I'll exfoliate, then we'll do a grapefruit and retinol mask – it's gorgeous and creamy.' She turned back. 'Ready?'

The expression on Nancy's face was nothing less than terror writ large as she gazed at her phone. Such terror that Patti found herself – momentarily and unusually – lost for words.

'Are you…' She felt shocked. 'Is everything OK?'

'What?' Nancy turned the phone over. 'Oh, sorry, yeah. Fine.' But like her tears, her lie was obvious.

'Are you sure, sugar?' Patti felt a bit shaky herself. It was her empathic nature again, she supposed, dragging her into Nancy's pain.

'Course!' Nancy gave a bright smile. 'That reminds me, Dez's had a right result with the Tigers sponsorship!' She was doing an epic job of pulling herself together now. 'The boys should get the away kit with the logos next week.'

'Amazing!' Patti had long learnt that part of good client care was knowing when someone didn't want to share. 'So, how's Dez's academy funding bid going?'

'Oh, great, thanks. All the backing's in place, and he should hear about that site any day.'

Forced into early retirement by the dreaded rupture of his left cruciate ligament, Dez was in the process of setting up a private football academy with a couple of old teammates.

'Outside Tunbridge Wells?'

'That's it. You know, Patti, I'm so glad it's working out down here. He nearly took that Derby County job, but I'm not a big fan of the north, me. All that rain.'

'Not sure Derby County's strictly north, Nance. More sort of… in the middle.'

'Anywhere above the M25 motorway's north, my dad always says.' Nancy managed a smile. 'I didn't want to be away from them. My mum and dad.'

Patti removed the cleanser and smoothed the exfoliator on. *And loving parents to boot: lucky woman!*

It must just be her overactive imagination (another attribute she shared with her great-aunt) telling Patti that something was amiss with Nancy. Honestly, what *could* be wrong in the wonderful world of wealthy footballers' wives – especially when you were married to a gorgeous guy like Dez?

His professional career may have been seriously shortened, but now he had his academy to focus on, and there was a lot of money to be made from parental dreams – an awful lot.

Everyone wanted their son to be the next David Beckham or Ronaldo.

It didn't matter that the actual statistics were appalling: that a boy had more chance of winning the lottery than playing professional football in the UK – less than a 1 per cent chance – despite so many kids growing up with that burning ambition.

'You must have got married very young.' Patti wiped the exfoliator off. 'Childhood sweethearts?'

'Shotgun wedding, babe. Aged seventeen, I was shooting with the photographer Ellen von Unwerth after a scout spotted me in a shopping centre in South London; by the time I was eighteen, I was up the duff with Hunter after I met Dez at Tramp.'

'Tramp?'

'The nightclub, babe. Classier than it sounds. And my dad would've killed Dez if he hadn't married me, so…'

Patti turned to dip her hand in another unctuous pot, thinking of her own first pregnancy.

'I see. And how is Dez after that… you know' – carefully she applied the mask around Nancy's perfect nose – 'the altercation with Neil?'

'What altercation?'

'Last night.' Patti felt a quiver of anxiety. 'Probably nothing.'

'Over what?' The other woman frowned.

'Oh, you know. Something and nothing – just a few words about what formation to play on Sunday.'

'Dez gets a bit frustrated sometimes. Thinks the boys could be doing much better, you know.' Nancy pulled a face. 'He's not always the most patient of men, my better half, you could say.'

The downside of being a retired footballer was – apparently – living out your sporting fantasies via your own kids: in Dez's case, two beautiful sons, for whom he had high hopes. And a three-year-old daughter, Chloe, whom *maybe* he'd push to the same extent on the pitch, though somehow Patti couldn't see it.

Dez struck her as old-fashioned; the kind of man who believed women belonged in bedrooms and kitchens – and on the catwalk, in the beautiful Nancy's case.

And honestly, last night's shouting match wasn't the first row between Dez and Neil. No, that had occurred a few weeks ago, during a friendly against another local team, the Eastdown Elite.

Declan, who played in the same winger position that Neil had been trying Dez's son Hunter out in, had been on the pitch, whilst Hunter was on the bench – which at the Tigers' home ground actually meant shivering on the touchline, and in the mud if it was wet.

Stalking up and down the line, Dez had let it be known – loudly – that he thought the other boy was lazy, whereupon Declan's dad, Big Feen – who'd taken a whole season to warm up to so much as attending a game, given the wariness of his travelling community – went to challenge him.

Immediately Neil had stepped in, defending the boy and drawing Big Feen away – offending Dez in the process with a remark about Hunter still needing to earn his stripes.

But as far as Patti knew, Declan hadn't attended training since, and Hunter was now playing in his position on the right wing, without any risk of being substituted.

'Dez thinks they ought to dump a bit of the dead wood, you know.' Nancy was talking from the corner of her mouth now, face tightening under the mask. 'To be in with a chance of a cup win this season.'

Dead wood? Patti felt this viscerally. Did they mean her Ethan?

'But I know Dez gets a bit full-on. Had competition drilled into him from a young age, you know.'

That had been obvious right from the start of the season, with Dez treading on Neil's toes, coaching from the sideline, throwing his weight around – much to the amusement of some parents, who believed Neil needed taking down a peg or two.

Not everyone approved of these tactics though, including Patti's husband, Sam.

'The team's about community, Pats, not cup games and glory-hunting,' he moaned on one of his few outings to the club. 'Dez should just concentrate on his academy if he's so desperate for wins.'

And the problem was only worsening as Neil became ever more belligerent, obviously feeling threatened, clinging on with everything he had.

6

Alex

Mid September

I could resist anything apart from my children's pleas, which was how I found myself standing in ankle-deep mud at the Tenderton Tigers football club a couple of Saturday afternoons later, watching what they called a friendly match – though at times it looked pretty *un*friendly to me. And that was without mentioning the grumpy mechanic guy who ran it, Neil – though he had thawed out a bit since our first meeting.

My trainers becoming more waterlogged by the second, I thought mournfully of my sturdy old walking boots, abandoned at home in Laurel Springs with most of my clothes when we'd left America so suddenly.

I'd had no choice but to turn tail, unable to meet the next month's rent.

What home would that be, Alex? What an idiot. Stamping a clump of mud off my trainer, I felt a huge flare of anger at myself.

But then Laurel Springs hadn't really been home either, had it, however much I'd loved it – for a while, at least. During all the years I'd followed Fraser's job around, it was the place we'd stayed in longest. Living in rentals throughout, we'd never put a deposit down on a house, nor any roots. It hadn't mattered to me. I'd had my own little crew, and I'd been happy enough to live like that: nomadically. It had been my way since my early twenties, after my parents had both died far too young, leaving my brother Gray as my only close relative.

And yet Laurel Springs had felt different somehow.

Sometimes, driving down to the sprawling palm-edged beach in the early morning to swim as the sun rose over the water, or sitting on the back porch watching another vivid sunset through the laurels, flooding the distant mountains, Fraser and I had chatted vaguely about the future. We would talk about settling back in the 'old country', as Fraser teasingly called it. But then we'd wade out into the surf, or open another beer and a bag of nachos, and it would be forgotten.

It was painful now to remember the children's excitement when we'd first arrived at that house in the hills; the two of them, much younger, rushing through the echoing rooms, arguing about who would get the best room.

Lying outside in hammocks in the gently sloping garden, we'd watch the mighty sunrises and sunsets; the bright little birds on the garden feeders, the chipmunks stealing the seeds; the odd racoon ambling down in the twilight to appraise our bins. We'd briefly lived the dream – and done precisely nothing about settling – or saving any money either.

No – I kicked myself metaphorically again – *I* had done nothing to make sure my beloved children were secure. I'd trusted Fraser, because I hated admin myself; I'd believed, given the nature of his work, office-bound, fiddling with numbers all day, that he must be good at it.

Or rather, I'd *chosen* to believe he was good at it.

Which meant, amongst other disasters, that now all we had was my sister-in-law's loan of her aunt's little house – a sister-in-law I had yet to meet properly – tucked away in a pretty village we most definitely didn't belong in.

And every day I prayed for my only chance to save us from real penury; every day I ran to check the post; my emails almost hourly. Still nothing from the insurance company. Still nothing from—

Stop, Alex! I screamed internally. *You can't expect anything from him.*

Stamping my way up and down the touchline to keep warm and hoping they'd put Harry on to play soon, I thanked God for small mercies: for the fact that my fears the children might stick out like sore thumbs in this quaint little village had been misplaced.

This child at least.

I should have known Harry's innocent charm would help him fit in anywhere. It was just a shame I wasn't finding it so easy myself.

On Friday, I'd picked my son up from school in the old Land Rover that Gray had bequeathed me, which was becoming precisely no easier to drive.

We'd gone to town to buy some uniform Harry was missing, fish and chips being my fairly useless bribe, given that it was a dish my innately American son had no real concept of.

'Why would you eat potato chips out of newspaper?' He wrinkled his nose as we pulled up outside the chippy. 'Sounds gross.'

'Chips in the UK are what you call fries, except bigger and fatter, and I'm not sure they do wrap them in newspaper these days,' I reassured him. 'I'm probably just showing my age.'

Inside, relieved to see that the newspapers in the shop were here for reading, I flicked through a stack on the window ledge as I waited.

The Tenderton Truth had a story on its front page about dredging the Raven's Pool, more commonly known as the Pool of Sorrow, the old lake at the Tigers football club (for lake, read large pond, I thought wryly, remembering the mighty North American lakes we'd camped around a few summers ago). The company responsible, apparently run by one of the club's parents, had dredged up a stack of bones, and, horribly, it looked like they were human, rather than animal.

'Plans to drain and cover the lake to make space for another pitch have been postponed,' architect Riker Bauer said. 'We'll have to find another way for the football.'

The news had come as a relief to local historians and witchcraft aficionados such as parish councillor Maria Desmond: *'Local archaeologists from the University of Kent have taken the bones away in the hope of being able to date them. We've got no reason to believe they're recent, although local police have been notified. Indeed, we think the Pool of Sorrow was used pre-eighteenth century for the ducking stool, long a highlight of Tenderton history.'*

A *highlight*? So weird.

Closing the paper quickly, I glanced outside at Harry, as if this article could somehow affect him.

But he was happily ensconced in his Marvel comic, grinning to himself. I watched him for a moment with a kind of awe. Since he'd arrived in England, he hadn't shown the slightest worry about failing; the notion didn't even enter the equation, apparently. He lived life day by day and in the moment, exactly as all the mindfulness experts said we should. If I could bottle his 'in the here and now' and sell it, I'd be a millionaire.

'Failure is not an option': who did that remind me of?

Fraser's scary father, that was who; a man who'd spent a lifetime polishing guns for a living. In retrospect, it explained a lot about Fraser's mixed emotions over work and play.

'Two cod and chips, one mushy peas, one gravy,' the bored cashier sang out. 'Salt and vinegar?'

In my new here and now, even fish and chips was a treat.

'Here you go, tiger.' I dumped Harry's portion into his lap. 'Share my peas if you like.'

'Yuck!' Harry pulled a face at the pot of bright green mush and waved the ancient Nokia phone his Scottish grandma had given him. 'I'm invited to Ethan's birthday party tomorrow.' Greedily he tore into the greasy chips. 'After training.'

The photograph of the old bones I'd just seen came to mind. 'OK.' I hid my own wince.

'Yeah, and his mom said for us to both come. Like, you too,' he added helpfully.

'*Us?* Hang on a sec.' Fat chip poised at my lips, I frowned. 'His mum?'

'Ethan said she'd met you some time.'

'Really?' I hadn't met anyone yet, apart from the old lady in the grocer's – and Neil, the grumpy mechanic, who also ran the football team.

'We have to get him a gift, right?' Harry pattered on, mouth full. 'Ethan.'

'That's nice,' I said absently, thinking how very un-nice it sounded. I didn't want to meet anyone; I just wanted to hide us all away – Harry, me and my daughter Iris.

Iris was arriving on Sunday morning, thank God, making the nine-hour train journey from Inverness to start school on

Monday – and not before time. If she stayed any longer with my cantankerous Scottish mother-in-law, she might just end up turning into the poor bear in *Brave*.

I needed Iris back where she belonged: to work things out with her; to see how she was; to try to soothe her over her dad's terrible fate. And to keep trying to convince her it wasn't *my* fault, what had befallen her father.

Perhaps, during the attempt, I'd manage to convince myself.

Yes, I thought now, stamping down the football pitch's sideline yet again for warmth, shoving my hands deep into my pockets: if I just kept my head down, I might get away without any explanation of what had brought us here.

'Hiya, babs! Good to see you!'

'Oh!' I almost jumped, so far away in my own thoughts was I. 'Hi.'

'Coming to Ethan's after?' A round, pretty face, smiling above a cuddly pink coat. Of course – the woman from the other week. The team manager Neil's wife, I presumed.

'Aha!' I tried to sound cheerful. 'So the famous Ethan's *your* son?'

'Yep, my little cherub's thirteen today, God love him, so we're having a little do at the clubhouse. The more the merrier, I say.'

'Um, I've really got to get back to…' To what though? I couldn't think of anything convincing to say. 'To cook the tea.'

'Tea as in dinner?' The woman smiled broadly. 'Ah, you won't be needing any when you see the spread we've laid on. And the cake. Or should I say cakes, plural. My mother-in-law must have stayed up all night icing.' Her smile suddenly looked fixed. '*Bake Off*'s got nothing on her, specially as she knew I'd ordered a posh one from town. I know the old mother-in-law jokes are awful, but really…'

She talked at such a pace, her voice sliding up and down the register in a sing-song accent, I could hardly keep up.

'Can't bear to be beaten, my dear ma-in-law. Never liked another lady loving her son… Oh, all right, Liz!'

'Patti!' A thin woman was striding towards us: red Canada Goose padded anorak, green Hunter wellies, short dark hair topping off an efficient, angular face. The type my brother would call a toff: officer material from his army days. 'Hello there.'

I almost wanted to click my heels to attention – and was it my imagination, or had the woman called Patti's smile become even more strained?

'Shame the match started so late today.'

'Yeah, I don't know what's up with Neil. Not really his best self, is he, poor fella. Good to see you too, Liz.' Patti slipped her arm through mine before I realised what she was doing. 'Coming up to the clubhouse for tea and cake with me and… Sorry, remind me?'

'Alex,' I said meekly.

'Alex is Harry's mum, Liz. He's just started training with us.' Patti pointed at my son, who was running around like a maniac on the far side of the pitch. I really couldn't tell if anything he was doing was useful to the team.

'Enthusiasm counts for everything,' a chubby, jolly-looking dad had said earlier with a grin, which I took as a veiled insult.

The woman in red just stared at us both.

'Alex, this is Liz, mother to the three Bauer boys. Could be a boy band with a name like that, eh?' It seemed like Patti was wittering from nerves. 'Liz is usually only around at weekends, aren't you, sugar? Big job in the City. So, shall we, ladies?'

'Sorry, but…' Liz checked an expensive-looking watch; a Rolex perhaps. 'Riker's been on a call with the financial broker, so he's taking over here, and I'm using the time to study my perjury case next week.'

'On a *Saturday*?' Patti pulled a face. 'No rest for the wicked, eh?'

'Hardly wicked. I'll send the boys up though, if that's OK?' Liz was already turning towards the car park, which was just in front of the frankly sinister-looking woods. 'And please don't let Maxi or Frederick have more than one slice of birthday cake. Riker's really worried that Maxi's been putting on more fat than muscle since Christmas.'

Riker… I recognised the unusual name from the article about the bones in the lake, which I'd driven past on my way up to the club car park. As I'd suspected, it was an unassuming pool, surrounded by old reeds; no sign of the tragedies its depths might be hiding. The stranger sight had been rows of old bottles outside the gates, full of unknown substances, some glass, some pottery.

'*Jawohl, mein Führer*,' Patti muttered under her breath as the other woman strode off. 'Oh dear, sorry. I mean, I *do* know it might sound a bit racist, like, given her husband's half German and whatnot, and he is a dab hand with an Excel spreadsheet, very handy for the club accounts, but honestly! He's a proper so-and-so round his kids, and I'm not even joking. Come on.' She manoeuvred me gently towards the clubhouse. 'Linda'll be cracking open the Prosecco by now, hopefully, along with the rest of the coven. God knows I need it after the week I've had.'

That at least was a sentiment I could agree with. Although the sound of a coven was alarming. Very seventeenth century, and yet another horrible reminder of the ducking stool, the bones in the lake and the old iron boots I'd spied last week near the churchyard.

What was it with this place?

What was it I'd not yet understood?

Conversely, the clubhouse was loud, warm and sweaty, full of people laughing, the chatter of football commentary, the swoosh and ping of pinball and fruit machines. There were medal walls, framed signed shirts and team photographs. A huge screen on the far side of the bar was showing a match that most of the men and some of the boys were staring at, as if they were expecting the Second Coming.

Most of the women sat on the other side of the room, younger children running amongst them as the mothers chatted over their heads, readjusting hair ties and shoelaces, doling out money for pop and chocolate, refilling their own own wine glasses amongst the odd cup of tea.

Behind them, a table groaned with cake and crisps. I watched two small girls solemnly select a bowl of Hula Hoops, placing it carefully between them before pushing a crispy hoop onto every finger. They ate each one at rapid-fire pace, then began all over again, until a small blonde boy arrived and tipped the snacks deliberately onto the ground with an angelic smile. One of the Bauer boys, I presumed; a little fair-haired replica of his mother, Liz.

'*Yoo-hoo!*' A ruddy-cheeked woman raised herself two inches from the plastic banquette to wave frantically at Patti. 'Over here!'

'That's Linda.' Patti dragged me towards the group of women. 'Your mate Neil's missus—'

'Oh – so you're not married to Neil then?' I was confused.

'Ha!' The look on Patti's face told me everything I needed to know. 'No, I've been spared that privilege, babs. I'd introduce you to my own husband, Sam, but he won't be available for the next hour.' She pointed across the bar to a pleasant-looking doughy-faced man scowling at the screen as someone scored.

'Oh dear,' Patti sighed, 'and now he probably won't speak again until tomorrow. Not that it'll make much of a change. Everyone, this is Alex.' She propelled me forward. 'Alex, this is my eldest, Luna.'

'Hi!' A young woman smiled politely. Somewhere in her early twenties, I guessed, as compact and neat as her mother, with two-tone brown and blonde hair and the most lustrous eyebrows I'd ever seen. 'Gran's just dropped the cake, Mum.'

'*Dropped* it?' Patti's pleasure was evident. 'Oh dear, *what* a shame.'

'As in dropped it *off*.' Luna pointed at the table behind her. 'She had to go – she's got Pilates in town. She'll pop in later, she said.'

'Course she did,' Patti said through gritted teeth, approaching the enormous iced cake her daughter was now photographing. It was crammed with tempting-looking layers of cream, iced flowers and unicorns interspersed with silver footballs, and bore the legend *Ethan: 13!!*

'I'll put the pics on the club Insta, Mum, if you like.'

'Ocean, don't eat that please, baby!' An ethereal-looking woman in purple tie-dye and a crocheted beanie pulled a chocolate mini roll from the lips of a tall, solid boy. 'It's got animal fats in it.'

'So?' the boy muttered mutinously beneath the slight shadow of a new moustache, looking like he wanted to punch her.

'So we love all our animal friends just like we love ourselves, don't we, Ocean? Which means we don't want to eat them.'

A scowling Ocean didn't look much like he loved anyone. 'It's just chocolate, Mum.'

'This is Meadow, and her son Ocean. Ocean plays in goal for us.' Patti patted the woman. 'Meadow has a lot of… causes, don't you, sugar? This is Alex, everyone. She's a newbie – she's just moved here, from… Where, Alex?'

Before I could answer, Patti's son Ethan tore up, an open-faced boy with his mother's brilliant green eyes. 'Can I have some money, Mum?'

'You know, Alex, I can sense you have travelled far.' Meadow gave me a fragile smile from beneath a rainbow-coloured fringe.

'Have a flapjack, Ocean. I made them, remember, so they're safe. So where did you begin, Alex?'

'Oh. Well, I was born in the East Midlands.'

'Wonderful, but I meant this last journey.' Her stare was scarily intense. 'To reach us in Tenderton.'

'Um.' I smiled back feebly, my desire to fade into the background sorely challenged. I had to say *something*. 'California.'

'Far out! I used to love hanging round the Big Sur before I had Ocean. And I had the most amazing time meeting my spirit animal with some ayahuasca in the Californian desert.'

'That's nice.' I had literally no clue what she was talking about.

'It's where I met Gandalf, fourteen years ago now.'

'Gandalf?' My mind was boggling. 'As in…'

'His origin name was Barry, but he was rebirthed as Gandalf when he became a shaman. I wouldn't do it now, of course. I mean, it's not safe to travel into spirit realms unless you're with a *real* shaman. And proper shamans are only ever Peruvian-born, I've since discovered, but anyway, welcome. There's room for all souls here.' Meadow nodded as she neatly plucked another mini roll from her son's bulging pocket and dropped it back on the plate. 'Carrot stick, anyone? They're from our very own garden.'

'Thanks.' I took a limp little orange stick. Was Barry aka Gandalf the boy's dad? I wondered, suppressing a smile.

Ocean refused a carrot, swore under his breath and stomped off to the group of boys watching the football match. Harry was one of them, I noticed with a mixture of relief and trepidation, fitting in as usual without any fuss.

'Not from the USA.' Meadow smiled again faintly. She smelt of patchouli and lavender. 'The carrots, I mean. No food miles here. You must miss moon-grown produce.'

My smile became less authentic.

'The good ole US of A, eh?' A tall man in an expensive tracksuit paused beside us, a handsome black guy who looked vaguely familiar. 'Why the hell would anyone leave the sunny skies of America for this hole?'

'Ah, Dez, don't be silly, like!' Patti shoved his arm lightly, her Welsh accent lilting strongly. 'He's only playing with you, Alex! This is Alex, Dez – she's just moved into the village.'

'All right, Alex.' He took my hand and leant over as if to kiss it, and I wanted to snatch it back in embarrassment. 'And *am* I playing, Patti?' He smouldered at the three or four younger mothers on the edge of the group, all very dolled up in tight little dresses or off-the-shoulder blouses, gathered round an ice bucket of Prosecco. 'What do you reckon, ladies?'

'Course!' they chorused merrily. 'We know you, Dez!'

It was obvious Dez was a total wow with the mums.

'Ah, but honestly, we all love Tenderton, don't we, team?' Patti implored them.

The woman called Linda gave a drunken thumbs-up and lurched for the bottle, nearly pitching face first into a plate of cheese sandwiches, which Patti moved quickly whilst catching Linda's shoulder with her other hand.

'Linda's lovely, but her little girl's not well; she hasn't been since birth,' she murmured over her friend's head. 'And now it looks like poor Lindy may have had *one too many*.' She mouthed the last bit.

'I would too if I was married to Neil.' Dez awarded us both a devastating smile. 'Wouldn't you, babe?' He sauntered off to the bar before anyone could answer.

'I'm sure I recognise him,' I muttered to Patti.

'Well, he *is* kind of famous.' Thrusting a plastic glass into my hand, she slopped warm Sauvignon to the brim. 'Dez Fullerton, ex-Wolves striker. And that gorgeous beastie' – she pointed at a beautiful willowy woman in the corner, gazing at her phone while absently stroking the unruly tawny hair of a small girl beside her – 'is his wife, Nancy. Model, I'm sure you can tell. I had her in the salon recently.'

I assumed that wasn't a sexual boast. 'I'm afraid I know literally nothing about football, so I've never heard of Dez Fullerton,' I shouted over the hubbub – at the exact moment someone turned the music off.

The whole bar turned to look at me, horror inscribed on their faces, whilst I stood, mouth open, my face turning scarlet.

Behind the bar, the handsome, if rather hairy, barman grinned through his beard and spoke into the microphone he was clutching. 'Hello, folks! This seems a good moment to welcome our most famous club member, Dez Fullerton, to pick the winner of the September raffle.'

A grinning Dez walked up to the bar, giving me a sly wink as he passed.

Five minutes later, Harry caught me surreptitiously pouring my warm wine into a fake potted palm.

'Mum!' He looked shocked. 'The wine might kill it!'

'I reckon it'll be OK. Want to make a move, kiddo?' I could still feel the sting of shame of my shout across the room.

'Can I stay?' he begged, his brown eyes big and puppy-like. 'Please! I can walk home – it's not far.'

'Oh, I don't know, Hal.' I was reluctant on more than one count. 'You don't know the area yet, and I think you'd have to go through the woods to get back. It's already getting dark.'

'Not the Whispering Woods!' the chubby-faced dad mouthed dramatically. 'You might run into the Hell Hounds.'

'Don't tease, Tony! The woods *are* a bit bewildering if you don't know them, but I'll bring him home after if you like,' Patti offered. She looked tired, I thought, and like she'd had enough of the whole event. 'It's no trouble, sugar. I pass yours when I drop Josh anyway.'

'Please, Mum.' Harry batted his eyes at me again.

'Well… only if you're sure, Patti.'

'No bother.' She gave me a thumbs-up. Across the bar, her pretty daughter was laughing with the nice barman. It seemed like a safe sort of place, a convivial buzz in the air. And Harry did deserve some fun, after the past year.

'And can I have some money please?' he wheedled.

Tentacles of dread clamped my chest. Money. 'Course.' I scrabbled in my pocket. 'Just haven't been to the bank for a few days, so…' I dropped a couple of pound coins into his warm hand. 'Love you,' I told the air as he shot back to the other boys, gathered round an old fruit machine.

'I'm so glad you came, Alex.' Patti hugged me before I could avoid it. 'If Harry gets signed up, you can join the coven. Give me your number, and I'll add you to our WhatsApp group.'

'Great.' I put my coat back on. 'Thanks so much for inviting us. I'll return the lift, I promise.' And I rushed to the door, pretending I couldn't hear Patti's second request for my number.

Much as I was touched by her warmth and enthusiasm – and I really was; it was the nicest anyone had been to me for months – I had no intention of joining any coven.

As the cold fresh air hit me outside, I thought of the old bones and the ducking stool with a shudder.

Mist had begun to gather all along the edge of the woods – the Whispering Woods – as day slipped into night. When I'd arrived, I'd parked the Land Rover beside other cars, but now it stood alone near the looming trees, which looked like they were floating behind the car park as tendrils of mist crept through them like smoky fingers.

There was something nameless but intensely intimidating in the air; something about the height and thickness of the trees, the twisted trunks just visible as I hurried to the car; something ancient and mythical and utterly uninviting. The surface of the dark pool by the gates was also seething with mist now, and the strange bottles stacked along the wall no longer glinted, the weak autumn sun having given up for the day.

Lost in my thoughts, I jumped when a man with a poker-straight back and slick hair appeared from nowhere. In shiny boots and an expensive quilted jacket, his nod was abrupt, as if his head was on a spring. 'Hello.'

Surprised, I nodded back, whereupon he flashed me an unexpectedly pleasant smile. 'Riker Bauer. Excuse me.' He hurried on. 'I am late to meet my boys.'

As I reached the car, feeling a little more relaxed, Dez emerged from the clubhouse. Standing in the doorway, silhouetted by the bright light behind him, he waved.

Flattered despite myself, I raised my hand to return the greeting – just as a woman slipped out of the shadows on the other side of the car park and moved swiftly towards him.

I dropped my hand quickly, feeling daft.

It wasn't me he'd been waving at; it was the other woman.

And as I climbed into the Land Rover, suddenly the penny dropped. Of course! Dez was the man I'd seen getting out of the white sports car outside Primrose Cottage a couple of weeks ago.

And the woman he was talking to now, up close and personal, an attractive black woman with intricate hair, wrapped in a leopard-skin coat, who had cast a quick look over her shoulder as she arrived… well, she most definitely wasn't his beautiful blonde wife Nancy.

7

Patti

Ethan's birthday: Virgo, moon waning

Patti hadn't enjoyed an iota of Ethan's party, which wasn't entirely surprising given that the moon was moving towards Libra, unbalancing the most balanced of star signs.

Not even seeing Eth's happy little face when he got the UEFA Championship tickets she'd saved up for had made her feel any more cheerful.

Worst of all – and she couldn't quite put her finger on why it felt so different these days – the atmosphere in the clubhouse had once again been grating.

Linda had got absolutely plastered – a regular occurrence these days. Sam had been typically morose after his home team, Millwall, had lost badly, therefore rendering him the host with the absolute least, barely able to raise a smile. And finally, that blasted cake from her mother-in-law had trumped it all. Patti's own horribly overpriced offering had just looked pathetic in comparison. Worse, she was aware she'd probably offended her best friend Hazel Calliste, Josh's mum, and owner of the Black Cat Café, by not asking her to make it. Perhaps that was why

Hazel hadn't turned up for even a quick Prosecco, leaving Patti to drop Josh off at the café after the party.

Patti knew she ought to have baked something herself; everyone knew that was what counted, the home-made touch, like perfect mum Nadiya from *Bake Off*. But time was a commodity she simply never had any more; especially since Sam had been laid up with his bad back, losing his foreman role at the new-build apartment blocks in town.

If Patti didn't keep things going, there was a chance the whole family might go under. Along with the everyday household expenses, there were Luna's uni fees and Ethan's subs and kit, and worst of all, the business rates on Beauty Bound had just been raised again.

If the landlord also put up the rent in January, Patti would be struggling to keep going. As it was, she might have to let her junior go – which would not only be heartbreaking but entirely exhausting.

If she was honest with herself, seeing Dez at the clubhouse earlier had been a high point in a bad day. He'd been as charming and attentive as ever, and although Patti didn't like his bolshie attitude on the sidelines, she couldn't help adoring his charisma.

At one point, cheered by his charm, she'd *almost* relaxed, admiring pictures of Meghan Markle with Luna and the girls. But then she'd overheard boring Riker Bauer – who'd finally dragged himself away from his broker to arrive in his stupid padded Barbour like some posh farming gent – berating his son Maxi.

'Didn't you achieve that running time?' His voice was as hard as his eyes. 'You did it last week, didn't you?'

'My calf was hurting,' Maxi muttered, not meeting his dad's gaze. 'It's really sore, Papi.'

'Ah, Maximilian, that is a shame. An ice pack and extra time on the treadmill before school then.'

'Riker!' Patti had detached herself from the other women. 'Good to see you. Are you telling Maxi how well he's doing?' She smiled at the boy. 'Isn't that right, Sheila and Neil?'

'He's a super-star forward.' Little Sheila from the tuck shop had brought in the fizzing candles for the cake. She'd once been a wow at the club herself – when they'd actually had a women's team, for about five minutes. 'So nimble.'

'Yep,' Neil agreed staunchly, suppressing a belch from his pint. 'The way he dinks the ball over the keeper, pure class every time.'

'Thanks.' Patti took the candles from the small woman. 'I bet you miss playing yourself, don't you? You were all set to be the next… Who's the American ladies' captain with the blue hair?'

'Megan Rapinoe? Pink hair right now, I think. Well,' Sheila said, as resigned as ever, 'I'm busy with work, so it's fine.'

Serving in the tuck shop? It wouldn't do for Tenderton women to get too modern, Patti thought sourly. Along with every other mother at the club who'd watched the women's team disband, she knew women's football had been banned by the FA until 1971. Britain had only had a professional women's league since 2018 – and Tenderton was firmly stuck in the last century.

'Yeah, he's a great little striker,' Neil was telling Riker now. 'We love having him on the team. He'd give Ronaldo a run for his money, eh, mate? You like playing up front, don't you?'

'I don't mind,' Maxi said, but he flushed with pleasure.

For all his belligerence sometimes with the parents, Neil was really good with the kids. 'Cake, babs?' Patti offered the boy a slice.

'Good to hear.' Riker attempted a smile. 'Hey! Don't be silly, Maxi.' The boy pulled his hand back guiltily from the monumental cake Patti *hadn't* made. 'You can't get your speeds up with too much fat. And then we can't be so proud of you as we are!'

When they left soon afterwards, Maxi dawdling behind his dad, the dastardly little Frederick on Riker's shoulders, and big brother Thomas (an efficient centre forward in the under-15 team), Patti felt a sudden wave of sadness for Maxi, the sweetest of the three brothers.

'Do you think he's a bully?' she murmured to Sheila, who'd appeared again at her elbow to help tidy up. 'Riker?'

'I think he's the type who likes to be in charge. He put a bid in to be manager last season.' The younger woman scooped up the broom she'd come to collect. 'You didn't hear that from me though.'

Leaving Sam to pay the bar bill with her credit card, and to pack up his mother's blessed cake (hardly dented, it was so huge), Patti had rounded up her charges.

Desperate to get off her feet, she'd dropped Josh back to the Black Cat Café, and the nice new boy, Harry, back to his mother, Alex, a woman Patti hadn't worked out at all yet. Pleasant enough, she supposed, but aloof and difficult to warm to. Plus, she'd definitely ignored Patti's request for her phone number earlier.

Good word, 'aloof'.

Her bloodhound nose told her Alex was hiding something. Where was the dad, for instance? She'd been tempted to ask Harry in the car, but it wasn't her business, not really. More importantly, she didn't want to upset him in front of the other boys – or unsettle herself when, tonight, she had some rare hours to herself.

Ethan was having a last-minute sleepover with his best mate Davey, Neil and Linda's son, which doubtless meant the boys would be up all night on the Xbox as Neil watched footie highlights in his den into the early hours and a drunken Linda collapsed into bed. Their little Angel was at her respite carer's, always a green light for poor Linda to unwind – recently, rather too avidly.

But Ethan being away meant Patti would get a lie-in for a change, and that was well worth a grumpy child the next day. Her own daughter Luna had gone straight out to town, clubbing with her college friends, which always put the fear of God into Patti, given what had happened when Luna was sixteen – a slow, persistent slide off the tracks until the school had had to intervene.

The new club barman, Mike, who looked like he'd taken a bit of a shine to Luna, was possibly going too. He seemed the reliable type, unlike the young men Luna normally fancied, which was some solace to Patti, though she didn't like his tattoos.

Sam had arrived home, dumped the cake in the kitchen and sulked off upstairs, still mortified by Millwall's defeat, so for once, the living room was all Patti's.

Easing herself out of her too-tight skirt – what was it with middle age and waistbands, and why did no one warn women this was going to happen? – she donned her joggers with relief.

Pouring herself a large vodka and lime, she was already happily immersed in an episode of *Married at First Sight* when her phone started buzzing on the table behind her.

She ignored it. These few precious hours were hers to enjoy without distraction.

But within minutes, the phone was vibrating like it had a life of its own. Patti dragged herself up to check it wasn't one of the kids.

'Oh my God!'

The club WhatsApp group was blowing up, it seemed.

Guys, have you seen this on Tenderton Community Treasure??
Who would do this? Who would say this?
And then – silence.

As she scrolled through the thread to see what they were reacting to, a text message from Hazel pinged onto Patti's screen.

Patti! Can you believe it? I so hope this isn't true!! Poor Linda! Call me ASAP. PS sorry I missed the party, work was mad.

Taking a big sip of vodka and a deep breath, Patti clicked on the link posted into the group.

What she was looking at didn't make much sense at first.

A video of some description: a head in silhouette, no face visible; an eerie voice echoing out of nowhere, like a continuity announcer from beyond the grave.

'*Welcome,*' it was saying. '*Come closer and let me tell you a secret about someone you might know...*'

Chilled, Patti automatically did as she was told, putting the phone right up to her face to read the tiny text now displayed, along with a load of old photos and a YouTube clip by the looks of it, the strange robotic voice-over sounding in her ears. Within seconds, she had spluttered her drink all over the screen.

Jesus wept. Could what she was reading and watching possibly be true?

And if it was, what did it mean for the future of the Tigers?

Tales of Tenderton

SHOCK HORROR! There's an old-fashioned racist in our midst ☹ In the days of old, before social media existed, believe it or not, there were other ways of spreading vitriol and hatred. An old football fanzine, *Valleys of Britain*, has come to light, prolific contributor one Neil Forth, or 'George & the Dragon', as he liked to be known back then. Worse: Neil is the manager of Tenderton Tigers U14s, but he's also an ex-member of the evil racist fascist group the National Front, who now have links to the most recent British fascistic twattery, Terry Fowler's supremacist group EDN.

Have a look at these photos of the 1977 march… Teenager or not, Neil Forth was there. Watch this YouTube clip: it proves what a racist he really was… It all goes to show that the supposed benevolence of the U14s Tigers football manager is very definitely in question…

Neil's George & the Dragon articles include:

- BOYCOTT THE SPAR ON BRIDGE STREET, TAKEN OVER BY POLES!
- GO BACK WHERE YOU CAME FROM – What us Brits deserve, fighting to keep small businesses afloat amidst a deluge of foreginers! [*sic*]
- BRITISH AND PROUD TO BE – Join us on the March of all Marches to support the writes [*sic*] of British workers. Immigrants should stay out! We need people to go home so we can look after our own.

So, for more updates on the evil machinations of your friends and neighbours, sign up to the *Tales of Tenderton* vlog and we'll send you news straight to your inbox as we get it!!

8

Alex

Monday

'Well, that's put the cat amongst the pigeons, hasn't it?' Patti Taylor rolled her eyes at me from my doorstep. 'Got time for a quick coffee?'

'Um, well…' I hesitated, not wanting to seem rude, and having no idea what she was on about. 'It's just…'

But she was already inside. 'I've got an hour before my next lady, so I thought I'd pop in. Didn't get your number at the weekend. Not interrupting, am I?'

'I was just going to do some work.' A big fat lie: I'd made a few calls, then had struggled uselessly over my website for the past hour. But Patti wasn't really listening anyway, I realised.

'And also, have you *heard*?' she was asking as I followed her fluffy pink coat into the minuscule living room.

'Heard what?'

'Goodness!' Her eyes swept the functional room. 'Can see you've just moved in, babs. Mrs Grable took all her stuff, did she? You need a few knick-knacks, don't you, brighten things up a bit? I've got a couple of pictures in our garage I could lend you. Lovely one of a beach at sunset.'

'Oh, thanks, that's kind, but honestly…' I stopped, unsure what I really wanted to say.

'It's no trouble, sugar. And oh, I know! I've got a gorgeous lamp that my ma-in-law gave me for Christmas, in the shape of a swan. I've not got the room for it, more's the pity.'

I didn't know how long we were staying, that was the real point. Didn't know if I could ever see this place as home.

'I see you put your witch balls up.'

'Witch balls?'

'To ward off the evil eye.' Patti pointed at the glass baubles in the window. 'Protect you from the witches that used to roam here, apparently. They used to fill them up with pee in the bad old days.'

'Euch!' I felt slightly horrified that I'd hung them now. 'I didn't realise what—'

There was a loud thump and a creak of floorboards above us, and the ceiling light flickered.

'Ah!' Patti lifted her head and shut her eyes for a second, as if she was listening, clutching her coat tighter.

Baffled, I gazed at her.

'Mrs Grable always said the good spirit protected her against the haunting.' Patti's eyes snapped open again. 'It must be here for you too!'

'Haunting?'

'Yes. Of the Pool of Sorrow. What they call the lake in the club grounds. Not really a lake, mind, more a big sort of pond, isn't it?' she added, echoing my recent thoughts. 'Where they used to take the poor witches to drown them.'

'Oh.' I remembered the article I'd read in the chip shop. 'Oh dear.'

Patti grinned. 'It's just old wives' tales really. Or should I say old *men's* tales! They liked to keep the women in their place, those old codgers. That Witchfinder General, and those terrible prickers.'

'Prickers? You're losing me, Patti!'

'Pricks who used prickers! Sharp needles shoved in to test the witch's mark, you know, like a mole, or a wart. And if the poor women so much as squeaked, that was it. They'd shown their guilt.'

'Horrible—'

Another creak – and a definite footstep above us.

'Goodness, sorry!' Patti glanced up at the ceiling again, and then back at me, eyes narrowed. 'Not a ghost then. Special friend? Sorry, I didn't think.'

'Ha, no!' I couldn't help myself; I smiled back. 'That's Iris. My daughter. She got in late, on the last train. Very tired. Very' – I dropped my voice – 'teenager-y. You know. Likes her sleep.'

'Oh, don't they just! Where did she come from?'

'She's been staying with her grandma for the last month. We were all there for a bit.'

'In London?'

'No, Scotland. Inverness.'

'Ooh, very exotic.'

'Not sure about that. Very cold and damp, more like.'

'Is it? Never been that far north myself. So where's your…' Patti's brilliant eyes flicked to my ring finger, and she hesitated, but she was committed already. 'The kids' dad?' she ploughed on.

One part of me admired her audacity; the other part felt my stomach dive.

'Gone.' The word came out too abruptly; blunt and solid as a truncheon round the back of a skull. Round *my* skull. That was what it felt like every time I said the word, or even thought it. 'Died. At the end of…' I swallowed. 'Last November.'

'Oh dear, I'm so sorry.' Now those kindly green eyes filled with tears. 'God, that's a terrible shock for you all. Ill, was he? Ah, and your poor children. I'm so sorry,' she repeated.

The bathroom door banged.

'Yes, thanks, you said.' I knew it was sorrow that made me curt and waspish. 'But we're dealing with it. Honestly, please don't pity us – it's fine. The kids will be fine.'

But I don't think either of us believed it.

It was testament to Patti's phlegmatic nature that she didn't immediately do a runner at either my brusqueness or my undoubtedly bereft face but persevered instead with the idea of coffee. I didn't really deserve it, I knew, given how stand-offish I might have appeared, but the truth was, I was scared of making friends here.

And yet it was time to move forward – I also knew that.

'C'mon, I'll take you to the Black Cat, introduce you to my best mate Hazel. Fill you in on the gossip.' She patted my arm. 'You're not going to believe what's been going on in Tenderton. I'm sure I don't. Or do you know already?' She looked almost hopeful, I thought, that I didn't.

'No. I'm clueless about everything Tenderton really. Apart from the obsession with witchcraft.'

'Grab your coat, why don't you. I'm parched.'

There was something about Patti's persistence, something in her kindness and warmth, that dissolved my last defence. 'OK.'

The truth was, I'd been so alone, missing my few girlfriends in California. FaceTime and Skype just didn't cut it. And I'd been out of the UK for so long, I'd lost touch with most of my old mates here.

Apart from the odd call to Gray – back in West Africa again with the charity he and Stacey worked for – I'd barely spoken to anyone apart from Harry for weeks.

Well, and now Iris, though of course that was an effort in itself – a bit like a one-way conversation with a resistant wall.

'Thank you.' I fought the hot sting of tears – also a perpetual theme in my life. 'I'll just…' I hurried upstairs. Patti was nice – she seemed genuine, at least – and I really could use an ally right now.

I knocked tentatively.

Iris, no surprise, was back in bed, the duvet pulled over her mop of hair, her bashed and beloved skateboard leaning against her rucksack, its underside scored with scuffs and the many stickers she'd added over the past few years.

'Just popping out for a quick coffee and provisions.' I tried to stroke her head, but she shot away from my touch immediately, wriggling down in the bed.

'Won't be long, baby. Anything you want?'

Silence.

'Fancy a doughnut – or I know! A chocolate eclair? There's a nice little bakery on the high street. You love eclairs, don't you?'

Silence.

'Iris? Or how about a nice croissant? Then later we could check out the local skate park.'

'Jus' g'way.' The mumble came from deep beneath the covers.

'You OK though?' I was definitely trying too hard; desperate for a sign that it was all right to leave her.

'*Ma!*' The word was like a bullet. 'Go *awaaay*!'

I withdrew from the bed, stung but not surprised. 'I've got my phone if you need me, OK?' I paused at the door. 'When I get back, we'll make a plan, shall—'

A pillow whistled through the air towards me, and I ducked just in time. Closed the door softly behind me, resisting the childish temptation to slam it.

Iris: mired in her grief; not herself since that terrible day when Fraser hadn't returned home. Since the police had arrived with the worst news we would ever receive.

The bigger problem now was my fear around what she knew; of what had been going on between us before his death. I still wasn't sure.

But *I* knew, and I felt my own guilt that I hadn't realised how bad things had been for him; how low he'd got.

That was the cold, hard truth I had to live with.

9

Alex

Ten months ago, Laurel Springs, USA

I woke, sweating and bewildered, in the early hours, the night bleeding into dawn.

The dream had been terrible: a cougar snatching a baby Iris from her crib and sprinting into the trees with her whilst I struggled behind, my legs heavy as lead.

I opened my eyes to a dim light flickering through the slatted doors that led from our bedroom out to the side porch.

'What time is it?' My voice was cracked, my mouth dry from the air conditioning. I'd never got used to sleeping with it on, but Fraser was worried about snakes here in the hills. It wasn't safe to have a window open, he always said.

'Early. Dawn,' he whispered from the doorway, pulling on his old camouflage jacket.

'Are you going?' I sat halfway up in the bed.

'Yep. Go back to sleep, princess. I'll see you tomorrow night.'

'Fraser.'

He paused in the doorway. 'Yeah?'

I gazed at him for a long second, muddled thoughts swamping my dazed brain.

'Have fun.' I slumped back down onto the pillow, articulating none of them, loathing myself for the rows we'd had recently.

'Ta. Oh, and I'll take the dog. See you, princess.'

I heard the click of Nova's claws on the wooden floor; the front door shut and the garage open.

I knew he'd gone to get his guns. I'd hated for a long time – for ever, in fact – how much Fraser loved those weapons. How he cleaned and polished them lovingly, like they were his children, and, since we'd been in the USA, killed wild animals with them for sport.

It was part of him I didn't get; a part I really didn't like, that we argued about intermittently. It was his Scottish blood, he would say, his Celtic blood; he'd grown up in the Highlands, stalking deer with his dad, beating pheasant and grouse for the big estates, for the landowners and the aristocrats, while he and his pals had gone poaching at dusk for a stag to sell at local markets, using guns instead of cruel traps, or snares for the game.

This was no worse.

This weekend, Fraser had actually wanted to take Harry to initiate him, but I was unequivocal, telling him there was no way – only over my dead body.

And although he had then thought better of it himself, how desperately I would come to regret using that line.

Now I heard the soft *thunk* of the garage door coming down again – the car port, as the Americans liked to call it; the purr of the Lexus out on the road a few minutes later. Rich must have pulled up at the end of the drive, waiting for Fraser.

I recognised the sound of Rich's car from his last few visits; it was new, bigger, quieter than the old station wagon: an expensive hybrid.

I felt a terrible skittishness, anxiety traversing my skin too fast. My fist beneath the pillow clenching in an involuntary act.

I wished at least he'd left Nova – Nova was *my* dog, lying faithfully outside the bedroom door, not allowed in by Fraser but always there. Guarding me.

The faint whump of a car door slamming.

Fraser hates not driving himself; that was my last coherent thought. He hates being a passenger.

I lay down again, and although I thought I wouldn't, I soon drifted back into a messy broken sleep.

More than anything else, Fraser hated not being in control.

The following afternoon, I was distractedly emailing an editor about an updated page for a travel magazine I was late submitting, in between shelling peas and chopping onions for a risotto – very fancy, my friend and neighbour Bobbi would say, 'You ol' fancy schmance,' topping our coffee up from the filter pot – when I heard a familiar yet eerie whining.

The dog, on the back porch, panting frantically, her tongue lolling, her eyes filmy, her thick coat matted with dry earth and burrs.

'Jesus! Nova.' I rushed to the screen door, pushing it open as she collapsed. 'What's happened to you, girl?'

Nova, part dog, part wolf, we always said. Creature of the Native Americans; Fraser's other beloved, although I had bought and trained her.

Fraser must be back early, I thought.

But it wasn't him who arrived next.

It was the police.

For all my time living abroad, I had never got used to the sight of cops with guns.

I'd rung them after Nova returned; after I couldn't contact Fraser.

None of his group were answering their phones; not him, or his friend Rich, nor their partner in crime and manager Ernie.

All the phones went to voicemail – either out of range or out of battery. I rang Rich's wife Janine, but she was away, and her phone was off too.

Their boss Ernie's PA was pleasant and unconcerned: they'd probably just gone so deep in the mountains they had no signal.

The police had said they'd check with Mountain Rescue and come to take a statement if there was no news, but they didn't sound worried either.

'We've had no incident reports,' the officer said. 'Try not to fuss, Mrs Ross. They've probably just gone out further than planned. Happens all the time. They'll come back when they're good and ready.'

'But the dog has come back – alone,' I said flatly.

They were still indifferent. 'Dogs are like homing pigeons – they follow their own scent. But OK, we'll send someone when we can.'

'Boys will be boys' was the definite insinuation, and I felt a visceral stab of anger.

I was out the back, tending to Nova, when the police officer arrived.

'I'm sorry to bother you.' I felt ludicrously apologetic, but I couldn't help feeling the animal looked haunted, somehow. 'I'm sure they've just gone higher up the mountain than originally intended, but I'd like to be sure.'

'What *was* the plan, Mrs Ross?' The officer scratched his bald spot with the end of his pen, clearly disinterested.

'They went hunting, a few of them from Fraser's work, Pacific Insurance. Boys' trip, you know.' Fraser's boss Ernie had his finger in many pies; he'd done a huge property deal recently, which they'd all bought into. 'Celebrating shares in a property in…' My mind went blank. 'A massive deal,' I went on stupidly. 'Somewhere in the south, maybe?' It was completely irrelevant, of course, but it suddenly felt terribly important to remember. 'Texas?'

'I'll put another call in to Mountain Rescue, see if there's any update,' the officer said. ''Scuse me a mo.' He wandered out onto the porch, muttering into his buzzing radio.

Chatter chatter chatter, Bobbi went mechanically – but watching the policeman's back, I began to feel a chill, despite the warmth of the late-autumn day. Fall, as they called it here in the States.

Pride before a fall, a fall in…

I was losing my mind.

I returned to my chopping, just for something to do, staring mindlessly at my poor dog, now panting on her mat. She'd eaten a few scraps, drunk a ton of water, but she didn't look right.

She kept gazing up at the door and whining.

I'll phone the vet in a minute, I was thinking absently as the cop came back in.

'I expect they just got carried away, right, Officer?' Bobbi's voice trailed off.

I looked up from my frantic onion chopping. I looked at the man's face – and I saw in an instant that he knew something I didn't want to hear.

Most of all, in that endless and confusing day, the single piece of clarity I retained was being infinitely relieved the children were both at school.

Thank God, I thought: *thank God they're not here to hear this*. Yet.

To hear that Fraser was missing; that they'd located the rest of the party but without my husband.

My guilt was huge. However much I wanted it to be different, it never could be. If I wished for ever that I'd got out of bed that morning, in that pearly-coloured dawn, it would still never happen. It was too late to change my actions.

I waited by the phone, pacing and pacing, details coming through: that he had fallen awkwardly after a landslide of shale from a higher peak; lost his balance, fallen off the sheer rock face, Rich had tried desperately to grab him, but to no avail…

Eventually I heard the worst.

I spent the next hour throwing up, alone and frantic. Bobbi picked up my children, my poor bereft kids, from school and brought them back with her girls.

Terrible tragedy: a hunting accident, the local press reported. *Fell down the ravine after a small landslide in pursuit of his prey… another member of the party badly hurt with fractured arm and ribs.*

But even then I didn't suspect the other, alternative truth.

When I visited Rich in the hospital, days later, alone in his private room, strapped up and bandaged, his loquacious wife Janine down in the cafeteria fetching coffee, he told me, wincing with pain, how shocking it had been watching Fraser fall into nothingness like that.

He told me how devastated he felt that despite his best efforts, injured himself, he couldn't save my husband.

I looked at him and I knew he couldn't comfort me, and I couldn't help feeling that somehow Fraser's death was all my fault.

That if I had tried to stop him going out that morning – or at least if we hadn't been rowing the night before, if he hadn't been so constantly stressed about targets at work, if I'd been more clued up or understanding about his monetary fears – things might have ended differently.

But it was too late.

Regret. The bastard child of hindsight and loss. That was what I knew I would live with for ever.

10

Alex

Monday

'All right, Patti!' The young waitress smiled as we walked into the warm café. 'Usual, is it?'

'Yes please, babs.' Patti was obviously a regular at the Black Cat. 'And Alex will have a...' She looked at me encouragingly.

'Just a black coffee please.'

'This is Hazel's place.' Patti nodded at the curvaceous woman behind the counter, on the phone, taking a long order by the sounds of it. 'She's got Josh, who plays centre back for the Tigers.'

As I followed Patti to a table in the middle of the room, Hazel waved at us, rolling her eyes and pointing at the phone as if to convey the person on the other end was vastly irritating. And with a jolt, I realised *she* was the attractive woman in the leopard-skin coat whom I'd seen at the club, out in the car park with Dez.

'Centre back means nothing to me, I'm afraid,' I admitted. 'Looks like I've got a lot to learn.'

'You *what*?' Patti's smile was nice and neat. 'You don't know every position on the pitch? Centre back just means he's a defender.'

'Aha.' I felt almost embarrassed. 'But yes, I'm still none the wiser about football.'

'Good Lord, an Englishwoman who hasn't been subjected to endless and deadly weekends of football all her life? To squeezing into football stands and freezing her bits off every Saturday afternoon?' Patti was really hitting her stride now. 'To drunken FA Cup finals that end in piles of vomit, tears or fist fights – or worse, nervous breakdowns when the home team loses?'

I shook my head. 'My dad and brother were more into cricket, and my… Harry's dad, his game was ice hockey. And baseball, after being in America a while.'

'Ice hockey, is that right?' Patti said comfortably as the young waitress unloaded our drinks from her tray. 'Ta, babs. Sounds very exotic. My dad was more into rugby, I have to say, typical Welshie, but my brothers love their footie too.'

I stirred my drink, pointlessly, to give my hands something to do. Fraser had been far from exotic, and yet when we first met, when I'd got a job on the campsite in the Scottish mountains after university, he'd seemed wild and rugged; an adventurer with whom I'd shared a love of nature and the outdoors, something I'd inherited from my parents.

Both of us were consumed by wanderlust, and life had seemed infinitely possible and glamorous for a while. Before I realised there *was* no wild glamour in emergency insurance, the career path my new husband had, to my enduring surprise, eventually chosen to take.

'What star sign are you, sugar?'

I was wrenched back to the present. 'No sugar, thanks. Just black for me.'

'No, what *star sign* are you?' Patti regarded me through narrowed eyes. 'Let me guess, you're a—'

'A Leo. Just.' I tried to sound like I was interested in astrology, though I very definitely wasn't. 'Nearly a Cancerian, I think. Something about cusps.'

'Hmm, that makes more sense. I wouldn't have had you down for a Leo.' Patti spooned so much sugar into her hot chocolate I nearly winced. 'Very extrovert usually. But your rising sign matters more.'

'Extrovert?' I repeated slowly. 'No, I can't say that sounds like me.'

'Ladies! On the house.' Hazel arrived with a slab of fluffy Victoria sponge. Sticking her biro into her intricate pile of dreads, she perched on the edge of the table, swinging her foot in its chunky Doc Marten. 'Sorry I missed the party, Pats, I was so swamped on Saturday I couldn't get away. Josh had fun though.'

'No worries, babs,' Patti said comfortably. 'But you were missed.'

I stirred my coffee uneasily. Hazel was definitely lying about not being there, and I didn't really want to guess why. I was just relieved she hadn't seen me in the car park that afternoon.

'So what do you reckon to all the to-do, eh?' Now Hazel really perked up. 'Can't say I'm totally surprised to hear that Neil's an out-and-out racist.'

'I don't know, babs, but no doubt about it, he's going to have to step down.' Patti sliced the cake in half neatly. 'It's not really fitting, is it? Not for the manager of the team.'

'Not fitting to have been a member of a racist party? I should coco.'

'And I can't get a squeak out of Linda at the moment. She's totally gone to ground. I'm a bit worried, you know.'

'Poor Lindy.' Their eyes met knowingly. 'But who's going to take over if Neil's out?'

'Dez, I should think, wouldn't you? He's been angling all season for it.' Patti pushed half of the sponge towards me. 'Though I bet Riker's got his eye on the prize too. Has done since he managed to get half the players sacked last season. All that complaining about the standard…'

'Oh, that Riker winds me up. He's so bossy on the sideline, shouting at the poor kids all the time – *Do this, do that!* Josh loathes him. He's a proper bloody—'

'Don't say it!' Patti raised one perfectly manicured hand, and I hid my own bitten nails under the table. 'Even if we *are* all thinking it. You'll only be as bad as Neil if you do.'

'Hardly.' Hazel looked indignant. 'And I mean, good God! I knew he might have the potential to be a bit right wing, but honestly, I had no idea. What an arse!'

'Sorry, but,' I dared to interrupt now, intrigued, 'what exactly is Neil meant to have done?'

'I wouldn't expect *you'd* be surprised.' Patti ate some cake with great delicacy. 'You saw a bit of his temper the other week, didn't you? When he asked you to move your motor?'

'Yes.' How could I forget my heart nearly stopping when I heard the pounding at the door? I cleared my throat. 'So what's he been up to then?'

'It only turns out that our dear manager, our friend Linda's best beloved…' Patti paused for dramatic effect, and dropped her voice. 'It only goes and turns out he used to belong to the National Front.'

'For years, by the looks of things.' Hazel gave her dreads a regal push upwards, her anger clear and crisp. 'Member of all sorts of untoward groups, the absolute *bastard*.'

'Oh wow. That sounds… bad.' I crumbled a bit of my cake. 'So how did you find out?'

'Because *someone*' – Patti's eyes were bright – 'has made it public. Very public.' She dragged a phone out of her pocket, extending the screen to me. 'Get a load of this little lot.'

A video, on pause, entitled *Tales of Tenderton.*

'Just click on it, sugar.'

'Oh, I can't bear to watch it again.' Hazel picked up Patti's empty mug and plate with a clatter. 'It makes me too cross when I see what he's been up to.'

Halfway through the shocking and strange little clip, I was vaguely aware of the café door opening and a dark-haired man entering.

'Awful, isn't it?' Patti murmured as it rattled to its sad end.

'It's pretty horrible, if it's true. But who made it?'

'Hang on a sec.' Patti frowned at me. '*If* it's true?'

'Well.' I felt uncomfortable under her scrutiny. 'I suppose I'm just thinking of, you know, the whole notion of fake news. I know it might sound a bit Trump-like, but it does happen.'

'Oh.' Patti frowned. 'Well, yes, I suppose there is that, but—'

'And the area I work in, it's not hard to construct things like that.'

'What area's that then?'

'Graphics. I was a… I'm a graphic designer.' Who desperately needed to get a job, and soon, though I refrained from asking if she knew anyone who needed someone like me. 'It's pretty easy these days to mock things up on computers.'

'It's definitely not fake.' Hazel glared at me, coming to wipe our crumbs up. 'Meadow's mates with that bloke from the bike shop, who went to school with Neil. He says it all stacks up from what he remembers of him back then.'

She stomped off to the counter.

'I'd better get back.' Conscious of the mounting tension, I felt for my purse. 'Don't want to leave Iris too long.'

'Put your money away, babs. It's on me.' Patti pushed her phone towards me. 'And put your number in, eh?'

'Oh, sure.' Obediently I picked it up. Patti wasn't giving up on me, I realised, and in a way, it was a relief to be told what to do. It took the onus off me for once.

'How old's your Iris then?'

'Fifteen.' Carefully I entered my number and passed the phone back. 'Fifteen going on fifty.'

'Oho, you got one of those too, have you? Starting at St George's, is she?' Patti's phone blipped as soon as it arrived back in her hand.

'Yes, tomorrow.' I didn't say Iris was meant to have started today, but had point-blank refused to get out of bed. Some things just weren't worth sharing. 'She needs to get back into it, I think. She's missed a bit, what with being in Scotland.'

But halfway through this sentence, looking at Patti's face, I saw I'd lost her attention.

'Oh dear,' she breathed. 'Oh good Lord.'

'What's wrong?'

'You too?' Hazel waved her own phone from behind the counter. 'Don't like the tone of this, I must say. No one's safe.'

'What is it?' I was curious.

Patti flipped the screen so I could see the message. *Who will be next in Tenderton? No one's secret is safe till it's all out there…*

'Oh.' I shivered. 'It's a bit… threatening.'

'Isn't it just.' Patti pocketed her phone decisively. 'But let's not give the idiots the time of day, whoever they are. Sorry, babs, you were saying – about your girl starting school. They love it really, don't they? For all their moaning, they need to be with their mates.'

'Guess so.' A distraught Iris had absolutely loathed school by the end of our time in the States; she'd almost stopped going at all. And of course, she didn't have any friends here in Kent. Yet…

I cast up a silent prayer. 'Anyway, I'd better get back. Thanks so much for the coffee, Patti. Hope they manage to sort the' – I glanced at the counter, where a man was talking to Hazel, and dropped my voice – 'the problem at the club.'

'Ah, well, if those dads have anything to do with it, I'm sure it's all in hand already. They're nothing if not competitive; they'll be lining up to take over. Which reminds me, is Harry coming to training again on Saturday? He'll need to sign up properly if he's going to actually play, but I expect you know that already.'

'Thanks.' I knew nothing. 'I'm sure he'd like to come, if he's allowed.'

'Course he's allowed, babs. He's very welcome. I don't know if he'll get many games this season, mind – not that it's up to me – but he can definitely train with the others.'

'Great.'

'Seems like a lovely kid. All right, Jack.' She nodded at the man, now on his way out with a coffee. 'Don't see you round this way much these days.'

'Patti.' He nodded back. 'Nope. I'm not here if I can help it.'

'Too many memories, eh?' She winked at him.

'Something like that.' His wry smile was crooked, I noticed, as my own phone pinged. I glanced at it: Iris, demanding Diet Coke and crisps.

'Better go.' I stood. 'Thanks again, Patti.'

At the door, I caught up with the man called Jack. In a black parka and jeans, he was lean, a bit taller than me, dark hair shot with grey, tousled, possibly expensively, though it was hard to tell.

'New to Tenderton?' He held the door for me. 'Settling in?'

His gaze was very direct, I thought uncomfortably; his hazel eyes heavy-lidded but penetrating.

'New, yes.' I passed under his arm, noting the scar on his right cheek. A deep one, old and healed.

'Don't stay too long.' Outside, he let the door go behind us. 'Or you'll get stuck.'

'Oh. Well, I only just…'

But he'd gone, leaving me goldfishing to myself as he sauntered to the corner and out of sight, whistling under his breath.

All things considered, I felt remarkably put out.

11

Patti

Saturday 26 September: Libra, with Pluto retrograde

After the vlog incident, no one had been sure if training would go ahead on Saturday. But according to last night's message from Neil, apparently it was business as usual – although it remained to be seen who would actually turn up.

In the club car park, having dropped Ethan off, Patti sat in her old Ford Fiesta, nursing her thermos mug and watching the Tigers manager stride out of the clubhouse in his old tracksuit. With a net of balls over one shoulder, plastic cones in the other hand, everything about his body language screamed anxious defiance.

Well, Neil *was* a Taurus – she'd double-checked earlier – so his bullish nature would make sense.

None of the boys had emerged from the changing room as, butterflies in her belly, Patti texted the coven, including Hazel, Liz and Nancy, to say she'd arrived. Despite her words in the café the other day, Patti had agreed with the other mothers that it was politic that they spoke to Neil first, before the dads. More hormones maybe but far less testosterone.

Although she *had* still asked Sam to accompany her, as backup.

'My sciatica's really playing up, love,' he'd replied as she bundled Ethan's kit into his bag. 'It hurts too much to move today. Sorry.'

He was always claiming that these days; another reason for their dwindling sex life.

Dwindling?

Who was she kidding?

Totally dwindled was more accurate.

On top of Sam's lack of solidarity, her friend Linda had avoided her all week. On one hand, Patti understood this, but on the other, it was frustrating. Everyone kept asking her what Linda thought about the awful vlog about Neil, and if it was all true, and had Linda known all along about her husband. Patti could only imagine that Linda was reeling, like the rest of them – though with rather more reason to feel deep embarrassment; and yet she also wondered if everyone who enquired about her was as morally pure themselves as they might like to pretend.

People were nervous; the vlog post was undoubtedly a double-edged sword. It brought a thrill of the old *Schadenfreude* – there but for the grace of God go I – but also a terror *they* might actually be next.

Truthfully, though, Patti was relieved she'd not seen Linda, because what on earth was she going to say to her mate if the accusations turned out to be true? And right now, she could see no reason why they wouldn't be.

It was all there in black and white on the screen, along with a set of photos of an angry mob protesting in Trafalgar Square – in the late seventies, by the looks of the terrible denim flares – disgusting, racist National Front placards held high. Honestly, though, it was hard to see if the tiny pale dot of a face in the crowd, circled in red, was Neil or not.

The car's clock flicked to 9.55 a.m. as Nancy's silver X6 swung past, pulling up by the clubhouse. Training started in five minutes – and by the looks of it, some of the lads hadn't turned up at all.

Patti's sigh was deeply felt. All she really wanted was a day off: a day to herself, without work or kids or this kind of extracurricular rubbish. She'd spend it with her feet in the whirly spa, doing her moon chart for next year and listening to *Astral Weeks* by Van Morrison, or maybe a podcast, those funny middle-aged *Fortunately* women...

'Hey, Neil!' Riker Bauer came striding down the path to intercept the manager, who'd stopped to check his phone, no doubt pinging with parental excuses.

'All right there.' Neil picked up the cones again, attempted to walk around Riker towards the pitches.

'I want a word.' Hands on hips, Riker stood in his way.

'Can it wait, mate?'

Patti, despite her personal lack of love for Neil, felt her own hackles rise as she heard Riker bark, 'I can't believe you'd write such bullshit or march for white rights.'

'No,' Neil agreed, his face reddening. 'And I didn't.'

'You didn't? It was all made up?'

'Well, the thing is—'

'So that's not you in the photos?' Riker's wife Liz, the lawyer, had joined him now. Side by side the couple stood, very neat and efficient-looking in matching quilted jackets, as if they were models for an advert for fell running or some other dull but wholesome activity. 'Or in the YouTube footage of that march?'

Patti had a sudden vision of the Bauers' bedroom, of them engaged in athletic, efficient sex.

Good Lord! What was wrong with her, constantly imagining other people's sex lives?

She watched as Neil tried to circumnavigate the Bauers again.

'No. Well, no, but…' He trailed off hopelessly. They'd blocked his way.

'If that's true, and it's not you, you can sue for defamation of character,' Liz said briskly. 'I would.'

'Yeah, well, I'm definitely thinking about it.' Neil's chin jutted forward like a boxer, only one who was waiting to be punched. 'But right now, we need to get on with training.'

'Ha!' Dez appeared out of nowhere now, in his best Wolves tracksuit. 'Sue *who* though?'

Patti didn't believe the suing thing for a moment. She knew full well that the Forths didn't have that kind of money for a start. The garage did all right, but Linda earned almost nothing as a teaching assistant at the local primary school, and they'd just had an extension built on their fifties house on the village outskirts, with a wet room and a ramp for Angel's wheelchair to access the garden more easily.

'Kids on the pitch?' Neil swung the footballs back over his shoulder.

'Er, I don't think so, mate.' Dez's tone was almost conversational as Patti eased herself out of her car, shutting the door quietly. Her hope that things wouldn't turn nasty was an entirely hollow one, she saw now.

'See you back here at twelve.' Neil stepped round Dez. 'Hunter's been playing really well, I meant to say.'

'Mate.' Dez shook his head sorrowfully. 'You must realise you need to take a step back. For the time being, at least.'

'No way.' Neil's chin jutted even further, if that was possible. 'This is my club.'

'It's the boys' club, isn't it?' Liz narrowed her eyes.

'Well, yeah, sure, I just meant—'

'And I dunno about you lot' – Dez looked at the Bauers, both with arms folded, then over at Patti – 'but I don't want some bigot training my kid. It's not like racism's not a huge issue in sport already. Just look at Rio and Anton Ferdinand's campaigns, or Marcus Rashford getting trolled, or Lauren James's recent abuse. I mean, the list's endless.'

'You're right, it's terrible.' Patti soothed Dez as Linda hurried up the path, handbag swinging from her shoulder. She wished Nancy would hurry up, but she still hadn't joined them, though Patti was sure she'd been in the BMW's driving seat. 'But as far as Neil's concerned, Dez love, nothing's actually proven yet.'

'What's going on?' Linda was a mixture of wary and angry. 'Leave Neil alone, yeah?'

Dez looked at Patti, all suggestion of flirtation gone, fury flashing in his dark eyes. 'You mightn't be bothered about this racist idiot…'

'I'm not racist!' Neil blustered.

'… but some of us have good reason to be.'

'You mean because you're…' Liz hesitated.

'Black? Yeah, say how it is, babe. Some of us have had to put up with this crap all our bloody lives.'

'It applies to me too. I'm an immigrant, if you like.' Riker moved nearer to Dez, who was almost hopping with anger now. 'So what you supported, Neil, is against me too.' When he got heated, Riker's syntax went a bit funny, Patti noted absently.

'What do you mean, *if I like*?' Neil shook his head vehemently. 'I don't have a problem with immigrants. I took on Declan and Mikhail didn't I?'

'Oh, big of you,' Liz snapped. 'One Polish kid, and Declan's from the travelling community, not an immigrant at all.'

'You know what I mean.'

'No, I don't actually.' Liz pursed her lips tight.

'I think you do have a problem,' Riker said bluntly. 'That is why you took so long to play Maxi up front.'

'That's complete bollocks.' Neil's eyes were bulging with disbelief. 'He just needed to build his confidence on the pitch, that's all. And he's British anyway, isn't he?'

'He was born in Munich,' Riker snapped. 'He has a German passport.'

'Excuse my French, but that's not the fucking point, is it? The point is, if you have no problems with race, Neil' – Dez's anger was threatening to burst out now – 'then why join the National Front?' He took a step forward. 'If you're not a racist, why would you even think of it? Everyone knows they hated black people. Hated anyone not white—'

Nervously Patti looked at Riker. If Dez lost it physically with Neil, which looked increasingly likely, who was going to hold him back? She cast a quick glance at the BMW. Definitely no Nancy; just a younger man she didn't recognise, tallish and slim, light brown hair pushed back from his face by a thin band. Leaning on the bonnet, grinning at his phone, he was apparently oblivious to what was happening.

'I think we should all calm down, yeah?' She put a tentative hand on Dez's arm. 'Let's go inside, talk about it sensibly, in the warm.'

'No way!' Riker said petulantly. 'Neil, will you resign?'

'Everyone has mistakes in their past,' Linda chirruped, her face beginning to change colour from pasty white to red above an unflattering beige polo neck.

'Linda!' Neil snapped.

'Mistakes? Aha – so you admit it then!'

'Dez,' Patti tried again, 'how about a cuppa?'

'Don't be stupid, Patti.' Dez threw her hand off impatiently. Much taller than Neil, he was imposing; frightening even as his fury grew. 'Be a proper man, mate, and do the right thing.'

'Which is *what*?' Neil was almost, but not quite, quivering, though whether with fear or rage it was hard to tell. 'I've put my heart and soul into this club, and I'm not a racist.'

Thank God! Patti was relieved to see Tony Burton's carpet-fitting van pulling into the car park – Declan, the new boy Mikhail, and Tony's son Tony Jnr squashed in the back.

'Step aside, obviously, and let someone else take over.'

'What I want to know' – Linda stepped forward now, in front of her husband, her wide face mottled with emotion – 'is who posted this, and why. What was the point of it?'

'It doesn't matter, does it?' Dez spat. 'The point is the information's all there, plain as day. They've done us all a favour, whoever they are, and right now, you need to do one, mate.'

'All right, people?' Tony bowled over in his work gear. 'What's occurring?'

'Sorry, Chloe needed a wee.' Nancy finally appeared with the three-year-old in her arms. 'Dezzie, calm down, darlin', would you?' Her French-braided hair was as immaculate as her white jeans and Timberlands. 'It's not worth getting this upset, yeah?' She nudged her husband gently. 'We said that, didn't we, remember?'

'*What?*' Dez looked at his wife like he couldn't think who she was, but he didn't shake her off as he had with Patti.

'I don't want you to get so upset,' Nancy said quietly. 'It's not worth it. It's just Sunday League.'

Everyone bristled at that.

'But I *am* upset,' Dez mumbled, reminding Patti of her son Ethan when he felt someone – usually a teacher or his sister – had done him a great injustice.

'With respect, Mrs Fullerton, I disagree.' Riker bowed his head to Nancy. 'It *is* very upsetting. I myself am shocked at the content of the video, as is my wife.'

'And you're not the only ones.' Hazel had appeared now too, dragging a surly-looking Josh behind her. 'It's absolutely flipping disgraceful! And Maria's not letting Kyran come back till this is cleared up.'

'Patti?' Linda around wildly for support, whilst Neil just looked like a belligerent bulldog who'd been force-fed a wasp: stuck between anger and tears.

'But do we know it's true?' ventured Tony, looking a little nervous. Dez and Riker were both much taller and angrier than him.

'Why don't we all go and have a sensible chat about it,' Patti repeated, but it was pointless. They were all so cross and unwilling to listen – and mostly she could understand why.

Only… Alex's words chimed somewhere in the back of her mind. *Fake news.*

'A chat? Over my dead body,' Dez snarled.

'Dezzie!' Nancy gestured at their daughter Chloe, happily waving at her brothers and pulling on her mother's plaits.

As oblivious as their little sister, by the looks of it, the two Fullerton boys were kicking a ball around with Maxi Bauer. Hazel's son Josh escaped his mother's grasp to join them.

'I'm not going to put up with it.' Hazel crossed her arms. 'It's bad enough always feeling like an outsider, but this is despicable.'

'Nor me,' agreed Liz Bauer. 'Frankly, if you don't step back, Neil, until this is sorted—'

'No way.' Neil was going redder by the second. Finding a hanky in his pocket, he wiped his sweaty forehead.

'You're not welcome here, mate, haven't you got the message?' Dez hopped from one monogrammed Nike trainer to the other. 'Sling your hook!'

Tony started to mutter something about giving people chances, but Neil had already dumped the net of footballs on the path.

'Have it your way. I'll step back while you sort it, and you lot can take over training. Perhaps then you'll see how much effort I put in. How much time I give up.'

Patti realised with a lurch that she was actually feeling bad for him.

'No one's saying you don't work hard for the club.' Liz Bauer sounded so patronising, Patti almost winced. 'But you must understand, Neil, it's not good for the boys to be associated with this kind of vitriol.'

'Who's behind this, that's what I want to know.' Linda was crying now, fat tears running down her puffy face, looking round at all of them pleadingly. 'Why have you got it in for Neil? For us!' Her son Davey – named thirteen years ago for Neil's idol Beckham – stood behind his mother, looking mortified beyond belief. 'Neil just cares about the boys, that's all.'

Patti saw Ethan emerge from the clubhouse, gazing at his phone.

'Eth,' she called, 'why don't you boys go and do a… a warm-up?' she improvised.

''K.' He shrugged. 'C'mon, Davey.'

Davey was torn though, looking from his parents to Ethan and back again, until Maxi Bauer slammed his ball into the wall right behind the group of adults, almost grazing his father's arm.

'Maximilian!' his father snapped. 'For God's sake!'

'Sorry.' Head down, the boy grabbed the ball and ran off to join the others, Davey following. They didn't seem very interested in all of this, Patti thought, as she watched them head towards the far pitch, jostling like puppies. Thank God for small mercies.

Neil gave a small groan and turned away.

'Go on, admit it!' Linda's cry was desperate. 'You've wanted to get rid of Neil for ages. Which one of you cooked this up?'

'Ah, that's not true, babs.' Patti tried to soothe her friend. 'Neil has been very much appreciated.'

'Not me.' Nonchalantly Dez kicked at a raised paving stone with his trainer toe. 'But I'm happy to take over as manager temporarily. Starting now, in fact.' He picked up the ball net. 'Louie's going to help me out. That all right with everyone?'

'Who the hell's Louie?' Neil expostulated as Alex's clanky old Land Rover pulled into the car park, offering a welcome distraction.

Nancy nodded her pretty head towards the muscular young man in white T-shirt and tracksuit lounging against her car. 'My naughty little brother. He's just been released from Millwall under-22s with a shoulder injury, so he's staying for a bit.'

He didn't look so little to her, Patti thought, as he caught her eye and smiled shyly.

'Know your stuff, don't ya, Louie?' Dez swung the net over his shoulder. 'Right, well. We got a cup to win, yeah?'

'I don't believe this.' Swearing under his breath, Neil stomped off to his van, followed by a sobbing Linda.

'Oh dear.' Patti exchanged an uncomfortable look with Hazel. This was not what any of them had signed up for.

'Get on with you.' Riker whistled to his sons as if they were dogs. 'Meet me at the corner at twelve thirty-five sharp, OK, and we'll go on to the gym. Come on, Frederick.' He put his hand out for the youngest, now busy killing ants with a sharp stick. 'Hurry now.'

Honestly, Patti thought irritably, he really was so very… Germanic sometimes.

'Hey!' Skinny Harry Ross jogged up, wearing an LA Lakers tracksuit. 'My mom says sorry I'm late.'

'Better late than never.' Dez was cheery, all anger apparently dissipated now. 'Let's do it, yeah?'

Clapping an arm around Harry's shoulders, he flashed Patti a devastating smile, which made her knees feel a bit trembly. She watched him stride off towards the pitches, followed by his lanky brother-in-law, hood up now and still grinning at his phone.

A screech of rubber drew all eyes to the car park gates.

Neil, revving madly, Linda mopping her eyes beside him, before he bombed off, too fast, away from the village.

And that, as they say, was that.

Except it wasn't. As it turned out, it was only just beginning.

12

Alex

As I arrived to drop Harry off, the argument between the gaggle of parents outside the clubhouse was immediately obvious.

Behind them, the woods loomed dark and large and impenetrable, more imposing than ever on this dull autumn day, and I felt a shiver of unease.

Dressed in what looked like pyjama bottoms and an anorak so enormous it swamped her, Patti was trying to placate the group of people gathered around the balding manager, Neil. From the hysterical gesturing and his expression, along with the tears pouring down his wife's face, it wasn't hard to guess what was going on.

This sort of scene was exactly what I didn't want to get involved in. I remembered similar things from my own rural childhood: parochial village politics and back-stabbing; whispers in the grocer's shop. And yet I had to let Harry join in with team sports; it was vital for his well-being to make friends quickly, to be part of a community.

'Are you sure you're OK to walk back with Ethan?' I kissed his warm freckled cheek, savouring both his familiar smell and the fact that he still let me do it.

It was something Iris very definitely didn't allow anymore.

'Course!' Grabbing his water bottle, he jumped out of the car to be met by that handsome footballer guy Dez.

'Don't go through the woods though,' I called lamely after Harry. I wasn't exactly sure why – I'd grown up in the countryside myself, but these woods felt different. They seemed forbidding and unfathomable, as if they held their own trouble, too near the supposed Pool of Sorrow, which had seen so many deaths. I had the uneasy if daft idea that if he went in, my son might never emerge again.

'Good to see you, Alex,' Dez called, and I felt my face heat up like a teenager as I returned his smile shyly.

As Harry ran to join the boys already halfway across the first pitch, I backed the car up hurriedly, doing my best to avoid eye contact with any of the other parents, apart from a quick wave to Patti. I knew I would need to start being more friendly soon, but to be honest, right now I had more pressing things on my mind.

This morning had started badly. To my great dismay, I'd received another email from the American insurance company, saying they were still dotting the Is on their investigation for the claim on Fraser's life policy.

They promised to be in touch again forthwith – which was meaningless as far as I could tell, and what they'd been saying for the best part of six months.

It was starting to look like a very real possibility that they wouldn't pay up. If the money didn't come through, and soon, I didn't know what we'd do. We couldn't live at Primrose Cottage for ever.

After I'd read the email, hand trembling on the keyboard, I'd sent a hesitant and businesslike one of my own to Fraser's best friend and colleague Rich, outlining what had happened – or rather, not happened so far – with the insurance, and asking him to please call when he could. I was hoping he'd have more sway with the company than I did – plus he was in the right country.

We hadn't spoken in person since I'd flown out of LAX airport three months ago. I didn't know if I felt more nervous about the fact Rich might not get back to me or the fact that a tiny part of me was horribly keen to hear his voice.

A mixture of bribery and bossiness got Iris out of bed and into town, though I was congratulating myself less by the time we left the coffee shop on the busy high street.

I'd been hoping that being away from the house might give us a chance to chat properly: that Iris would tell me more about staying with her grandma in Scotland; that she might open up a bit about her grief – how she really felt about the loss of her dad – and that I might be able to explain that I was grieving deeply too, whatever she might think.

Honestly, it seemed like Iris had taken a national diploma in moaning since she'd hit puberty – particularly at me. But when we lost Fraser, *everything* changed.

Always a daddy's girl, she had stopped talking altogether. Utterly traumatised, she had even given up moaning – unlike my mother-in-law Fiona, a woman unhappy with her lot in life, and with whom Iris had chosen to stay on the banks of Loch Ness, rather than come straight to Kent with me.

Ostensibly the visit was just until I'd sorted out Iris's school place, but there was a less palatable truth: the fact that my daughter seemed to hate my guts right now, preferring her grandmother's company. A link to her father, I tried to placate myself.

Yes, Iris appeared beyond furious with me for things I didn't quite comprehend – other than that I was the remaining parent. *The wrong parent*, a little voice muttered in my ear.

I was also hoping she'd understood she really did have to start school properly now – not just the half-day she'd done last week. I wasn't taking any more excuses. I just needed to persuade her that she'd make friends; maybe find someone who shared her love of all things skateboard right here in Tenderton...

But even a caramel brownie and a large mango smoothie hadn't helped Iris's mood, whilst my own black coffee was probably one too many this morning.

Jittery and increasingly on edge as I tried in vain to coax a single word out of my daughter, I was met with either the top of her head as she toyed with her phone or a hostile gaze if I demanded an answer.

'Let's go to the shoe shop then.' I tried hard not to bang my mug down in frustration, but it wouldn't have mattered if I had. Baseball cap back on, Iris was already halfway out of the door.

As I caught her up on the pedestrianised main street, dodging shoppers, my own phone pinged. I pulled it out without thinking.

'God, Mum.' Iris rolled her eyes. 'Are you an addict or what?'

'What, honey?' I looked up. 'Oh, sorry.'

'Can't you just put it down for a second?' Mimicking me, I realised too late. 'You're, like, addicted to that thing.'

I grinned, willing to go along with the joke – until I realised she was deadly serious.

'I just thought it might be Hal.'

It wasn't; it was Patti. She was taking Harry back to hers with Ethan, if that was OK with me.

Drop in for coffee on your way back.

More coffee; more gossip. The nasty but riveting idea of another local being hauled over the coals of the horrible vlog...

And yet, female warmth too – the friendly kind, not the burnt-at-the-stake type.

'I'll just quickly…' Texting a swift reply, I heard a massive gasp beside me.

'*Oh my God!*'

'Iris? My phone went flying as I whirled round. 'What is it? Have you hurt yourself?'

'Dad!' A strangled cry, as if she'd just been garrotted. 'Dad!'

'Iris!' I shot an arm out to stop her, but it was too late. She was off, sprinting down the street, banging into people, one woman's shopping trolley going flying, oranges rolling under feet. She was a blur as I scrabbled on the ground for my phone, yelling her name. 'Iris! Wait!'

'She ought to be more careful!' The elderly woman, groceries spilt across the pavement, was deeply upset, despite my apologies. 'I could have broken my hip.'

'I'm so sorry.' Quickly I gathered as much of the fruit as I could, shoving it into the trolley before chasing Iris again, still apologising over my shoulder.

But she was lost in the crowd. Only her Dodgers cap was left, lying at my feet, battered and faded. Fraser had bought it for her at a New York game one Thanksgiving weekend, before she got so cross and he became too depressed for family trips. I scooped it up, navigating my way round a stall selling knock-off perfume to skinny women in ill-fitting anoraks, when I spotted my daughter again through the dwindling throng, skidding round a corner into a side street.

'Iris!' I shouted, not caring who was staring now.

Turning into the small alley myself, I saw her circling on the spot outside a little parade of shops, keening like the mourner she was, while a middle-aged auburn-haired man in a beige jacket hurried away from her in embarrassment.

A man I guessed Iris must have thought – must have hoped beyond hope – was her father; a man who was, of course, a complete stranger.

As Iris wheeled in confusion, a thin woman in a long floaty dress emerged from a small shop. She wafted over to my daughter and put her arms around her.

Out of breath, I slowed, expecting Iris to push the woman off in anger. But to my huge surprise, she let herself be led inside. I sped up again, calling her name loudly.

By the time I reached the shop, Iris had disappeared.

The shop was called At the End of the Moon, the dark blue front painted with silvery moons of all sizes and shapes, interspersed with gold stars, the windows hung with twinkly fairy lights and posters for local harp concerts and psychic readings.

One side of the window display held a small array of musical instruments: a ukulele, an acoustic guitar or two, a flute, all pretty dusty.

The shop seemed to be some sort of spiritual haven, and although it was far from my kind of thing, God only knew both Iris and I needed a slice of sanctuary right now.

A bell tinkled lightly as I stepped through the door, straight into a cloying fog of sweet incense, strange drifty music playing quietly from an old stereo in the corner.

Over Iris's head, the woman met my eyes, smiling faintly – and I realised we'd met before.

It was the ethereal Meadow, the hippy with the love of all things vegan and organic from Ethan's birthday party, mother of the Tigers' goalkeeper Ocean – two names I remembered because they were so outlandish.

'Welcome to you, Alex, and to Iris.' Meadow clasped large, bony hands before her in a prayer position, bowing her multicoloured fringe over them. 'Namaste.'

For the first time, I caught her northern accent properly.

'Hello.' I nodded back. 'Iris, I was worried.'

Iris didn't respond as, violet chiffon dress trailing behind her on the tiled floor, Meadow sat my daughter on a purple velvet chair in a tiny wooden booth in the far corner of the shop. 'Madam Zara isn't reading today, so you can be my fortune-teller if you like, duck.'

I really hoped she was joking.

'Thank you, but' – I checked my watch – 'we really ought to be—'

'Ocean,' Meadow spoke over my head, 'put the kettle on, there's a good lad. We've got visitors.'

The solid boy appeared through the sparkly bead curtain at the back of the shop. 'What?'

'Not what, pardon. Iris here needs a little pick-me-up, don't you, ducky? Get her a camomile tea please.' She turned to me. 'And one for you?'

'I'm fine thanks. Not training today?' I said brightly to the boy.

'We didn't feel it was appropriate, did we?' His mother spoke for him. 'All that toxic energy in the air.'

He shrugged. 'S'pose.'

'Too much for them.' Meadow dropped her voice as Ocean disappeared again into the back. 'Not good for their mirror neurons, in my opinion. We're waiting whilst they sort it out up there.'

'Ah.' I nodded as if I'd understood what she'd just said about neurons, but in fact wondering now if I should have let Harry go to the club. But he'd been so keen, and I did believe in my children having at least some autonomy. 'I really hope they do.'

'Me too. But of course it's not the only problem at the club. The spirit is still walking.' Meadow wafted across to sit opposite Iris, on the other side of a little table clad in black velour star cloth. As she gazed at my daughter intently, I saw Iris through the other woman's eyes: her round face beneath her ruffled auburn waves pale; her dark blue eyes huge and stunned by grief – and yet, actually, she looked far less angry than she had in a while.

I wanted to ask what Meadow meant about the club, but I didn't want to break this rapport between her and my daughter.

Slowly I took a breath, the air filling my lungs as I watched, hypnotised; the woman taking my daughter's hand in her bony, delicately hennaed one. Gently, she touched the single silver thumb ring Iris wore before turning her hand over.

'I sense your pain, young one. Let me see…' She studied Iris's palm. 'Hmm, you've just been on a long journey, I see.'

No shit, Sherlock, I wanted to say, but I managed to bite my lip.

As unbearable as it'd been to witness Iris suffering for the past few months, honestly, I was running out of ideas. I'd tried so hard to get her to talk, but she was too furious with me, even more furious than before when she'd refused point-blank to see the bereavement counsellor in the States. And now she was here, it seemed the time with her grandmother and cousins in Scotland hadn't helped either, despite my prayers.

If anything, Iris had arrived feeling worse than when I'd left her and Harry in the Highlands on my way to Kent. And whilst Harry still came to me for comfort, despite not being very forthcoming about his inner life, he was an open book compared to his sister.

But then Iris was very much her father's daughter, a girl who felt her emotions intensely but deep beneath the surface. Always fiercely independent, even as a small child, it meant she'd not let her guard down for a second about her despair – and yet the despair was evident.

'Tea?' Ocean trundled through the curtain with an ugly pottery mug, which he slopped down on the table. 'Oops.' He winced. 'Sorry.'

'It's fine.' Iris looked up, surprised. 'Thanks.'

I noticed his blush, as Meadow murmured, 'Get the rose petals, duck,' to him, Iris's hand still in hers. 'Very calming, we find, the roses. Reduce anxiety.'

Solemnly Ocean opened a small cupboard and passed Meadow a glass jar of scrunched dried-up old things.

Eye of newt, perhaps, or toe of frog?

And yet the energy around Meadow seemed clear somehow, almost resonating in the air, and I found I was suddenly torn between a desire to sit down and tell her everything, and a desire to grab Iris and run.

'Especially after a terrible loss.'

I shot a look at Iris, who very fixedly didn't meet my gaze. Meadow's intentions might be good – I sincerely hoped they were – but I felt less than relaxed.

But Iris looked the exact opposite to me. Hand resting in Meadow's, she seemed more comfortable than I'd seen her for days, weeks – months, even.

Leaning against a shelf groaning with crystals, picking up a book about spirit animals, I resigned myself to waiting.

'You really miss him, don't you?'

My heart jolted and I looked up. Was she talking to me?

But no, Meadow was intent on my daughter, now nodding piteously.

'Don't cry, young one,' Meadow murmured, and again, for all my doubts, I felt how compelling she was. 'Let's see.' She dropped Iris's hand and pulled a crystal ball towards herself. 'Here is a great chasm in the earth.' She gestured vaguely at the glass globe. 'And, ah! I must say, he's been on a momentous journey to calm, although his spirit is still troubled.'

Nausea swept through me.

'Thank you, but I really need to get back for Harry.' With clammy fingers, I shoved the book back on the shelf. 'Thanks for the tea. Come on, Iris.' I held out my hand.

'Mum!' Iris protested, her face dissolving back into the thundercloud it resembled so often recently. 'I'm not ready yet.'

'Iris!' I barked. 'Now!'

'She's very welcome to stay with me.' Meadow hadn't raised an eyebrow. 'I'll put her on the bus later. We don't drive, do we, Ocean?'

'Not yet,' I was fairly sure I heard him murmur.

'It's fine, thanks.' I grabbed Iris's hand and propelled her past the karma candles. 'We have to collect her school shoes anyway. That's why we came into Canterbury.'

'Ah, *school*.' Meadow sighed deeply. 'Yet more societal constructs that harm the youthful spirit.'

'Gosh.' I suddenly felt like screaming. 'Well, Iris is looking forward to it, aren't you?'

'No,' she said rudely. I'd walked right into that one.

'I used to home-school Ocean.' Meadow's fey smile was grating now. 'Less prescriptive, we found, wasn't it, ducky?'

'Maybe.' I caught a definite eye-roll from the boy as I dragged Iris to the door.

'Nice to meet you, Iris,' he said, and despite my frustration and angst, his gentle demeanour touched me.

'See you at the football club, I expect.' I smiled at him, and to my great surprise, my daughter almost managed a smile too.

'If you're going to St George's,' Ocean said to her, 'I'll see you there next week. It's not that bad.'

There was a pause as I held my breath, watching Iris adjust her cap. 'Cool,' she said eventually. 'See you there.'

'Great!' I beamed, and actually managed to take her hand in mine.

'Let's see about football, eh?' I could just hear the faint twang of Meadow's dulcet tones as we hit the street running.

It went without saying that Iris slipped her hand quickly from my grasp; was angry with me afterwards, grumbling that I'd humiliated her, then refused to talk as we collected her shoes.

When we got in the car, she turned the stereo up really loud, so I couldn't ask about the man she'd followed in the town centre. The man she'd obviously longed to be her dead father.

We drove along the dual carriageway in silence for a while, until I tried to say something about Ocean being a nice boy, even if his mum was a bit out there. But Iris just turned the radio up even louder, and without warning, I found my own anger building until I couldn't contain it any longer.

With a screech of tyres, I pulled the Land Rover into the next lay-by and stopped the engine, shaking with frustration. 'Iris!'

'What?' She folded her arms defensively.

'Just how long is this going to go on for?'

'As long as I want it to.' She stared out of the window at the nondescript day, the old car vibrating every few seconds as another vehicle blasted by in the next lane.

'You need to talk to me, honey. I don't get it.'

'Do you really think I'm going to talk to you after what you did, mother dear?' she hissed, venom dripping from her words.

'But what *did* I do?' I could feel the tears coming now, and I wasn't sure if they were hers or mine, but I did know her anger was so alive it felt visceral in the small space.

'*Doh!*' My daughter's pretty face was scrunched in fury as she turned to me, more furious than I'd ever seen her. 'Like, had an actual affair?'

'What?' My stomach plunged in fear. 'I didn't!'

'You did.' She was crying now, and she looked about five. My heart flip-flopped. 'I know you did, so don't bloody lie!'

'Iris, sweetheart, *how* do you think you know that?'

'Because. I heard.'

'Heard *what*, honey?' I was confused.

She didn't answer; just glared at me as another juggernaut went blaring past, and I realised suddenly how dangerously I was parked.

Quickly, hands shaking, I restarted the car as Iris turned up the stereo again.

What was it exactly she thought she knew?

She had been such a happy child; so full of energy and love and wonder at all the world had to offer. And then puberty arrived, and with it, Fraser's obvious stress when he took the last promotion.

Things quickly got harder. My sweet little girl became so angry, it was a shock to me. But not as much of a shock as it was to her father.

That was my fear. Her angst and my frustration – how much had they pushed Fraser to a limit he couldn't bear?

13

Patti

After the terrible altercation with Neil at the club, Patti had definitely *meant* to go straight round and talk to Linda, to check she was all right. But in the car home, the boys claimed they were starving. So instead, she had cooked a big fry-up and sat chatting about the first training session they'd had with Dez, who they all thought was absolutely 'sick'.

As she watched them hoover up eggs and bacon as if they hadn't eaten in weeks, her phone rang. Apparently the Clarins rep had got the wrong day and was at the salon to meet her.

With a big sigh, Patti went into work.

Arriving home around four, flagging now, she found a tearful Luna at the dining table, laptop open, head in hands.

'I was just going to pop to see Linda, babs. You OK?'

'Oh, Mum,' her daughter wailed. 'I really can't do this essay.'

'What's it about?' Patti felt her heart sink.

'What journalism means in the twenty-first century if the newspaper industry dies out. It's, like, totally doing my head in.' Luna turned her woeful face up to Patti. 'Please don't leave me, Mum.'

*

Some hours later, sloshing with tea and chocolate, neck rigid from sitting still for so long, Patti was just wondering if a vodka and tonic might help Luna's essay flow better when a Facebook notification pinged up on the laptop.

It was quickly followed by another, and then by the sound of Patti's phone chirping in her bag.

Luna clicked on the link.

'There's another one,' she said slowly, eyes scanning the screen.

'Another what?' Patti rotated her neck, hoping for some relief. Perhaps she'd do some massage training on Monday, get her junior to practise on her.

'That nasty vlog thing.' Luna's eyes were widening as she read. 'Oh. My. God!'

'What?' Patti felt the most awful rush of fear. 'Luna! Is it something to do with us?'

'Us?' Luna shook her head. 'No, course not, silly. But look.' She pushed the computer round so Patti could see. 'What a horrid photo.'

Patti stared at the screen: at a still of a woman sprawled on all fours, her bottom angled ridiculously in the air, smashed bottles of wine on the pavement around her.

Luna hit play on a video clip, but Patti's heart was sinking even before she saw the content.

She'd recognise those badly done roots anywhere, that unique haircut.

Disgraced manager Neil's wife, little Davey's mum – Patti's own oldest friend in Tenderton. It was Linda Forth.

Around 2 a.m., having proofread Luna's essay backward and forward – not one of her fortes, it must be said, having last written one herself around the age of fifteen – Patti woke to find herself fully dressed on the sofa, covered with a blanket, shoes off and neatly placed on the floor beside her. Luna, of course. She thanked God that her daughter was so much more together in her twenties than she had been in her late teens. It had felt like touch and go for a while back then.

A massive snore cut through the quiet: Sam. She could actually hear him through the ceiling.

Picking up her phone, she saw the multitude of notifications, and for a breathless moment, the panic built. But there was nothing from Linda. Nothing from the new and presumably unwitting star of the *Tales of Tenderton.*

The video had been a shaky clip of Linda barrelling out of the village store around seven o'clock in the morning, chased by the owner Mrs Marshall, the chase ending with Linda hitting the box hedge at the edge of the frame and falling heavily to her knees – whereupon several bottles of alcohol, presumably hidden under her coat, smashed on the ground.

Patti knew Linda's drinking had got worse recently, but she hadn't realised quite how bad it was. Since seeing the awful vlog post, she had rung and texted her friend several times – to no avail. *I'll definitely see her tomorrow*, she promised herself, hauling her tired bones off the sofa. She'd pop round to the Forths' house before the game.

And yet she couldn't help it – Patti felt the relief of those as yet untouched by public ignominy. Whoever had created this poisonous vlog had it in for the Forths, that was clear, and maybe that would make it easier to work out who was behind it. And maybe, just maybe – it would end there.

But right now, all Patti could think of was more sleep.

At the top of the stairs, she turned right automatically, to the spare room, instead of left to her own bed. She could really do without Snore-fest tonight.

14

Alex

When I collected Harry from Patti's neat little cul-de-sac on the way back from town, he was full of beans – unlike his big sister, now sulking in the back.

'I've been asked to play tomorrow! But Davey's not going to.' His cheery face became solemn. 'He says he can't till his dad comes back to the club, even though Dez said it was all calm.'

'I see. Is Davey Neil the manager's son?'

'Yeah, he's called after David Beckham, and he's real nice,' Harry said. Sometimes I found it hard to believe I had children so Americanised. 'But he's also pissed about what's happened.' My son shot me a quick glance beneath his lashes to see if I was going to scold him for swearing.

'Is he?' I let it go. 'Why is that?'

'He says Dez has been after his dad's job since he came here.'

'Has he now?' I glanced at Iris in the mirror; headphones jammed on, busy picking at her green nail varnish.

As I pulled up outside the cottage, glad to be able to park easily for once, I heard the ping of my email.

I prayed it was an answer from Rich…

*

Within hours of me giving my number to Patti, I'd been added to the main Tigers WhatsApp parents' group: a meet time and a kick-off time for tomorrow's match were now being announced.

Unsure how I felt about being drawn in, still, for the first time since moving into Primrose Cottage, I felt a little differently about being in Tenderton.

The children both pottering upstairs, I built a fire in the sitting room's boxy grate, put some music on our cheap dock and added spice to the big pot of stew I'd been tending for the past day. I'd made pumpkin pie for old times' sake for afters, and for once, the room actually felt cosy. Firelight flickered on the ceiling, catching the glass baubles that I'd left hanging in the window. Why not have a little more protection from evil spirits? I thought wryly.

Yes, it was beginning to feel a little like home – and more so when Iris actually deigned to come and eat with us for the first time since she'd arrived.

Perhaps our row in the car had cleared the air a little, even if it was still unresolved. Whatever the reason, I was so glad to see her at the table, I wasn't going to question why.

After supper, we watched an old Marilyn Monroe film together, *Some Like It Hot*, that made both the children laugh – at least when Iris wasn't looking at her phone. She had always loved the old black-and-white Hollywood films; we used to watch them in America on cool wintry Sundays, sitting in the den that looked onto the garden, under the tartan rugs my mother-in-law sent over every Christmas. When Iris was still happy to spend time with me regularly.

As the film finished, Harry dashed up to finish some maths homework, but Iris stayed on the sofa beside me, searching for something on her laptop.

I didn't dare move, for fear of breaking the spell. So I sat staring into the fire, listening to her fingers rattle across her keyboard, and for a blessed little while, I felt myself relax.

Later, when I went up to bed, she actually let me kiss the top of her head.

'Don't stay up too long, hon,' I said, and Iris semi-shrugged but didn't argue.

Halfway up the stairs, she called me back.

'I was thinking.' Laptop resting on her belly, she looked pensive. 'Can I get my own guitar?'

She'd played for a bit in America, in sixth grade, but she'd stopped when she got into skateboarding.

'Course.' I thought of the instruments in the window of At the End of the Moon. 'We could ask Meadow if she has one maybe.'

'OK.' There was a pause, and I was about to go back up when she said, 'Dad loved his old guitar, didn't he?'

'Yes.' I really didn't want to disappear down that particular memory lane tonight, but I realised how vital it was to allow her to talk about Fraser. 'Yes, he did.'

'Did you keep it?' She didn't look at me, but at her toenails, recently painted the same emerald green as her chipped fingers.

'Yes, of course. But it's in storage, honey.' Until I could afford to get everything sent over here. 'We'll get it soon, I promise. Do you...' I swallowed. 'Do you want to talk about your dad?'

'No.' She picked up the laptop again.

'OK.' I couldn't help feeling relief – and I knew better than to push anything with her at the moment. 'Don't stay up too late, will you? And put the guard over the fire when you come up.'

'Sure.' She didn't look up.

*

On the landing, I stopped to peer out at the winding river.

Despite my fears about money and the future, I was warming to the idea of belonging to something again.

I'd come to love the river in my short time here. It was strange, but I had the feeling that it somehow sensed my intrinsic sadness. But did it know that however deeply I was devastated by Fraser's loss, there was also a tiny part of me – and it sickened me to even dare to admit it – that felt freed by it too?

That was something I hoped no one would ever know.

Because it hadn't been good over the past few years – not good at all. He'd been promoted, and we'd been excited, but with more money came more stress, earlier mornings in the office, longer days, until eventually his mood seemed so low, I thought he must be struggling with some sort of depression.

But in a typically Fraser way, he refused to talk about it, or get help, despite the proliferation of therapists in California – 'It's normal, like having a good dentist,' my neighbour Bobbi had told me. Not for Fraser though; he'd begun to spend more time with 'the boys' than with me, particularly his great mate and colleague Rich, hiking and hunting at weekends to release his stress.

When he wasn't working, we'd go to the beach or the zoo or a skate park, but in the last few months he was tired, or grumpy, or distracted, and only occasionally would he take Iris out on the mountain bikes or go bug hunting with Harry.

Briefly I allowed myself to imagine what it would have been like to have moved to Kent together. I knew in my heart of hearts that it probably wouldn't have lasted, but that did nothing to assuage my guilt.

In fact, it only made it far, far worse.

The sight of the neighbourhood bats, sharp zings swooping through the dark at breakneck speed, interrupted my thoughts now, as somewhere nearby, vibrating in the darkness, came the comforting sound of an owl calling to its mate.

Out of the shadows emerged a silhouette: a big black cat, padding across the garden, jumping up onto the fence, the Whispering Woods tall and thick behind it.

For a moment, I was at the back door of my grandparents' farm – until, across the gardens to the left of me, my eye was caught by another movement, in front of the woodland.

A woman stood there, tall and straight, in a cloak and hood.

A deep shiver coursed through me as I blinked and stared – only now I looked again, I could see that no one was there at all. My overactive imagination, I supposed.

Still, I closed the curtains quickly.

In the middle of the night, haunted by my own dreams, I woke and could hear the broken panting of a dog at my bedroom door; a piteous whine, the scrabble of claws on a wooden floor.

Nova.

Bobbi had promised to look after her when we left America. But she'd messaged me the next week to say that Rich and Janine had taken the dog out hiking, as agreed, and were begging to keep her.

There was no way Nova could possibly be here in Tenderton. Much as I wanted to bring her to the UK, I couldn't bear the idea of her trapped in a cage in the dark on a day-long flight. She'd had enough trauma already.

Another whine.

Half asleep, I stumbled to open the bedroom door.

Nothing but shadows.

As disturbed sleep submerged me again, I could still hear the whimper of my beloved Nova, and it seemed to me, in my troubled dreams, that she was mourning her lost master.

15

Patti

Sunday, September's end: Libra

For once, to the mothers' relief, Sunday dawned dry, if also cold.

However dedicated you might be, there was little more miserable than standing in the pouring rain for seventy minutes – especially if your team was losing. And there was a fair chance of that today, the match being this season's first Kent League game against the Tigers' arch-enemies, the Kingley Knights.

Tension was already high, mutterings between the Tigers parents about the dastardly vlog, wondering who was behind it and who would be next, exacerbated by the long-standing rivalry between the two teams. A fair bit of player poaching had gone on over the years, and it was a matter of honour today that the Tigers should win, having lost all last season's games to the Knights.

The latter were what Patti's brothers would call a 'proper tidy little squad'. Their coach was a sinewy, aggressive man even more competitive than Neil, whilst the parents were, in Patti's opinion, badly dressed, rude and overloud.

At least all the Tigers had turned up today, apart from Ocean and Davey. Noting the latter's absence, Patti felt another lurch of guilt about Linda. She'd stopped at the Forths' house on the way to see if Davey wanted a lift, but no one had come to the door.

And yet there was a bigger turnout of spectators than normal, with Kyran's parents seeming particularly overjoyed that Dez had taken over. Kyran's dad Trev could be heard congratulating him: 'Just what we need, mate, at last, a proper coach!'

Alex arrived, Harry scampering in front of her.

'Hiya, babs!' Patti called. 'And Harry! How are you doing there?'

Dez came jogging up to Alex before the boy could reply. 'Thanks for answering the call to arms, babe.' Patti felt a jolt of envy. 'We're a few men down today. Hunter's knee's playing up so he's on the bench, and Ocean's not back, so Josh is in goal.' He didn't mention Davey, and Patti felt another twist of betrayal at her own treachery towards the Forth family. 'You all right, Harry?'

'Awesome.' The boy nodded eagerly. 'I'm warmed up already!'

'Ace! Go and join the others, OK? Just need to take the player details from your lovely mum.'

'Harry's really excited.' Alex handed Dez the FA form she'd filled in.

'Cool. He'll need some passport shots for his ID card, and then we're sorted. So, you're our Tenderton virgin.' Dez winked at Alex, and Patti felt a little stung. 'I'm sure there's a lot I could teach you.'

'Oh!' Alex flushed bright red.

'Hey.' Nancy's brother Louie arrived with a shy smile, a pile of player bibs over his arm. 'I'll start the warm-up, Dez, yeah?'

He's a handsome lad, Patti thought distractedly as the two men wandered off discussing tactical formation.

'You know I really favour the 4-4-2, but we'll try the 3-3-4 today that Neil's been playing them in,' Dez was saying, his arm

slung round his brother-in-law's shoulders. 'Change in incre-
ments, yeah?'

Honestly, Patti thought crossly, well aware of Alex's lingering
gaze. What *was* it with Dez and the ladies?

As the whistle blew for kick-off, the ever-uptight Liz Bauer
appeared in her voluminous Canada Goose jacket, which just
made her look even thinner. Patti sucked her own stomach in.

'Who's that?' Liz pointed at Harry, who was vigorously jogging
up and down the sideline with the other two subs.

'That's Alex's son, Harry. You've met Alex, haven't you?'

'Briefly!' Alex smiled at Liz. 'Before Ethan's birthday party
last week?'

Patti was bracing herself for an onslaught about Linda's terrible
disgrace on the vlog, but Liz had other bones to pick.

'Sorry.' Her angular face was pinched with cold. 'But I'm not
sure he should be playing. Your son.'

'Oh?' Alex looked embarrassed and Patti winced. Liz really
did come from the curt school of manners, so much so that Patti
sometimes wondered if she was slightly on the autistic spectrum,
like her own middle brother, who always told the truth, no
matter what.

'Liz…' she began.

'Why?' Alex sounded puzzled. 'Dez wanted him to.'

'Well, he's not officially signed, is he?' Liz took her role as
club secretary a little too seriously sometimes. 'We don't want
to get in trouble.'

'Shush.' Patti shot a look at the Kingley parents. They really
weren't people you'd want to mess with. Coming from one of the
poorest, most deprived parts of Kent, they were a tough crowd;

a mixture of mums dolled up to the nines, or with tattooed fingers, and scrawny dads with over-gelled hair, or motley-looking overweight ones, whose descending tracksuit bottoms displayed their bum cracks and beer bellies beautifully as they chain-smoked on the sidelines.

A few of the latter were sharing a joint down by their goal, although the play was in the Tenderton half now.

'But…' Liz looked irritated as Declan O'Connell thundered past with the ball, a Kingley defender tugging at his shirt. Just in time, Declan sliced the ball to Maxi, who managed to lose the winger hot on his own heels.

'Ooh, nice pass, Declan,' Patti called. 'Look, just leave it, Liz, eh? Harry's not even on the pitch yet. Let Dez worry about that sort of thing.'

'But it's vital to play by the rules…' Liz trailed off as Maxi clipped the ball with a deceptive back-heel kick and sent it soaring towards the goal.

'Lovely,' murmured Patti. 'Clever boy.'

The whole crowd held their collective breath, until the ball hit the crossbar, bouncing off into the undergrowth beside the pitch. The three women groaned.

'Oh for God's sake, Maxi! That should have gone in.' Liz went stomping off – to chastise her son presumably.

'Poor kids,' Patti murmured to Alex. 'You wouldn't want to be a Bauer boy. An hour before school on the treadmill every day, I hear.'

'An *hour*?' Alex looked appalled. 'God, I can barely do ten minutes. By the way, I keep meaning to ask, what are those weird bottles by the club gates? I nearly took out a tyre reversing over one the other day.'

'Oh, the witch bottles?' Patti grinned. 'Load of old nonsense. To counteract spells put on players, you put their hair clippings or their pee in the bottles. They're really old. Like, centuries old, I think.'

'Yuck.' Alex pulled a face as a huge gust of wind buffeted the two women. 'Sounds gross. Why does the club keep them?'

Patti pulled her coat closer. 'Not sure. Kind of lucky talisman, I guess. I'm not sure they're not actually a protected species. You know, like, listed or something' – she put on a posh voice – 'artefacts, darling,' but the rising wind was disconcerting her.

'Do they work?'

'About as much as the witch balls do!' She tried to concentrate, but the wind was really picking up now, and the trees had begun their eerie whispering. How vehemently she loathed the noise…

'I keep meaning to take mine down.' Alex clutched her bobble hat, threatening to take lift off. 'But I've got kind of attached to them.'

'Oh, Eth!' Patti was distracted by the sight of her son being surrounded by Kingley players at the far end of the pitch. 'Stand up, babs!'

'Open your eyes, ref!' Dez was yelling, but despite a massive dirty challenge from a Kingley midfielder, missed by the referee, somehow Ethan emerged through the opposition, having managed to hold on to the ball.

'Oh, *good boy*!' Patti watched him move down the field with intent.

'Press, boys, press!' The cry went up as Ethan zipped past another defender, crossing the ball through a sudden gap to Kyran. Patti found herself clenching her fists as Kyran took a shot from an audacious angle, right past the goalie – who'd just thrown himself in the wrong direction.

With a satisfying thud, the ball landed in the back of the net.

'Yes!' As one, the Tenderton parents went wild. 'Woo-hoo!'

'Way to go, Tenderton!' Harry hopped up and down on the sideline, his hair on end in the vigorous breeze.

'That's *exactly* what I'm talking about, Kyran!' Dez crowed. 'Great run, Ethan!'

Patti felt herself swell with pride as she watched Ethan's teammates excitedly jumping on him and Kyran. 'Nice teamwork!'

'Ha!' Alex grinned at her. 'So maybe those manky old witch bottles did help ward off the opposition!'

'Maybe.' Patti bit back a sigh. 'But I suppose it depends on whether you believe the witches were on the wrong team. Bad, you know.'

'Do you?' Alex looked curious. 'Think they were bad?'

'I doubt it. I mean, I do tend to think of the Wicked Witch of the West or "Hansel and Gretel" when I think about witches, but really' – she watched Ethan thunder back up the pitch, chasing down a Kingley centre forward – 'they were probably just herbalists and midwives, trying to help with their own remedies, don't you reckon? And the men wouldn't like that, the doctors, the Church and all that. Calling them witches might just have been another way of keeping them in their place— Hey!'

A Kingley player was clutching Maxi Bauer's shirt as he tried to get round him.

'Less of that, babs!'

'Is he allowed to hold him like that?' Alex frowned.

'I'm not sure *allowed* is the word I'd use.'

'I must say –' Alex watched as Maxi broke free and took off with the ball – 'I'm not sure I get the whole obsession with witchcraft here.'

'No, it's weird, isn't it?' Patti agreed with alacrity. 'But it was pretty rife in most of Britain, for centuries. And for whatever reason, Tenderton bought into the history of it.'

'It *is* kind of horribly fascinating, I guess,' Alex said as a flag went up, Maxi having passed the ball too hard, sending it straight off the pitch.

'And isn't that the trouble with all superstitions and good-luck charms?' The whistle blew. 'They become pretty seductive.'

Then Patti remembered poor Linda's shame, and how the drink had become so seductive to her friend since her daughter's prognosis, and she found that her heart was hurting with the sorrow of it all.

As the game went on, the atmosphere between the two sets of parents worsened until the damp September air was thick with friction, the earlier Kingley weed-smoking doing nothing for peace and harmony.

'So much for an autumn of love,' muttered Patti.

The increasing tension was definitely reflected on the pitch. One of the Kingley defenders received a yellow card for a handball. Soon afterwards, words ensued between a burly grandad and Kyran's dad Trevor about the Kingley player's hard tackle on Kyran.

None of it was helped by Dez's own temper.

For all his faults, apart from that one row with the ref at the start of the season, Neil had never allowed himself to get into what he called 'argy-bargy' with opposing managers. Pitch-side, he had been more Ted Lasso of Apple TV fame than Sir Alex Ferguson of Manchester United, who was infamous not only for winning the most Premiership titles of all time but also for kicking a football boot at David Beckham in rage.

But Dez definitely hadn't got the memo.

Striding up and down the touchline, swearing under his breath, he repeatedly ranted at the ref or the opposing linesman, and once or twice he even bawled out Tenderton's own linesman, Riker Bauer.

'Goodness, I hate it when our lot run the line,' Patti muttered to Alex. 'It always makes for trouble.'

'The line of what?' Alex looked confused.

'Touchline.'

'*Line of Duty*, you mean.' Patti's great friend Hazel had arrived in the middle of the first half, having left her daughter Cyn in charge of the café today. 'I'd rather not spend every single Sunday out here in the cold,' she muttered crossly. 'Got so many other things I'd prefer to be doing on a Sunday.' She caught the other women's gaze. 'What?'

'Like washing your hair, you mean?' Patti shoved her friend gently. 'Or hoovering, or picking your toenails?'

'Yeah, or pretty much anything.' Hazel raised her eyebrows good-naturedly, and they all laughed, but Patti knew she needed to talk to Hazel privately about the vlog; about Linda's drinking. Her addiction had been apparent for too long now, and they'd made feeble attempts to tackle it, but they owed her more: loyalty, and the duty of care that came with close friendship.

'Oof,' groaned Patti as the Kingley striker made an attempt on goal and missed by a few centimetres. 'Phew!'

Hazel's son Josh, playing in goal in Ocean's absence, booted the ball out to the wing, where it ricocheted off a Kingley midfielder, straight towards the mothers.

'Watch out!' They sidestepped neatly as Tony Jnr skidded up, bright pink in the face, and grabbed the ball from Patti's feet for a throw-in.

'Come on, you Tigers,' Hazel hollered, as if in reparation for her earlier moan, and Patti, joining the rousing cry, suddenly remembered why she didn't mind coming to football every Sunday, come rain or shine.

Until, that was, a mouthy Kingley forward ran through the whole Tenderton team with the ball and scored from the halfway line.

At half-time, as Patti unpacked orange halves and bags of sweets for the boys, Nancy arrived with her daughter Chloe, the pair of them resplendent in matching white fur jackets and new UGGs.

Nancy never wore the same thing twice, it seemed to Patti, tugging her own old jeans up and her faded Levi's sweatshirt down.

'Sorry we're late.' Nancy beamed as she picked her way through the mud. Those UGGs weren't going to be pristine for long. 'How's it going?'

'Pretty tight at the moment. One all, and a *lot* of aggro.'

Caught in the radiance of Nancy's smile, Patti ran her tongue over her own wonky teeth. Nancy *must* have had hers done: they were literally perfect. She'd briefly debated those invisible braces herself, but they cost a bomb...

'Had to wait for the courier from the agency.'

'Courier?' Hazel, swaddled in her mangy old leopard-skin coat from the village charity shop, looked intrigued.

'Oh.' Nancy blushed. 'Just a new ad I'm in. They sent through a load of merch for me – hair product and stuff. I might have some to share around—'

'Wow.' Hazel looked impressed. 'Nice!'

'What ad?' Alex asked politely.

'Shampoo.' Nancy flipped her blonde mane over one shoulder.

'Here, let me.' Louie prised the Tupperware box gently from Patti's grasp as Patti gazed at his gorgeous sister. He'd clearly been seconded to be Dez's wingman, which didn't surprise Patti really; Dez struck her as the type of bloke who didn't like to travel alone. But Louie seemed like a nice lad, dishing out orange slices and wine gums to the boys, laughing and joking with them about the alcohol content in the sweets before gathering the team for Dez's half-time talk.

'So you're playing like warriors who've fallen a-bloody-sleep in your trench, boys. This next half, we just need to attack, attack, attack – and not let up.'

Dez didn't half use a lot of battle imagery, Patti thought absently, texting Sam to remind him the second half was about to start. For Ethan's sake, she hoped his dad was on his way.

The boys were playing much better than in their last few games, and Ethan had really stood his ground with his opponent, despite the other boy being much taller. And he'd set up the Tigers' only goal deftly. About to wonder aloud to Hazel whether it was out of eagerness to impress Dez, she saw her friend's eyes grow bigger.

'Oh dear,' Alex murmured. 'That doesn't look too good.'

'What?' Patti's head whipped round.

'Oh my God!' Hazel swore softly. 'The state of her!'

Linda was stumbling across the car park towards them, and from the way she was lurching, and the dishevelment of the bowl haircut she'd sported since the 1980s, it was obvious she was very drunk.

'Sit here,' Patti ordered, having followed her stumbling, wailing friend around the clubhouse for the past five minutes, neatly shoving a stool beneath Linda's bottom before she hit the floor. 'What's happened?'

But Patti knew what had happened, of course.

'A good deal of gin, by the looks of it.' Old Mrs Jessop bustled in from the tuck shop with a steaming cup of tea. 'Don't you think?'

'Maybe.' The two women exchanged a glance over Linda's lolling head, slumped at the bar.

'There's a reason they call it mother's ruin.'

She was right. Linda did look ruined, her face soggy, streaked pink and white: almost like a rasher of bacon, Patti thought distractedly.

'Neil's ruined. I jus' can't believe they… no, *you*, that *you'd* all do this to him,' she slurred. 'It's 'orrible.'

'There you go, nice and strong and hot.' Mrs Jessop ladled sugar into the cup. 'This drinking isn't good for you, is it, dear?'

Patti wondered if the old lady had seen the online post showing Linda on her knees surrounded by shards of glass, and a steady stream of wine and gin. But Mrs Jessop probably didn't do the internet.

'Specially so early in the day. Have you eaten?'

'They've wanted him out for ages,' Linda moaned. 'All of you, been plotting. Know you have, don' lie.'

'That's just not true,' Patti protested as Mrs Jessop passed the tea. 'I've never heard anyone say they wanted him out. Ever.'

'Still, "a drunk man never tells a lie".' Mrs Jessop shook her white head sorrowfully. 'As they say.'

'Who says that?' Patti looked at the old lady sharply. Was that really helpful? 'And what about drunk *women*?'

'One and the same, dear.' Mrs Jessop's watery blue eyes were unblinking. 'Sheila,' she called down the corridor. 'Bring the lady a nice packet of biscuits – and the washing-up bowl from under the sink. Just in case.'

'I bet you're a Capricorn, aren't you?' Patti tried not to sound sour. Her mother was one.

'I might be.' The little old lady smiled. 'And then again, perhaps not.'

Little Sheila brought some Hobnob biscuits and the blue plastic bowl as Patti went to phone Neil, muttering quietly to herself.

Ten minutes later, a furious Neil burst through the bar doors.

'Thank goodness you're here,' Patti began. 'I'm a bit worried about Lin—'

'It's none of your business,' he spat. 'I can take care of my wife, thank you very much.'

'But, Neil, really—'

'Leave it! Come on, Lindy.' He hauled Linda off the stool, where she was swaying, face in her arms on the bar.

'Neil!'

But he refused to so much as look at Patti as he half led, half carried his wife through the doors, which caught in the wind and banged. Outside, he bundled her into the back of his van, their disabled daughter Angel sitting up front, playing on a Nintendo DS.

Patti felt sad for Linda, and a bit bad for Neil too. She knew what a good father he was, and how hard it had been for both of them with poor Angel in and out of hospital. But was the vlog right? Was he really no more than a terrible bigot?

Patti shuddered. She'd definitely done things in her own life she regretted, and she had secrets that someone could have a field day with. More than one secret, in fact, she thought, cringing at that awful night in Brighton. Honestly, the idea of someone airing her dirty laundry sent her into a cold sweat.

Hurrying out, hoping to catch the last ten minutes of the match, she noticed a motorbike pull up at the back doors of the clubhouse, the rider unrecognisable in black leathers.

One of the bar staff arriving for their shift, Patti thought, trotting down the path to rejoin the others.

But she'd only got halfway before something flickered across the Pool of Sorrow, just beyond the pitch, and Patti experienced yet another shudder of dread. It was a bird, most probably, wings catching the water – but a sudden image of Linda flashed into her head, body floating, arms out – and it was like the sky had just turned black.

At the final whistle, an elated Dez punched the air and yelled before shaking the ref's hand as if he was his new best friend; as if he hadn't been rollicking the man throughout the match. The guy was probably desperate to get away, thought Patti, watching the defensive body language.

Still, it had been a good win: 2–1 to the Tigers after a goal in the last five minutes set up by Maxi Bauer – to his father's restrained pleasure – and finished by Hunter, Dez's own son, who'd come on for the last quarter.

'For the glory,' muttered Tony Snr, who still felt some allegiance to Neil, despite his faults.

In the midst of the boys, Dez performed a jubilant sequence of dances, starting with Usain Bolt's victory move and finishing with the Floss, whilst Louie grinned beside him, the sweaty team gulping water or tipping it over their heads, all buzzing with pleasure.

Even the normally composed Nancy did a little jig with Chloe.

Swapping jokes and insults, the boys looked dazed and pleased, bundling into each other like the cubs they always reminded Patti of.

But Riker didn't look jubilant at all, despite Maxi's best efforts. He was obviously still put out after Dez's telling-off earlier, only scowling harder when Dez awarded Man of the Match to his own son, Hunter, who'd barely been on the pitch.

'Very bad form,' Liz muttered, finally putting her phone away. Patti doubted she'd seen more than a minute of the match, after Maxi's first failed goal attempt.

'Drinks are on us,' Dez announced loudly. He clearly believed that his leadership for one entire game was the sole reason for the boys' triumph. 'Me and Nance won't take no for an answer, will we, Nance?'

'Yeah, come for a cocktail,' said Nancy.

'Lager top,' Trevor joked, and everyone laughed.

In general, socialising had dropped off since last season, due to Neil's surly mood, and the fact the Tigers hadn't had a good win for ages. Today, though, everyone was enjoying the buzz, most of them wandering up to the clubhouse.

Still, Patti couldn't rid herself of the uncharitable idea that it was largely Dez and Nancy's minor celebrity status, along with their good looks, that enticed the other parents inside – along with the chance to gossip about the horrible vlog. Who would be next, or was it over? Had it just been about getting rid of Neil and his wife?

Hand clamped to his eldest son's shoulder, Riker could be heard scolding Thomas as he stalked up to the clubhouse; something about not pressing hard enough in his own under-15s game on the far pitch.

'You must have X-ray vision,' Alex joked to him, and Patti caught her eye.

Nothing ever seemed to satisfy Riker Bauer, including her husband's building skills – but that was another story…

In the noisy bar, Patti stood aside to make a quick call, a low flame of indignation burning that Sam hadn't turned up to watch

Ethan – yet again. She had an idea of why he hated coming to the club these days, but it wasn't good enough, not for their son.

Waiting for her husband to answer, she watched absently as the barman, Mike, handed a padded envelope to Dez.

'Package for you, mate,' he said. 'Just arrived.'

'Nice one.' Dez glanced down at it. 'I've been waiting for that. Run us a tab, yeah?'

'Sure thing! Have to get a card off you first though, mate.'

'No worries.' Dez was so triumphant, he wasn't taking umbrage at anything. 'And a double of your own poison, eh, fella?' He handed Mike a gold American Express card pointedly.

Listening to Sam's phone ring out, Patti imagined all her unpaid bills this month, glowing red on the shelf above the television.

'Actually, I'd appreciate your help with a little something else.' Dez gestured to Mike, and the barman leant forward to listen.

Behind Patti, two mothers were whispering about Linda's drunken antics. She bit her tongue. She didn't have the energy for a row, but she did wonder just how many people in this room had signed up to the evil vlog updates. She'd resisted the temptation herself, but she'd bet her last fiver most people here were on the recipient list.

'Patti.' Dez beckoned to her as Mike disappeared into the back of the bar. 'A bottle of your best bubbly, what do you reckon?' Before she knew it, he'd planted a big kiss on both her cheeks. 'Two bottles!'

The heady fragrance and the heat of a man were both so alien these days, Patti suddenly felt girlish and squirmy inside.

Her embarrassment was masked by the hubbub in the heaving bar, so busy now that little Sheila emerged from Mrs Jessop's lair to help pull pints. Patti always pitied Sheila on match days.

She'd been brilliant on the pitch herself, but Tenderton had been so backward in coming forward with women's football, the last coach had left the club at Christmas, after a huge row with the management.

'Not worth the hassle,' she'd told Patti as she'd packed up her car to leave. 'Turns out you can't teach misogynist old dogs new tricks.'

In one corner, Hazel and the rest of the coven were cracking open their first bottle of Prosecco, along with Alex, who looked relatively relaxed for once. Dez had poured some actual champagne for Patti, but her heart wasn't in it. She knew Ethan would pretend he didn't mind that his father hadn't turned up, but she'd seen his worried little face earlier.

Not always the strongest or bravest player, her son. Despite his bravura performance today, she knew he was scared he might lose his place in the squad. Without Neil to back him, that might be a reality. Picking up her glass, she wondered how soon she could take Ethan and slope off home.

The invisible sun was setting now, the wind blowing the clouds faster and faster as the evening drew in, the promise of a storm seemingly a very real one now.

'Oh my God!' Maria Desmond, Kyran's mother, shrieked suddenly. 'Look!'

All eyes swivelled to where she was pointing, towards the woods, the shadows of the trees bending and swaying ominously across the twilit pitch directly in front of the club.

'What?'

'I can't see anything, you daft cow!'

'Ow, that's my toe!'

'Oh – *I* see it!'

'Where? Oh my!'

At the edge of the woods, just shy of the dark shadows and the gathering storm, stood a slender figure clad in a long black cloak, head bowed, face hidden by the deep hood. Finer details were hard to discern from this distance – it was so murky out there now – but it looked like a woman, Patti thought.

'Oh my God – it's an actual bloody witch!'

'What? Where?'

As everyone rushed to the windows, the figure turned and melted into the trees – but a couple of the braver boys, including Hunter and Logan Fullerton, ran outside, to Dez's consternation. 'Come back, fellas,' he called to his sons from the door.

And it was too late: the figure had vanished.

Gulping at her drink, Patti found her heart was beating too fast for comfort.

'That was proper creepy!'

'She's come to find her dead lover.'

'Don't be stupid – it's just some nutter in fancy dress.'

'No, it's the witch from the lake. Look how she walked – she's got no bones in her.'

'Where *are* the bones then?'

'They were in the Pool of Sorrow.'

'Those woods are good for all sorts,' Trevor Desmond was saying lewdly as more boys appeared from the changing room. They gathered at the window in front of their parents, but there was nothing to see apart from the menacing trees and the mist that had begun to envelop them now the wind had started to drop.

Trevor, who ran a gardening business, had once held a fundraising talk at the club, explaining how the Whispering Woods had its own microclimate, making it more prone to misty weather.

But all Patti could think of right now was that mysterious figure – and how chilled she'd felt just looking at it.

'It was definitely the ghost from the Screaming Woods,' Hazel murmured, catching Patti's gaze. 'That's why I never go there.'

'Screaming?' Alex frowned. 'I thought they were the Whispering Woods?'

'They're both,' said Hazel ominously.

'What ghost?' Nancy looked nervous, checking her boys were near.

'Just a silly old legend, sugar.' But Patti drained her champagne, still feeling inordinately rattled. 'Pay no attention.'

''Scuse me, all!' There was a rap on the counter for quiet. Dez had just emerged from the back room of the bar with a huge bouquet, to take the microphone. 'Ladies and—'

'Ah, you shouldn't have, mate!' A tipsy Trevor nodded at the flowers, and everyone laughed, the apparition forgotten.

''Fraid you're not my type, Trev,' Dez replied, to much hilarity. 'So, ladies and hooligans' – cue yet more laughter – 'thank you so much for coming. Great result today, well deserved by my boys.'

'That's right.' Tony Snr toasted the air, and everyone clapped.

My boys? Good Lord, it was like Neil had never existed, Patti thought, shooting a look round the treacherous room. Even Tony had forgotten his friend now.

'I've got another little surprise for you all.' Dez made sure he bathed everyone in his warm gaze. 'A bit of a premiere, if you like. Mike, if you don't mind?'

'Premier League,' Riker joked – badly – and Dez appraised him for a moment, then gave a loud hoot of laughter, the earlier tension between the pair apparently dispelled.

'Something like that, mate,' he said, winking.

Mike switched the TV screen over from the Championship highlights to the AV channel, proud Arsenal tattoo on his hand, while Dez beamed at the crowd. 'May I present, as a special treat… Nancy's new ad!'

'Dez?' Nancy looked surprised. 'What are you on about?'

'I wanted everyone to see.' Dez toasted his beautiful wife. 'I'm so proud, babs. It's the start of a new time for us, isn't it? Finally settling in here, after all the moves we've had to make. The Fullerton Academy, named after yours truly' – he performed a mock bow – 'will be up and running before you know it, and I intend to take my Tenderton Tigers role proper serious till then.' He put his arm round Nancy, giving her smooth cheek a resounding kiss, just like he'd done with Patti a little while ago.

There was an audible 'Ah!' from the crowd, which drowned out the uncomfortable mutterings about Dez's role with the Tigers, while Nancy's shy smile warmed everyone's hearts – especially those of the fathers.

The TV flickered into life, and a hush fell as Nancy's face came into view on the screen, flushed and looking damp with sweat. Her long blonde hair tumbled across her eyes as she leant down to retrieve something out of sight. Her naked shoulders revealed that she was wearing only a strapless black bra.

'It's a bit out of focus,' Patti murmured to Hazel and Alex. 'Meant to be arty, I suppose.'

But the other women were still, eyes fixed on the screen.

'Um,' whispered Hazel, 'I'm not sure about that, Pats.'

Patti felt her eyes almost popping in surprise as Nancy's hand was seen moving across the frame.

'What is this, Dez?' Nancy's voice was shrill, fraught with stress. 'This isn't my ad! Turn it off, for Christ's sake! *Turn it off!*'

There was a horrified silence as over thirty brains computed what they were actually watching… Not a professional advert after all, but Nancy, semi-naked and leaning across the screen, apparently about to put a man's erect penis into her luscious mouth.

'What the *fuck?*' As a thunderous-looking Dez froze in shock, Nancy's brother Louie vaulted neatly over the bar and ripped the wires out of the back of the TV.

The screen fizzed loudly, then flickered to black.

There was absolute silence in the room for a moment but, as one, everybody turned to look at Nancy. She stood wide-eyed, white-faced and pink-cheeked – as open-mouthed as she had been in the final frames of the video, before the TV had juddered off.

'Mummy?' A tremulous voice broke the silence. '*Mum?*'

Hunter stared across the room at her, while the younger boy, Logan was turning puce, his own eyes huge with shock. Only their little sister Chloe was oblivious, down on the floor happily playing with strings of multicoloured beads.

'Baby…' Nancy stretched a desperate arm out to both boys. 'Hunter—'

But he turned and ran from the room, followed by his younger brother, now shouting something about 'disgusting'.

'I'll go.' Louie jogged back round the bar. 'Wait up, boys,' Patti heard him call as the door swung shut behind the three of them.

The wind caught it and banged it again: once, twice, making the room shake.

Then it was deathly quiet, until the barman whacked up the jukebox, and as Rihanna began to sing about anti-love, whatever that might be, the rest of the room breathed a sigh of collective and deeply uncomfortable relief.

In the middle, observed surreptitiously by everyone – however hard they pretended to be engrossed in their own conversations – a baffled-looking Dez had reached Nancy, who had scooped Chloe up from the floor. He muttered something in her ear, then, as an appalled Patti watched, Nancy shoved their daughter into his arms and tore away from him, dashing out of the doors after her sons.

Dez stood holding the child as if she were a small bomb, while all around him the parents kept pretending they weren't all riveted with excitement at this latest turn of events: at the gorgeous

Nancy's very sudden fall from grace; at another priceless piece of unexpected gossip in Tenderton.

Honestly, what the hell was going on in the village at the moment? There hadn't been this much scandal since the late nineties, when the local priest had turned out to be a cross-dresser called Deirdre.

'Have you seen this?' Hazel thrust her phone at Patti.

Alex glanced down. 'Jesus!'

'No, I'd say it's definitely *not* Jesus.'

A ripple went round the room as phones began pinging and vibrating; people dragging them out and gazing down at them in awed horror.

'Oh my goodness.' Patti stared at the screen in Hazel's hand: a still of a semi-clothed Nancy, emblazoned with the word LUST.

Stomach rolling, she looked away. She'd seen enough.

Now it was just a case of who would be next...

16

Alex

Would I have gone to the clubhouse for a drink if I'd known what would happen next? Did I want to subject my son to the ugly vagaries of adult life at the tender age of thirteen?

Definitely not.

As Harry came off the pitch, muddy but happy, my immediate instinct had been to scoop him up and leave; take him home and keep him safe with me for ever. This instinct had grown and grown since Fraser's death.

But I knew it would look churlish to not go and celebrate his win, albeit briefly, with the others. I wanted to be sporting myself, plus I was fast coming round to the idea of making a few more friends at the same time as the children did, and these women seemed nice. I used to have lots of friends – once. But now… well.

I was frightened of putting my faith in anyone these days, that was the truth. I wasn't sure the Tenderton vlog was easing that fear, and I hadn't even *dared* think what would happen if my own name came up, but Patti was so warm, and the others were friendly enough, so happily I agreed to go for a drink with them.

We left as quickly as possible after that terrible video had played out into the silence, once the police had talked to us all, Harry still agog at the very adult drama he'd just witnessed. Glancing at his face, a conversation came to mind that we'd had in the States, walking home from the school bus. He must have been about nine, immersed in reading an adventure story that described the main character as being someone's pawn.

'What do they mean?' he had asked. 'What's a pawn?'

'They mean like a pawn in a chess game, hon, being moved by someone else.'

Slight pause. 'But… is there another kind of pawn?'

'Oh.' I was taken off guard. 'Do you mean *pornography* porn?'

'What is that?' He looked slightly abashed, I realised.

'It's…' I considered quickly how I could best explain it. 'It's films of people having sex with each other.' We'd done the birds-and-bees talk briefly, but I could see this was deeply unsettling for my son.

'Why would anyone do that? Watch people having sex?' He flushed angrily. 'That's *disgusting*!'

Sometimes I longed for those days so fervently, I felt like I'd burst with it: the innocence, the time before the world corrupted my babies as they grew. Before Iris became so immured in grief and anger, and Harry became… less certain of himself, perhaps.

'You know that's really wrong, don't you, Hal?' In the Land Rover now, I indicated left out of the club. 'What we just saw. It's like… the whole sexting thing.'

'Sexting?' He looked puzzled. 'What, like sending girls sexy messages?'

'Girls – or boys, I guess. And, well, more like sharing images. Has anyone ever shared any naked pictures with you?'

'*Ma!*' he almost shouted, appalled. A driver behind us tooted their horn, revving their engine frantically.

It was Dez, I realised, in his little white sports car.

All right, mate, I muttered in my head, lurching out into a space in the traffic before he could beep again. His early friendly demeanour had entirely dissipated in the wake of the awful video; his face looked furious and bewildered in turn.

'Or' – in for a penny – 'has anyone asked you to—'

'Shut *up*!' Harry was bright red himself now, like poor Logan Fullerton had been just now in the bar, face aflame, staring at his mother in absolute horror. 'Just shut up, can you?'

But it wasn't a question.

I hoped Harry's own horror was because the idea was anathema to him, and not because I'd stumbled on some guilty secret of his.

Back in Church Street, I took some pride in managing to park the old car more efficiently than usual.

'Going to do a roast for supper, Hal. Chicken OK?' Chicken was all I could afford, and a small one at that. 'Apparently we shouldn't eat any more beef, Iris says, which is a shame, given how much you both love a burger.'

'Don't mind.' Harry, still refusing to look at me, tumbled out of the car to rush up the path.

To my surprise, Iris stood in the doorway, glowering at me.

'Nice to see you,' I said nervously. 'Harry won, did he say?'

'Good for Harry.' Her scowl didn't falter.

'Oh, and Ocean asked after you.' I thought she might be pleased, but her expression didn't change.

'Something you want to tell us, Ma?'

'No.' I shook my head. 'What's up? Can I come in?'

Blocking the door still, she turned back into the cottage, bending to pick something up. 'You tell me.' She shoved a bunch of flowers into my arms with a glare. 'What would Dad say?'

'Dad?'

'Yes, Dad. Your *dead husband*.' The words came out like pellets from the guns Fraser had loved so much. 'I knew it!'

'Iris—' I started, but she was already stomping up the stairs, and I knew from bitter experience that it was better to let her calm down before trying to talk.

I turned the flowers round to look for a card, the ornate foliage still tickling my chin as upstairs my daughter's bedroom door slammed. It wasn't quite the amazing bouquet of wild roses Nancy had been about to receive from Dez before the dreadful video (Hazel had scooped those up after the Fullertons had left, promising she'd look after them for Nancy), but it was a pretty bunch of stargazer lilies, daisies and red berries.

And I had no idea at all who might have sent them to me.

Quickly I scanned the street. No one around – as usual, in this sleepy little village – apart from a middle-aged woman dragging a stumpy dog behind her, and a man in a cap washing his bike at the end of the road.

And why would there be?

The card was small and buried deep in the middle.

From an admirer, it read simply. I didn't recognise the writing – but of course, I wouldn't. It had been written by the florist.

I stepped inside, bolted the door firmly behind me and leant on it.

For the first time in months, I felt the chill of real fear.

I wasn't clear why: the anonymous flowers and the unpleasant vlog posts – *Tenderton Tales* – were unsettling to all of us – though I guessed they were unlikely to centre on me, given that we'd only been in Tenderton since last month.

But one thing was indisputable: I felt scared.

17

Patti

'Call the police,' Dez had insisted when the stills from the video had gone live on the vlog. 'And delete this shit now – all of you!' In fact, he'd yelled it across the clubhouse, into the awful chasm of yet more silence after this second shock.

Thrusting his small daughter at Hazel to hold, he jabbed at his own mobile, seemingly oblivious to the fact that a weeping Nancy had now fled the scene along with their two boys.

Minutes later, Louie returned for the little girl, who was crying now too, and a ranting Dez bundled her over to him, shouting into the phone that he wanted to speak to 'the gaffer – NOW!'

Too much *Line of Duty* perhaps.

The last the other parents saw of Nancy was the top of her head, baseball cap on, her brother at the wheel of the big silver X6 as it roared out of the car park.

Dez, however, wasn't going anywhere until the police arrived.

'No one move!' he commanded after he hung up. 'The Old Bill are on their way. I don't get who would do this to me,' he raged, pacing up and down.

Patti rather thought it was being done to Nancy, or at the very least, both of them, but she wasn't going to venture that right now.

Up and down Dez strode, until Riker grasped his elbow and gently guided him towards the events room behind them.

'Let us sit down, have a chat. We will all delete it, yes?'

They were followed by kindly Tony Burton, who could be heard assuring Dez that it must be 'a misunderstanding, mate, and you're right to be angry, but there's always two sides to a story'.

Patti admired his courage in the face of Dez's fury.

Dez wanted nothing short of retribution apparently.

In the main bar, everyone else was aflame with the scandal. Whoever the evil troll behind the *Tales of Tenderton* was, the vlog had taken off, it seemed, and judging by the multiple pings on phones minutes ago, most of the parents were party to it.

'Who would do this?' went the whisper. 'Who'd want to shame poor Nancy like that?'

'The same person who wanted to bring Neil down?'

'Who'll be next?' Maria Desmond asked anxiously, whilst Hazel scrolled through her own phone so frantically, Patti felt sure something was worrying her friend.

'Envy eats nothing but its own heart,' Mrs Jessop could be heard murmuring to Sheila as they tidied the counter, ready to shut up shop for the day.

People did delete the stills, as Dez had requested, and yet there was the vague hint of an idea in the air – not spoken aloud, not yet – that the whole thing was, in some way, someone's just desserts.

Especially as the thing that no one was saying, or no one had said out loud *yet*, was that it very obviously hadn't been Dez in the video.

Fortunately, the police had been quick to arrive at the club – enticed by Dez's name perhaps, a few of those more disconsolate about Neil's sudden take-down had muttered.

'We'll be in touch,' a short, officious PC had told the remaining parents. 'To save you all waiting, please leave your names and numbers at the bar.'

Mrs Jessop and little Sheila were in the doorway when Patti left, fastening their raincoats against the lingering possibility of a storm.

'A rolling stone gathers no moss,' said Mrs Jessop, and Patti almost laughed, because what the hell did that even mean?

But there was something about Mrs Jessop she'd always admired; something about the gimlet look in her eye. She wouldn't let anything get past her, Patti imagined, and yet she was the type of old lady who made Patti miss the idea of her own mother.

The type she'd like on her side.

Sam was asleep on the sofa when Patti and Ethan arrived home. No surprises there, she thought, slamming the back door loudly.

She sent Ethan up to the shower and crashed around the kitchen ill-humouredly, with every intention of trying to rouse her apparently comatose husband – but in vain.

Bundling Ethan's muddy kit into the washing machine, she leant against it wearily, staring out at the wooded hill they lived in the shadow of. She was what her mam would have called dead on her feet, but she couldn't even slump on the sofa without moving Sam first. She was also starving, but the last time Sam had cooked tea was approximately three years ago. Still, the idea of starting a meal from scratch now was anathema to her.

Patti felt truly drained.

And then she thought again of the dreadful state of Linda yesterday; of Nancy's devastated face earlier as that intensely private video played into the stunned silence, and she remembered Mrs Jessop's words about envy.

She prayed with every bone in her body that she wouldn't need someone on her side soon.

Ethan appeared in his pyjamas as Patti was digging around for the pizza menu. All shiny and damp from the shower, he looked so cuddly that she wanted to clutch him to her, but she knew he'd just say 'gerroff'.

'Takeaway tonight, eh, sugar?' She settled for ruffling his hair. He still seemed young for his age sometimes, she thought, compared to a couple of the other boys, who'd grown several feet in a season, it seemed, with attitude to match, but right now, she was clinging onto Ethan's immaturity: her remaining baby. 'Special treat, you played so well today.'

'I didn't really.' He was downcast.

'Well I thought you did,' she said stoutly. 'You set up that goal beautifully.'

'Hunter Fullerton said I'm weak.' Ethan's bottom lip was starting to tremble. 'He said I played like shite.'

'Did he now?' She let the swear word go, all things considered. 'Well, he's a little—'

'Patti!' Sam's voice came warningly.

'Oh, so you're awake finally, are you?' She rolled her eyes. 'Hallelujah!'

'Hunter said that Dez's gonna drop me now he's in charge, and Kyran wouldn't talk to me cos he said I did a late tackle.'

'But you won – and Dez's going to do no such thing.' Patti looked at her son's pale little face. 'Even if it was true – and it's not – it's not up to him. He's not officially in charge, he's just standing in while Neil… while they sort things out.'

'But Dez is, like, a *pro*!' Tears were gathering in Ethan's eyes now. 'And if he doesn't want me, no one else will.'

'Hey.' Patti grabbed her son's chin gently and tipped his face up to meet her eyes. 'Of course he wants you. He's lucky to have you on the team.'

But the tears were already spilling down his cheeks, and she felt her own heart twisting.

Good Lord, it was meant to be *fun*, wasn't it; about team spirit, not breaking kids' hearts and winning medals. On top of the competition though, Patti had a sneaking suspicion that Dez was there with a very personal agenda.

But whatever that was, it certainly didn't include watching his wife engaging in sexual acts. For all Patti's admiration of Dez, there was something about the way he'd ordered everyone around in the clubhouse after the awful video that she'd found deeply irritating.

'Come on, baby, let's get our pizza, yeah?' She waved the menu at her son. 'Extra cheese and pineapple on a fat crust?'

'No way.' Ethan, still snivelling slightly, shook his head. 'I'm on a d-diet.'

'A *what*, Ethan Taylor? Over my dead body you are!' Outraged, Patti stood in the middle of the living room like Wonder Woman, hands on hips.

'Don't be so stupid.' Even Sam reacted now, hauling himself up to sitting.

'You're skinny as a rake,' Patti added. Which wasn't *entirely* true but wasn't that far off either. They were all starting to broaden a little now, these boys she'd known since they were tiny, filling out and becoming more muscular. Even Ethan, though she might not want to admit it.

'Louie said it's good to drink protein shakes if you want to burn fat.'

'Louie?' Sam shook his head. 'Who the hell's Louie when he's at home?'

'Dez's brother-in-law,' Patti replied. 'You'd meet him if you bothered to come to the club. Seems like a nice lad.'

'Louie was signed to Millwall when he was eleven,' Ethan said wonderingly. '*And* he had a trial for Chelsea.'

'And was let go when he was twelve probably,' Patti scoffed. She hated the whole academy system with a passion; not least because Ethan had never had a look-in, not a sniff of a scouting, unlike a few of the other boys, Maxi Bauer and Kyran included. And Dez's own boys, of course.

It had become obvious this weekend – before the latest scandal unfolded – that Dez's big ambition was his own private academy. So what was the Tigers? A hobby? A way to get free advertising? Right now, Patti wasn't sure how she felt about that, given what Ethan was saying.

'No,' Ethan said. 'He's still signed to Millwall under-22s.'

'Oh yeah?' Sam perked up at the mention of his beloved club. 'The Lions, eh?

Typical.

Patti grabbed the phone, biting back her irritation.

Honestly, before Dez and his beautiful family turned up at the end of last season, moving into one of the big houses on the gated Dewdrop Estate, everything had been fine at the Tigers. There was rarely any drama, if you didn't count one dad throwing his pint over another, and a mum who'd run off with the under-12s coach after a friendly tour in Spain. Too friendly, it turned out. Oh, and the girls' team being shut down in the middle of last season because there wasn't 'enough call for it' – despite at least one player being scouted by the junior England women's team.

Although of course all that was before Neil had been outed as a racist and his wife as a drunk.

'So, no extra cheese, yeah, Eth?'

But to Patti's growing frustration, Pizza Pizazz said she was looking at an hour's wait.

Zonked out in front of *Britain's Got Talent*, Ethan and Sam clutched their stomachs in high drama, claiming starvation, and Patti felt the escalation of irritation: a familiar climb in her chest. She was expected to solve the problem, and arguing with Sam about why he couldn't take over was just too much in a difficult day.

Irrationally furious with everyone – with the pizza place, with Sam for being so endlessly useless these days, and with her mother for moving to the Gower sixteen years ago and never offering a toast soldier of support, not even when Patti had terrible PND after Ethan; but most of all, right now, with Neil Forth and now Dez sodding Fullerton for upsetting her son and the whole applecart – Patti grabbed her coat again.

'Fine. I'll fetch it myself.'

Stomping down the pavement, fists balled, buffeted by the wind that had only sidled off for a while, she aimed a surreptitious kick at the neighbour's car, parked too close to her neat if ancient yellow Fiesta. She followed it with a whispered 'Yaa!' at their ginger feline fluffball, sauntering with insouciant intent towards her flower beds. 'They're not for you, buster, so do one!'

Feeling ever-so-slightly better as the cat fled in high dudgeon, she sped out of the modern cul-de-sac she still couldn't quite believe she lived in.

A few years back, Sam had worked on a neighbouring site for the developers, so they'd been able to bag one of the first houses, moving up in the world, leaving their council house on the wrong side of the Kent–London dual carriageway. It had been so exciting, and Patti could still remember Sam scooping her up like a new bride and carrying her in. Now, though, his back had gone, so there was no lifting, no nothing at all anymore. And with a big mortgage came monthly financial stress...

In the shadow of the hill, she was halted by the temporary traffic lights on the corner. Red, obviously, despite not a single car passing her. She drummed her fingers on the wheel. She might be exhausted, but she was also brimful of nervous energy after the weekend's bizarre events.

Turning Blondie up loudly on the stereo, she reversed so fast the car wobbled, then, without thinking too hard, turned and took the woodland way.

Normally she avoided this route; the road was long, twisty and narrow, and the street lights ran out as soon as it merged into the trees. In the dark woods, it was hard to avoid the pockmarked surface that no money was ever spent on.

But the real truth, though Patti wouldn't admit it, was that she avoided it because she just hated woods generally, hated not being able to see the sky at all times, and these local ones even more because of the old stories about the women who'd lived there, fleeing from the 'witchfinders' in desperation. Silly ghost stories, of course, just myth, and completely ridiculous, but unpleasant nonetheless.

Much like the story of the great dog that roamed the Kent meadows, one of a pack known as the Hell Hounds. Also ridiculous, but—

Out of nowhere came that weird vision from the salon – the body floating face down in the pool.

Patti clutched the steering wheel, blinking hard, desperate to clear her sight.

Oof! The car hit a pothole so hard she almost bit through her tongue. Good Lord, she'd forgotten how bad this road really was; so bumpy the car was actually rattling. But at least she could see—

She hit another crater, turning Blondie down to hear the exhaust pipe clattering with an unnerving jangle. Then something pale flew out of the trees, and she closed her eyes in terror, yanking the wheel too hard, so the car skittered off the road and up the grassy verge—

Cwack!

She jolted to a great shuddering halt.

About ten seconds later, she dared to open one eye to find she was almost face to face with the gnarled trunk of an ancient tree. Shocked, she didn't move; simply sat stock-still for a moment, sensing the precarious angle of the car and wondering what the hell that ghostly thing that had flown out of the trees had actually been.

An owl, she was sure… Just an old owl.

But her fear didn't abate. It was something primal, something deep-rooted. She wasn't conscious of where it came from or why; she just wanted to get out of there quickly, back to the light.

Nervously she pushed her door open.

'Damn damn *damn*!' To her dismay, she was stranded halfway up the narrow verge. Worse, her phone had absolutely no signal.

Cautiously she clambered out to inspect the damage. But as she stepped onto solid ground, the noise began.

She didn't know where it was coming from – she could hear but not see it – but it got louder, ever closer, until it was battling over her own panicked breathing, caught in her throat.

Suddenly, from nowhere, eyes snapping yellow in the headlights, a beast hurled itself from the trees, howling and salivating, baring huge jaws. Instinctively, Patti covered her head and ducked.

'Come here!' A male voice was shouting somewhere far off in the trees.

It took Patti a moment to realise the voice wasn't talking to her.

'Get back here NOW!'

No, he was calling the animal.

Whimpering, the huge dog slunk back towards its owner.

'Vinnie, you absolute sod!' A figure appeared out of the trees. 'I'm so sorry. Are you all right?'

Patti managed half a nod. 'Fine,' she croaked.

'Here.' He offered her a hand. It was Louie, Nancy's brother, she realised: breathless and covered in a faint sheen of sweat, as if he'd been running, fast. The dog, an Alsatian, she thought, was now on a lead, standing obediently by his side.

Mortified, pretending she hadn't seen the proffered hand, Patti uncurled herself; pushed herself up with what she hoped was a semblance of dignity, hands planted in moss and ferns to do so.

'He's still so young, he's over-friendly.'

'Friendly?'

'That or overprotective. He'd never have hurt you though, I promise.'

'No,' she said faintly. 'I expect not.' It was true, the animal hadn't so much as touched her; she'd just nearly had a heart attack was all.

'I bring him out here to let him off the lead, do a bit of wild running with him; he's got that much energy. There's not normally...' Louie glanced around. 'I mean, no one's here usually.'

The trees were thick, and the night was dark, the only light the beams from Patti's car as she brushed herself down.

'No, well, I wasn't exactly planning to be here myself.' She gestured at the car, the left front wheel of which she could see now had skewed off at a strange angle.

'Oh dear,' Louie said. 'That's not looking too clever.'

'It's very oh dear,' she agreed sadly. 'Don't know how I'm going to move it.'

'I'll give you a lift.' He indicated the track behind him. 'My car's up on the main road.'

'I'm meant to be fetching a pizza,' she said absently, and he grinned at her.

'No worries. I'll take you. Least I can do after…' He inclined his head at the entirely placid dog.

Patti's thoughts had become strangely tangled, and now she felt less worried about the dog being free and more concerned about whether it was sensible to walk further into the woods with a young fellow she hardly knew. But what choice did she have?

'Thanks,' she said simply. 'I'd appreciate it.'

Leaning into the Fiesta, she turned the engine off and picked up her bag. Before the lights died, she caught the swirl and dance of the woodland night in their beam – the tiny insects, the mouth of the path through the trees – and for a split second she was back in her teens, running free on the Welsh coast in the cold country air she'd taken for granted, the pure lungfuls of it; the wild camping, and the partying in the forest the year she'd gone to beauty school.

The year her mam had married the dreaded Nigel, he of the hands and—

'Coming?' Louie's voice broke through her memories, and she gave a great shiver, staring into the void where the track met the trees.

'Sure.' She pulled herself up to her full, admittedly short height and, slamming the car door, turned to him. 'Lead on, Macduff.'

They had to walk close together because of the darkness, and the narrow path, the dog following meekly behind. In the densest part of the Whispering Woods, the wind couldn't reach them, and it was still and quiet, apart from Patti's heart, still hammering fast from the fright. At first, she couldn't concentrate on anything apart from putting one foot in front of the other, but eventually she became aware of other things around her. The sound of her own breathing steadying; leaves rustling, a distant hoot, the smell of damp bracken. The smell of Louie; of washing powder and sweat – a different kind of scent to that of her own males.

When they reached his car, Louie opened the boot, clicking his fingers at the dog, who jumped in with no protest, a big lick of muscle and fur.

Sitting up front beside Louie, for the life of her Patti couldn't think of a thing to say – and then realised she was so exhausted, she didn't care. Just the idea of trying to sort out her abandoned car made her more tired. She'd ask Sam to deal with it – but normally, of course, it would be Neil who'd tow and fix it.

What was the best thing to do? she wondered, staring out of the window absently as her old estate slipped by on the ring road. Did she turn her back on Neil and Linda, given the demonic vlog, abandoning her old friend in her time of need? Or did she pit herself against the opinion of the masses – except what *were* those anyway? Was Neil now totally persona non grata, as the posh people liked to say? Who was going to be the ultimate judge of what the vlog said he'd done; what was the official path forward at the club? Patti had little faith in the powers that be. Maybe they'd forget Neil's crimes in the face of Nancy's disgrace.

Except Neil was going to have to atone for his sins, wasn't he, and face up to the consequences of his actions, even if they were long ago?

'We're here.' Louie nudged her gently, and Patti realised with a jolt that they must have been outside the pizza place for at least a minute or two.

'Oh, sorry.'

'You were a million miles away.'

'I was just thinking…' She changed tack abruptly. 'How's things at home?'

'Home?' He looked confused.

'Nancy and Dez, I mean. After… you know. This afternoon.'

'Oh yeah.' He reddened. 'Well, not great, you know. Dez is fuming. He's gone to London actually. And Nance…' He trailed off miserably.

'What?'

'Dunno. Kind of both furious and really embarrassed, I suppose. Says she'll never be able to go to the football club again, for a start.'

Patti considered this for a second. 'Well, I must say I've been wondering how it actually happened. Do you know? I mean, do *they* know?'

'How it *happened*?' Louie looked faintly appalled.

'Oh no, sorry.' Embarrassed herself now, she qualified her question. 'I mean, how it came to be in the DVD player. Or in the clubhouse at all, for that matter.'

'Oh, I see.' He was relieved. 'Well, Dez reckons it was one of his enemies. Turns out the bike courier was booked anonymously, not from Nancy's agency at all, as Dez thought.'

'*One* of his enemies?' Patti was curious. 'How many's he got?'

'Dunno.' Louie's friendly face closed. 'It's not the kind of thing we've ever really talked about.' His discomfort was evident.

Patti was dying to ask him if he knew who the man in the video was, but that would just sound nosy. Which it was, frankly – and yet, of course she *was* intrigued. Obviously the whole episode was completely humiliating. But at the same time, there was a tiny part of her, she realised with a thump, that was jealous.

Good God, Patti Taylor, have a word with yourself! Jealous of a woman who, beautiful or not, had just been revealed to all and sundry as about to put a… a cock in her mouth…

Patti fumbled with the door, swinging herself down onto the pavement as if Louie could read her awful mind.

'I'll wait,' was all he said, calmly.

But it must say something about her own sex life, she thought sadly, pushing her way into Pizza Pizazz; or rather, her absolute lack of sex life. She couldn't even remember the last time…

'Order for Taylor, please, babs,' she told the girl behind the counter. The girl nodded, shooting a quick look out of the window at the big car that purred outside, Louie nodding along to the thumping bass he'd just turned up.

She probably thinks I'm his mum, Patti thought, watching the girl adjust her ugly cap, in case he looked in, presumably. She pulled her coat collar up against the savagery of feeling suddenly old. And inside, she felt herself wilt a little bit more. It was becoming obvious to her now that she was actually losing the plot.

But then Louie looked at her from the car window and gave her the sweetest smile. And somehow, on the way home beside him, clutching the nice warm pizzas on her knee, the smell of baked dough and cheese in the air, Patti felt much cheerier.

Or at least she did until she walked in and found that her menfolk had got bored of waiting and had raided the freezer, cooking everything they could find for themselves before retiring to their respective bedrooms, leaving her all the clearing-up to do.

18

Alex

Monday

I'd thought Iris would continue with the huge fuss about starting at St George's that had gone on all last week, but a message pinged on her phone on Sunday night that made her face light up.

I knew not to enquire too enthusiastically, especially as she was still furious about the flowers that had arrived. I'd given them to our elderly next-door neighbour anyway.

But when I gently asked who had texted, Iris was actually happy to share for once. It was Meadow's son, Ocean, apparently, asking if she wanted to meet at lunchtime.

They'd been texting, it seemed, since we'd left the shop last Saturday, swapping numbers with some sleight of hand I'd missed. He had a band, Iris said, looking almost proud, and had invited her to hang out in the music rooms at school.

Originally she'd been reticent about getting a lift that first morning, but when I said I was taking Harry anyway, she deigned to come too.

'Tomorrow though,' Harry announced from the back seat, 'can I walk with Ethan and Josh?'

'Sure,' I said, just glad that he had these new friends.

At the school gates, I thought I saw Nancy dropping her son Hunter. I wanted to offer my… what? Condolences? Empathy? But by the time I'd found a parking space and hurried to catch her, the big silver car was gone.

Driving across the green on the way home, I passed that horrible contraption: the very basic chair attached to the long wooden plank. On a whim, I parked and got out to look.

Nearing the railing around it, I could read the inscription scratched into the side – *Thou shalt not suffer a witch to live, Exodus 22:18* – and I felt a wave of nausea and sorrow just looking at the ugly thing.

Patti had explained that the local council had elected to keep it as an artefact: a reminder of the evil men could do to one another, and how not to return to those days. But I just thought it was loathsome. The evil men did to women would be more apt: and why *was* it nearly always women who suffered these fates? I thought of Patti's words about midwives and herbalists, and how they were blamed for wanting to help; but also how easily people blamed others when they were scared for themselves – or in the old days, perhaps, for their own souls.

Getting back in the old Land Rover, it all made me think of Nancy's poor humiliated face in the clubhouse yesterday.

Women rarely, if ever, seemed to release revenge videos of their sexual encounters with men, so why the other way around? Or rather, why was it not the guilty men held to account, instead of the women being disgraced and reviled?

The faces of Nancy's irate young sons sprang to mind, as did the devastation to the whole family. Thirty seconds of footage that could never be wiped from the minds of anyone involved, including the innocents; a snapshot of time they'd have to live with for ever.

Walking up my little path, I thought that I'd like to offer Nancy some support. I wasn't sure how to go about it, but I could get her number from Patti, and—

On the doorstep, something crunched under my foot.

A button. I picked it up: dark grey and not one I recognised. Maybe off one of my old shirts, or a skirt of Iris's?

And then again, maybe not. I pocketed it anyway.

Inside, I resisted the temptation to lie on the sofa and watch daytime television, instead forcing myself to the table that now served as office, meeting place and family restaurant. I switched on the computer I'd just bought. It was second-hand, but still something I could ill afford.

A few of my American colleagues had promised to keep using me, despite our relocation; it made no difference to them if I worked remotely. But I was in desperate need of new contacts and new jobs in the UK – and soon, if we were to keep our heads above water.

At the table with pad and pen, I was halfway through compiling a list of companies to approach when I heard a creak upstairs. The overhead light flickered on, off, on again.

It was just the old floorboards settling, and the ancient electrics, I knew that, but still I realised, with a huge shiver, just how freezing I was.

The cottage was usually chilly and damp, unless the seventies heating system was clanking away, but I kept it off when the kids weren't here. It was another extravagance I could ill afford. But now my hands were almost blue with cold. A draught was definitely blowing from somewhere nearby.

Peering into the kitchen, I realised that the casement window was ajar. Odd. Maybe one of the kids had opened it. As I leant over the sink to shut it, a face appeared on the other side of the glass. I pulled my hand back as if I'd been burnt, stepping back straight onto something that hissed loudly at me.

My own cry was audible, echoing in the almost empty kitchen.

The black cat leapt up onto the sink, slunk through the open window and blinked at me, before pouring itself off the sill and through a crack in the fence.

And there on the other side of the glass, a tousle-haired man stood waiting for me to collect myself.

'Sorry.' He didn't look the least bit contrite. 'I did knock.'

'Really?' I tried not to yell at him. 'I didn't hear.'

As my pulse slowed, I realised that he didn't look like he was about to murder me, and that we'd met before.

'Shall I go back round…' He pointed, and then disappeared.

It was exhausting being the new girl in town, I was coming to understand. Everyone was both new and then not so new, my brain having to work extra fast as I kept zipping through my mental Rolodex of faces.

As I turned the heating on for a treat, to soothe myself, a knock came from the front.

Opening the door, I was still groping for why he looked vaguely familiar. And then it came to me, though in what order, I wasn't sure afterwards, as he extended his wallet at me. He was the man from Hazel's café, who'd walked off while I was still talking. And the thing in his hand was a warrant card.

Apparently, he was a policeman.

Feeling like a boundary had been violated from the get-go wasn't a good place to start any sort of acquaintance.

And even though the man, whose full name was Jack Stanton, according to his ID, gave me a calm and precise explanation of his credentials – a detective sergeant from the police station in Tunbridge Wells – I couldn't stop struggling with the fact that he'd scared me so badly in my own home.

Still, I let him in, assuming he'd come about poor Nancy and the revenge porn at the club.

'Do you want a cup of tea?' I offered. It was against my better instincts, but I was still desperate for warmth; yet more desperate for extra time to pull myself together.

'A coffee would be good, ta.'

'I'm out of coffee, I'm afraid.' Exactly why I offered tea, I stopped myself retorting. Play nice. 'Have you come about what happened at the club yesterday?'

He looked blank for a moment.

'With, you know, the…' For the life of me I couldn't remember their surname. 'Nancy and the new manager guy. Dez.'

'The footballer?' Jack Stanton had a look in his eye that indicated he very much knew what I meant. 'That's right. We'd like your take on it.'

'It was pretty shocking.'

'Yeah, I can imagine,' he agreed. 'Nasty business. I'll take some details.'

'What is it you want to know?' I pulled my jumper sleeves down as far as they would go, so he couldn't see my hands trembling.

'Just whatever you remember, anything you noticed.'

I wasn't sure I could be much help, but I gave him details of the afternoon as best as I could. He took a few cursory notes, but I couldn't help feeling his heart wasn't in it.

'Do you have a view on this type of thing?' I asked eventually, feeling exasperated.

He raised an eyebrow. 'On what?'

'On revenge porn obviously.'

'I wouldn't call it that, personally.'

'No? What would you call it then?'

'A liberty.' He pushed his dark hair back reflexively. 'Of the highest order. It's a growing problem. It'd help if people would teach their daughters not to share nude selfies.'

'Nancy's a grown woman.' I felt the hot bite of anger. 'And teach our *daughters*? What about teaching our sons not to share them?'

'Yeah.' He gazed at me inscrutably. 'Well, that too. You got boys, have you?'

'A boy and a girl.'

'I've only got daughters, and I've taught them this in no uncertain terms, Mrs Ross.' He fished some nicotine gum from a pocket. 'Truth be told, I do find girls can be a bit silly sometimes. Naïve.'

Was he *trying* to rile me? Afterwards, I despised myself for losing my temper, but lose it I most definitely did. And I was further goaded by feeling the whole time that Jack Stanton was laughing at me – though not in a nice or amused way, but sort of contemptuously, from one side of his face. A bit like that Batman villain Harry loved so much.

'Thank you for your opinion,' he said calmly, as my rant trailed to an end. 'I doubt you're wrong. But with the internet as out of control and unpoliced as it is' – I sensed him suppressing a sigh – 'there's bugger all we can do most of the time. We just need to teach our youth the way to go about things. Boys *and* girls.'

'OK. But like I said, Nancy's an adult, and capable of making her own decisions. And it still backfired on her.'

'Yeah, sure. But on top of the online image abuse Nancy Fullerton suffered – and we've asked everyone to delete the photos and not share them' – he stared at me for a moment, as if I might be considering sharing them personally – 'there's a growing concern about what we can police. There's photographic theft and harvesting, "sextortion"… all sorts going on, and the laws aren't changing fast enough to keep up. The less people record digitally right now, the less abuse can take place.'

'Right.' I considered his words more calmly now. 'But it's just… it's always women having to take the blame. It's always *us* having to not share a picture or not wear a short skirt, or not have one drink too many. Or not walk home alone through a dark…' *Wood*, I was going to say, but I changed it to 'estate'. I didn't want to think about the woods. 'Who is the onus *really* on?'

'Big words and all that aside, I reckon that's a debate for the philosophers, ain't it? I've barely got time to solve the crimes.' He put his pad away. 'My friends in the States tell me you lost your husband last year.'

'*Lost* him?' I almost laughed. God, he'd dropped that into the conversation like a small bomb and then stepped neatly away. 'He… he died, yes.'

'How?'

'In an accident.' I wanted to punch Jack Stanton squarely on the nose. I stood and walked to the window, took a breath. 'He… fell.'

'I'm sorry.' In the window's reflection, I could see his half shrug. 'I didn't mean to upset you. I am sorry for your loss, truly.'

'Thank you.' I bit down any other rejoinders as I turned back to him. 'But what do you mean, your *friends*?'

'I mean' – he met my eye – 'the FBI.'

'The FBI?' I was confused. 'Are you joking?'

'It only came to my attention because unfortunately it looks like a few of your late husband's colleagues might be in some trouble.' He suppressed another sigh. The man seemed truly exhausted. 'His old firm in the States is being investigated.'

'Really?' For some reason, my stomach turned to water. 'But what's any of this got to do with Nancy?'

His gaze was too oblique to read. 'Well, nothing obviously.'

'Right.' I gazed at the baubles in the window, catching the ceiling light that gave a small electric flicker in response. 'So how exactly can I help?'

'They'd just like to know if you are or have been in touch with a man called' – he pulled out his pad again – 'Richard Leonard?'

'Richard?' I felt my chest tighten. 'Fraser's colleague Rich?'

'Sure, Rich, if you like.' Jack Stanton shook his head almost sorrowfully. 'Do you know him?'

And in amongst all of this confusion, my strange turn of thought was: *God, I'm just grateful Iris is at school.*

'Don't disappear off.' Stanton stood up, drawing our meeting to a close, having taken a few perfunctory details about the company Fraser had worked for. 'I'll be in touch.'

Don't bite, Alex, I thought, but my irritation overwhelmed me. 'Please, don't rush.'

'Cheers, Mrs Ross.' He almost grinned. 'I'll see myself out.'

Given that he only had to walk three metres to the front door, it wasn't much of an offer.

Thoroughly unsettled, I watched from the window as Stanton peeled off another piece of gum and got into his black Audi, already on the phone.

Who was he talking to, and what was he saying?

As he drove off, I paced the room furiously. I was no longer cold; my cheeks flamed with anger and shame.

Why did he want to know about Rich?

And, maybe worse, what *exactly* was it Jack Stanton thought he knew about Rich and me?

But of course, there *was* nothing to know…

Not really.

Eventually I picked up my bag and left the house, to walk to the old red phone box I'd seen round by the church.

But when I got there, I discovered it was now a mobile library, full of old crime novels and self-help books about clean soups and healthy eating.

With Stanton's words in my ears, I didn't dare go back and use my own computer to email. I needed to find a payphone. That or an internet café and an anonymous computer, so I could feel safe about what I said.

I couldn't leave any sort of trail, especially with this nasty vlog on the go.

I didn't want to give anyone any sort of dirt on me or mine.

Iris hating me was punishment enough for my one fatal mistake.

PART 2

October

19

Patti

October: Libra in opposition with the new moon

By the start of October, the whole 'Is the club manager a terrible racist and what do we do about it if so?' debacle should have been sorted, but although the racism allegations had been escalated up to the league welfare officer, he was still in the process of looking into them.

This delay meant Dez was still in charge of the coaching for now.

The good news was that the under-14s' winning streak seemed to be holding, and that was like nectar to the honeybee that Dez as a manager was turning out to be. He was lapping up the victories over the past month left, right and centre, and fantastic as the results might be for the team, the fact that Dez appeared to be taking absolute credit for everything – as far as Patti could make out – was less endearing.

Last week the local press had even turned up for the cup game against the Eastdown Elite; not one but two newspapers – one from Canterbury, the other from Tunbridge Wells. The latter had included an in-depth interview with Dez about his own track to football stardom: *It was my mum who was the power behind the throne*, the article read, the royal analogy striking fear into many Tenderton hearts. *My dad disappeared off the scene when I was 10. We lived in proper deprivation in Deptford till I got signed at 16. And that meant I could buy my mum a house when I was 18 – everything she deserved. I still strive to make her proud daily.* A touching sentiment, if it was to be believed.

The *Canterbury Herald* had gone one further and published a photo of Hunter's winning goal – of *course* it was Hunter – alongside a big profile of his dad Dez, describing in detail the plans for his new football academy.

It was this last that had raised most eyebrows, causing rumblings amongst the other parents. Was Dez just using the Tigers as advertising for his own ends, people were starting to wonder; to garner publicity for the academy, which wasn't long off opening now?

In the meantime, the investigation into Nancy's leaked video seemed to have ground to a halt. No one quite knew how to refer to it – *was* it revenge porn? And if so, *whose* revenge? Was she having an affair, or was it old footage someone had got hold of to bring the couple down?

Most pressing seemed to be how it had got into the clubhouse in the first place. Dez thought the courier had been bringing Nancy's advert from the producers in London, but it seemed most likely that the DVD had been switched before it arrived. The police had taken details from all the parents who'd been there at the time of Nancy's humiliation, but no one had any more information or knew what would happen next.

Nancy herself had yet to return to the club, although Louie was often at training alongside Dez. The boys really liked him – he was nearer their age than any of the other managers, and a good laugh to boot.

But something wasn't right in the state of the Tigers, that was becoming clear, and the poisonous vlog was always in the back of people's minds. Who would have their private life, their most intimate secrets, displayed next?

No one knew that either – they just knew the vlog was going from strength to strength.

It was most unsettling.

Sam hadn't managed to fix the Fiesta's wheel after Patti had to abandon it in the woods, although he had at least given it a try – largely so they wouldn't have to pay anyone else, Patti suspected.

But asking Neil to tow it to his garage had at least given her an excuse to visit Linda.

At the Forths' house, Angel, who managed to open the door after a long wait, said Linda was in bed. This wasn't a good sign, in Patti's opinion, given that it was only two o'clock in the afternoon.

'Has she not got out, sugar, or has she just got back in?'

'Not sure.' Angel used all the energy in her wasted limbs to manage a shrug, and Patti wanted to congratulate her but also knew how patronising it would sound. 'I was out with Gran.'

'Is your mam OK, babs?' Patti gazed down at the girl in her wheelchair, hoping for a little insight, but Angel seemed more interested in getting back to *The Vampire Diaries*.

'I'll tell her you came round.' She conferred a nice smile on Patti that also said, *And now please leave.*

When Patti reminded Ethan later that he was meant to invite Davey round for his tea, the boy shook his head.

'He won't come,' he said glumly. 'He's not talking to any of us right now.'

The following week, Patti left work early to take Ethan's water bottle up to the new week-night training session Dez had added to their schedule, along with a healthy nut-based snack, Ethan having eschewed all crisps and chocolate since Dietgate.

Keeping a nervous eye on Dez, busy team-talking the boys in his usual bullish Alex Ferguson manner, telling them how good he knew they could be but how they had to live up to his expectations to make him proud, Patti managed to ask Louie quietly how Nancy was doing.

Louie rolled his eyes. 'Not great.'

But there was worse news.

The horrible *Tales of Tenderton* vlog appeared to be blossoming, and there was still no sign of who might be behind it.

Over the past few weeks, increasingly damning pieces on various Tiger parents had continued to be published online, and the vlog seemed to be getting a little more sophisticated in its make-up. It was becoming a weekly, if not daily, habit to check your inbox for the latest instalment, all of which were now inlaid with a *Deadly Sin* tag. Even if you hadn't signed up yourself, someone else would share it with you, so the whole village, even those without internet, was party to everything that went online.

The parents were often horrified at what they read, but the bigger problem was, some of the posts were undeniably entertaining – to the extent that a certain arm of the club had almost come to look forward to the vlog going live.

Except, of course, for when it affected them personally.

Mild-mannered Tony Burton had been outed as signing the petition to pull down part of the Whispering Woods for a new estate so he could make some money from being rehoused, despite the fact that he was an active and vocal member of the tree-planting 'green' committee in the village.

Kyran Desmond's mum Maria had apparently been shagging a local Tory councillor for the past few months, despite being both married – to Kyran's dad Trev – and a Labour councillor herself.

The Polish lad Mikhail's mum, Halinka, was apparently another contender for *Cheat of the Year*: despite having benefited from the UK's hospitality and free state education for her three little angels, she'd been using her brother's address to get daughter Rona into the nearby grammar school, a place hundreds of kids were fighting for. *ENVY strikes*, crowed the vlog post.

And Declan O'Connell's family – the boy from the travelling community – were being hauled over the coals for so-called 'puppy farming'. His mum, Kezia, a robust woman with a friendly face and child-bearing hips, had been caught out when a black Labrador puppy she'd sold ran in the rain, displaying the mottled coat of a mixed-breed mutt beneath the dye she'd used.

But Patti's own guilty favourite had been the video of the ethereal Meadow, owner of the spiritual crystal and palm-reading shop in town and lover of all things organic and pure, which had showed her leaving a branch of McDonald's shovelling two Big Macs into her mouth, one after the other, fumbling with fries like a woman possessed, all swilled down with a big can of Monster energy drink from her macramé handbag. The subtitle on this one was *GLUTTONY*.

Patti felt terrible that she'd derived any pleasure at all from it. She knew, irrefutably, that the vlog was beyond creepy and toxic. Worst of all, it meant they were all being watched by someone nearby, someone gathering more and more dirt on them whilst everyone waited anxiously to see who was next.

Mutterings on the touchlines got louder every week, the parents ever more divided.

They might be winning games, but the trust was gone. No one had faith in anyone anymore. A couple of boys had been removed by their parents, although they were by and large the players mainly on the bench anyway, and Davey Forth only turned up intermittently. They were starting to lack numbers as a squad, but

Dez was also on the lookout for new blood, constantly trialling new players, which made many of the original team nervous.

And of course, Patti lived in fear of what might be revealed about her own family, who so far, thank the Lord, hadn't appeared on the vlog. Surely, though, it would only be a matter of time before they too were included? Every day she prayed it wasn't her turn, but she knew something had to give – and soon.

Perhaps the usual Christmas bash would be a good place to mend bridges. Only Christmas was a couple of months off, and given how things were going, Patti wasn't sure they'd make it that far.

The team might be inching nearer the cup for the first time in three years, but whether anyone would actually be talking to each other by then remained to be seen.

20

Alex

Sunday 4 October

The Tiger mums' WhatsApp group began to ping one evening whilst I was making supper.

Despite my financial fears, to my surprise we were all continuing to settle into village life. I liked the pace of it, I found, though I still didn't like the climate much, and the children seemed to be doing all right.

But I had very real worries still: namely that Iris had been speaking to me even less – if that was possible – since that bunch of flowers had arrived, despite my best efforts to make amends for a crime I'd inadvertently committed. I'd never discovered who the flowers were from, but they seemed like the least of my concerns.

Alongside my daughter's continuing wrath, I was still waiting for answers from America – most importantly, about the payout from the insurance company – so I could start to plan for our future.

At the club earlier, there'd been a particularly hostile game during which two parents had had a heated row when someone else had asked if Neil was coming back soon.

'Why would we want that bastard back?' Kyran's father Trev, in a particularly bad mood – presumably fuelled by his wife Maria's recent infidelity – had snapped at one of the other dads, who'd retorted, 'Because he's done so much for the boys? Everyone makes mistakes.'

They were placated by that nice kid Louie, Nancy's brother, making a joke, and then good old Tony bumbling over, but some of the tensions were becoming so fraught, they were untenable.

Why don't we go all out for the do at the club? It could really bring people together, Patti suggested on the mums' thread. *Make it a bigger bash than normal?*

We could have a pre-Christmas party, early December? Raise spirits as well as drink them? Have a raffle too, Hazel responded. *Santa lists, that sort of thing?*

The very thought of Christmas made me feel a bit sick, the last one having been one of the lowest points of my life. To add to that, I wasn't sure how I was ever going to get back on track with Iris.

The few highlights of Tenderton included seeing Harry so enthusiastic: discovering a 'whole weird bunch of British bugs' to input on his favourite app, while also getting involved with the football club. Personally, I was happy to have some women I might tentatively call friends now.

How about Halloween instead? I typed. *Kids usually love it, and it's a chance for everyone to dress up & go a bit wild.*

Just how wild, I wouldn't have been able to predict though.

Living in the States, I'd come to enjoy Halloween, with Iris and Harry always going big with their trick-or-treat costumes. I wasn't sure if the Brits celebrated it the same way nowadays; it definitely hadn't been a thing when I was younger.

But Halloween seemed like good harmless fun for everyone.

Unless you got tricked, of course.

Iris in particular loved fancy dress, and helping her create a good outfit would give us something to bond over.

Like that, the lawyer Liz pinged back, ever brusque. *Gd idea.*

We could have a fancy-dress competition, and some traditional games – you know, like apple bobbing, I added, enthused.

Yeah, and what about a hog roast? someone called Kezia wrote. Her name rang a vague bell from the *Tales of Tenderton* vlog. *My old man can do you a knock-off pig.*

Ooh, said Maria. *And a fire pit? Or a bonfire?*

The floaty Meadow had still not returned to the club, claiming the energy was too bad. And although Ocean had been back in goal again at the last game, I did wonder about the row at home that might have preceded his appearance.

Nor was Meadow on WhatsApp – she didn't do social media, it turned out – but when someone told her about the party idea, she offered to do some fortune-telling if we wanted.

'What do you reckon, Hal?' I asked over supper.

Harry had been signed to the team officially now, much to his joy. Louie and Dez said he was a 'nice little player, if a bit untamed', and though I knew Patti worried that poor Davey Forth hadn't returned to the team, I was relieved to see my son having fun.

And for all her unrelenting anger with me, Iris had at least made some friends locally. She'd started singing backing vocals with Ocean's band, and she'd picked her subjects for A levels – all sciences. My clever girl: she'd just announced she wanted to become a doctor.

'We need one in the family, Ma, don't we?' She'd peered gravely over a textbook one evening, as if everything was normal between us, and I was so warmed by her words, I went to hug her.

But as I reached her, she turned away, giving me a literal cold shoulder. We still weren't allowed to touch, it seemed.

Also on the downside was the feeling that I might not have heard the last from Jack Stanton, although I prayed hard I had.

My attempts to research what he'd told me had been foiled at every turn, an internet search turning up nothing apart from the pain of seeing Fraser's name still listed on his old firm's site. I thought about emailing them to ask them to remove it, but it seemed so final somehow, I just couldn't bear to.

On a Skype call, my old friend and neighbour Bobbi said she'd heard nothing about any scandal either.

I started to wonder if Jack Stanton had been trying to wind me up.

But what definitely wasn't imaginary was my need to earn more money – soon.

One email I *had* received recently was from my brother Gray in Africa to say that his wife's aunt, Mrs Grable, was in need of ongoing medical care, meaning they'd probably have to sell the cottage to pay for it – and possibly quite soon. *Sorry, but better consider this a tentative warning*, he added.

If Fraser's life insurance payout didn't come soon, we were really up the creek, with only broken paddles for company.

And every time I thought of this, my own feelings of responsibility were hauled into the light. Along with not having a pension or savings, there remained the fact that deep down, I thought Fraser's terrible accident might have been my fault.

No one else had ever said that, but it was what I lived with daily. That if he hadn't been so down about everything, if I hadn't missed the signs, he'd have been paying more attention on the mountain that day.

Or worse still – my very worst fear – he might not have let himself fall to his death deliberately.

I needed someone to tell me that hadn't happened – and there was only one person who could.

21

Patti

Friday 9 October

Flat out in the salon midweek, Patti had been more than surprised to receive an invite via text to Nancy Fullerton's house on Friday night.

She couldn't help herself; she was *very* flattered.

Patti hadn't seen the model since her dreadful humiliation in the clubhouse that awful Sunday, but she'd warmed to the younger woman on that one visit she'd made to Patti's salon.

Patti was further flattered – although even more surprised – when she realised, after making discreet enquiries with Hazel and Alex, that her friends hadn't been asked as well.

On Friday afternoon, she washed and blow-dried her hair specially, put on her favourite and most expensive dress – bought for a cousin's wedding a few years back – and rang herself a cab. The Fiesta had not survived its trip to the garage – another nail in the coffin of the Taylor finances – and she wasn't going to bother asking Sam for a lift. He'd claimed all week that he was busy job-hunting, and far be it from her to let anything get in the way of that miracle. He'd actually announced the other day that he was thinking about retraining.

In what? she had wanted to snap back. *Being a lazy arse?*

She did try to understand that perhaps Sam didn't feel very good about himself, but he didn't help the situation by constantly ignoring her, leaving all the housework to her, not to mention letting himself go physically, lying around in stained T-shirts, ripped tracksuits or too-tight jeans.

'There's a cottage pie in the fridge and peas in the freezer.' She sprayed herself liberally with the remnants of her Christmas perfume and waited for her husband to say she looked nice.

'Ta.' Sam barely blinked, immersed in an online search.

Sighing, Patti texted her daughter Luna instead to ask her to do the food, and then felt cross with herself for being so predictably stereotypical.

Don't worry actually, she added. *Not your job.*

I'm out for tea anyway, Luna texted back. *Going to Cyn's pop-up at the Black Cat with the girls.*

Hazel's own daughter Cynthia was running a monthly pop-up dining experience at her mother's café. Patti wondered absently if Luna was planning to see that new guy again – the nice lad from the clubhouse bar, Mike. She approved of him; he seemed a stable presence for her once-erratic daughter.

The apple never falls far from the tree, eh, Patricia, she heard her mam sniff with disdain.

Well, Ethan could do tea; he was old enough, and Patti needed to hone his domestic skills anyway.

She popped her head round his bedroom door.

Sprawled in his old Ben 10 beanbag on the floor, her son jumped and then swore, turning his phone over quickly so she couldn't see it.

'*Mum!* You should knock first.'

'Sorry. Are you on Facebook?' She frowned.

'Facebook's dead.' He rolled his eyes. 'It's for old people.'

'Is that right? So what *were* you looking at?'

'Nothing.' He had picked up his phone now and kept his eyes firmly on the screen.

'I'm off now.' She pushed her suspicion down, hard. 'Can you heat up the pie for you and your dad, babs?'

'I'm not hungry,' he muttered.

Good Lord, she hoped it wasn't some horrible pornography site he was addicted to. She had strict parental controls on the internet, but kids these days were so savvy.

But she was late already, and this was not the time to start an inquisition.

'And finish your homework, yes, Eth?' she told the top of his head. 'Then it's all done, and you can just chill tomorrow after training.'

'Mmm.' Just like his dad though, he barely looked at her.

Honestly, Patti thought sadly, making her way downstairs, if it wasn't for Luna being at home at least *some* of the time, she'd never talk to anyone in this house at all.

Perhaps it was time to get a pet.

Twenty minutes later, the cab dropped her at the gated entrance to the Dewdrop Estate.

As she straightened her dress, clutching her bottle of Prosecco, a terrible clanking noise neared and a vision in patchwork rattled round the corner: Meadow, astride her old boneshaker.

'Hey!' She juddered to a halt.

'What are you doing here?' Too late, Patti hoped she didn't sound hostile, but she also sincerely hoped Meadow wasn't—

'Been invited for a drink.' Removing her rainbow-coloured helmet, Meadow dismounted. 'Bit weird, but I've been wanting to check out the ley lines over this way for ages, so it's a good excuse.'

She was wearing strange tie-dye trousers and an awful rust and brown jacket. Patti glanced down at her own smart little dress and heels, and suddenly felt horribly overdressed. Had she misjudged this evening?

'Ley lines?' She pressed the buzzer on the gatepost.

'Prehistoric lines, powerful earth energy, you know. Where humans have trodden paths since time began.'

'Oh,' said Patti stupidly as the electric gate swung open. She wondered if Meadow knew the crotch of her baggy trousers was down round her knees. 'I see.'

'I think Perry's Hill and the old convent of Our Lady of Lourdes lie on one.' Meadow pushed her bike through. 'The convent was a white witches' haven before the Church took it over, according to local legend, and Perry was a giant-slayer extraordinaire.'

'Hang on – Perry's Hill?' The hill Patti lived in the shadow of, behind the cul-de-sac on the edge of Tenderton. She'd never known who Perry was, or why he'd had a hill. 'He was a giant-slayer?' The gate clanged shut behind them.

'So legend says.'

'And you, er... you actually believe in that?'

'Not sure about giants, but I know the witches existed.'

'*Actual* witches?'

'Depends what you mean by a witch, my friend.' Meadow's nod was enigmatic. 'These days, there are enough in Kent to form many covens.'

'But we already have a coven.' Patti smiled brightly. 'At the club.'

Meadow wasn't listening. 'And of course there's the old house in the woods.'

'Is there?' Patti thought uncomfortably of the night she'd almost smashed the car into a tree. 'I didn't know that.'

'Where the great white dog abides, and the woman in the water. That's how the legend of the Hell Hounds started.'

Patti tried not to snort in disbelief. 'You don't actually believe in the Hell Hounds, do you?' But suddenly she remembered first meeting Meadow a few years back at the club, and a weird warning Meadow had made then…

Meadow looked at her. 'A word to the wise, Patti – they're not something to mess with,' and Patti's desire to laugh was quelled in her throat. 'Just as you should not stare into the Pool of Sorrow.'

'Oh.' What odd-coloured eyes the other woman had, one being a slightly darker blue than the other.

'Don't mess with the covens either.' Maybe it was just the dim light of the drive that made Meadow's eyes look so strange. 'You wouldn't want to upset the sisterhood, would you?'

'Oh no,' Patti agreed, chastened. 'Of course not.'

It was cold now, and she wished she'd worn her warm coat, as together they trudged up the drive, passing a fountain that gurgled in the middle of the clipped front lawn, a naked cherub looking very coy as water gushed from his mouth and his—

Given the reason they might have been asked round, Patti thought it better not to comment, especially as she'd noticed a camera at the front gate; it gave the disquieting sense that someone was listening.

'Ever get the feeling you're being watched?' she whispered, gesturing subtly at another camera, angled at the door they were approaching.

Meadow glanced at it but didn't reply. But then, in all the years Patti had known her, the woman *had* never displayed a smidgen of humour.

Patti thought of tortured souls in the woods and old convents, and the latter made her shudder. She'd attended a Catholic primary school herself; she'd never forget the feeling of a ruler across her palm, or the glare of Sister Beatrice. She thought of witches, and the figure they'd seen from the clubhouse on the day Nancy's video was played, and she felt that prickling sense of unease again, the one she'd had intermittently since she first saw the vision of the body in the water all those weeks ago. She was relieved when Meadow pressed the doorbell, shivering as the breeze picked up: she'd dearly like to be inside now.

But the tune the doorbell played – 'Nessun dorma' – was in such stark contrast to the conversation, it broke the tension, and Patti failed to contain her slightly hysterical laughter.

Meadow, on the other hand, just cocked her head to the side, looking grave, as if she was going to sing along.

Beneath a brilliant moon, fully risen now, the modern white house they waited in front of was squat but long, with strange castle battlements, out of keeping with the rest of it. A balcony stretched along the entire front of the house, huge stone lions guarding the front steps – though Patti was pretty sure she'd seen the same ones at the local garden centre in the summer.

To their right was a double garage, Nancy's X6 parked in front of it; to the left, a huge expanse of lawn, lit with solar toadstools along its edge. In the dim evening light, Patti could make out a giant trampoline, a set of goals and a small pink electric car abandoned by an immaculate flower bed.

'Good Lord, it's amazing, isn't it?' No longer laughing, Patti clutched her bottle tighter, wishing she'd splashed out on champagne rather than cheap fizz.

'If you like this sort of thing.' Meadow leant her ancient bike against her thigh – a bike that looked frankly ridiculous in these environs – and fingered the air. 'There's a very strange energy though. Can you feel it?'

'Girls!' Nancy flung open the door. 'Lovely to see you – so glad you could make it.' With a quick glance down the drive, she stood aside – 'Come in!' – then shut the front door smartly behind them.

They followed her perfect bottom in its cherry-red track pants, the glimpse of a tattoo just visible on her coccyx ('*Tramp stamp*,' Patti imagined her mother muttering), across a hallway fragrant with floor polish and into an enormous lounge. Lit with scented candles and clever mood lighting, it was full of fur rugs (fake, Patti hoped), multicoloured beanbags and an L-shaped tiger-print sofa longer than Patti's entire garden, a well-thumbed copy of Charlotte Brontë's *Villette* on one corner, face down and open.

One wall was inset with a vast fish tank, full of tiny tropical flickers, while the corner housed a semicircular bar, complete with popcorn machine and hot-pink velvet barstools. Neon swirly lights announced that it was *Dez & Nance's Bar*, a jolly painted sign below assuring visitors it was also *Where Everybody Knows Your Name*. On the far wall, there was a painting that looked like an Old Master, while a huge photo of the family grinned down from the nearest: the five of them laughing together in a white studio. The result was a little like they were floating in space.

The whole room was a big clashing mess of style and taste, but it worked – and it also made Patti feel overwhelmed by an emotion she couldn't put a name to.

'So, girls.' Nancy sashayed behind the bar. 'Name your poison!'

To Patti's surprise, Meadow's eyes had immediately lit on the bottle of Grey Goose vodka in the crammed row behind their hostess's head.

'I'll have a double of that' – she pointed – 'with three ice cubes please. As long as they're made with filtered water?'

'Of course, sweetie,' Nancy assured her. 'All filtered here.'

'Too much fluoride does terrible things to the brain.' Meadow looked sad. 'Can I use the loo please?'

'Second on the left,' Nance said as the terrible doorbell sang out again, and Patti realised that her dreams of an intimate evening getting to know Nancy better were over. 'Just past the gym.'

In the hallway, feet could be heard running down the main stairs. Glancing out, Patti saw Louie, in running shorts and a vest top, a dark grey whippet close behind him. He took the last steps in a leap, his bare muscular arms shining in the low light.

Very deliberately, Patti turned to study the fish tank; tiny dashes of colour flitting off at her approach.

'All right, ladies!' a voice said loudly from the doorway. 'Party time, is it?'

More surprises as the robust Kezia O'Connell, mum to the Tigers' winger Declan, strode into the room in a long denim skirt and chunky boots.

'Well, isn't this a bit of all right?' Her huge hoop earrings swung in the mood lighting as she gazed around the room. 'Don't mind if I do!' Her voice had a West Country burr, Patti noted absently as Kezia plonked a four-pack of Strongbow cider down on the bar. 'Thanks for asking me.'

Come to think of it, Patti wasn't sure they'd ever really had a proper conversation. The O'Connells lived out of the village on the neat caravan site near the flyover, and Kezia rarely came to the boys' matches, probably because she usually had several younger children holding on to her skirts.

'Kezia!' Nancy bounded round to kiss both her cheeks, reminding Patti of a gazelle. 'So glad you made it, sweetie. And Halinka – lovely to see you too!'

Behind Kezia, a painfully thin woman with brightly hennaed hair appeared, dressed in double denim, pulling a packet of Silk Cut from a cheap silver handbag.

'OK if I smoke?' she asked. Mikhail's mother was a croupier at the big casino in town, and the woman recently revealed to have lied about her address to the council. 'I have one only an hour,' she said, as if the smoking police were on hand.

'Course, sweetie. Go nuts!' Nancy smiled at someone behind Patti as she handed Halinka an ashtray. 'Can you open the doors, Louie darlin'?'

'No worries.' Louie met Patti's eye. 'Hi! How are you?'

But Patti's voice was apparently stuck in her throat as the young man opened the huge bifold doors. She looked at his strong back, at his shoulders as he flicked the top locks, and she was suddenly aware of a tremor of something.

Nancy's hands clapping girlishly brought her back to reality.

'Tell you what' – a ratty little dog skittered to Nancy's feet and she plucked it up with one hand – 'let's *all* go out, shall we?'

Drinks in hand, the women trooped out onto the terrace, followed by the elegant whippet that had been trailing Louie.

The huge full moon was in its ascent, a strange feeling of anticipation in the air, chilly enough to tempt the women to the pastel-coloured blankets stacked by a statue of Bambi.

As the others cooed over the baby deer, clad in sparkly fairy lights, Patti's eyes were drawn by the enormous hot tub, glowing blue on the right of the terrace. Without warning, that body floating face down flashed into her head again, its arms out in desperate supplication, and a sense of freezing dread drenched her, almost as if she'd just been doused in cold water herself.

Picking up a mint-green blanket, Patti draped it over her shoulders, but her hands were still trembling as she sat.

'Be nice to Pele,' Nancy said to the chihuahua, setting it down as Halinka lit the candles on the table.

The poor whippet – Pele – made futile attempts to get the handbag dog to play, but every time it got too near, the tiny one snapped at its nose with ferocious little teeth.

I know just how you feel, thought Patti sadly. *Poor Pele.*

'Nice dogs,' Kezia said, and everyone looked at her. 'Don't worry, I'm not gonna try and sell you one!' She grinned, not the least bit abashed. 'I love dogs, me, and we don't farm 'em. I just… I had to earn money, yeah? Got a lot of mouths to feed.'

'We understand that,' Nancy said softly. 'Dez would be properly sympathetic, wouldn't he, you fluffball?' She clicked her fingers for the chihuahua. 'Poor Gazza, *you* don't love other dogs, do you, darlin'?'

'Pardon me if I don't quite believe your old man'd get it.' Kezia raised an eyebrow. 'I mean, living in *this* palace!'

'Believe me' – Nancy met her gaze calmly – 'this is not where Dez came from. Nor me. He's worked his arse off to get here.'

Patti fidgeted, aware of a sudden tension in the air.

'If you say so,' Kezia sniffed.

'I do,' Nancy said mildly. 'I know footballers seem to earn silly money, but Dez's mum worked three jobs to bring her kids up, alone.'

'I hear that. And I don't care what people say, *I* did what I had to.' Kezia's sanguine mask slipped. 'Big Feen's had a few issues recently with work, and I needed to feed my little lovers.'

Her kids, Patti presumed she meant, rather than actual lovers. 'Of course,' she heard herself agreeing with alacrity.

'I get it, really.' Nancy scooped the little rat away from the whippet's increasingly desperate attempts. 'Off you go, Pele.'

Looking very sorrowful, the whippet slunk inside.

There was no sign of the big Alsatian, and Patti realised suddenly that Meadow was still missing in action, along with Louie. He'd opened the doors and promptly disappeared. Probably had a hot date in town…

Clutching her vodka and lime, Patti still felt chilled to the bone, despite the blanket.

Kezia broke the silence. 'So, lush as this is, mate, something tells me we're not here to admire your garden. What's the occasion?'

'No occasion really.' Nancy stroked the little dog's head. She was obviously lying. 'Just wanted to get to know you all a bit better.'

'I like house very much,' said Halinka. 'And this is funny.' She pointed at the toadstool solar lights. 'Make like, how you say, magic?'

Nancy grinned. 'If you're lucky maybe.'

'We look at garden?' Halinka arched pencil-thin brows.

'Course, sweetie, go nuts.'

Patti, still swigging vodka to calm her nerves, considered the different forms of magic women had used over the centuries. Whether it was witchcraft and spells, or crystal balls and palm reading like Meadow, or the astrology and star signs she herself loved (her latest horoscope had warned her that this month was bad for matters of the heart), all of them were just about survival, weren't they? All were ways of getting through the world, fielding pain and sorrow.

Patti glanced at her glass. *Good Lord*, she thought, *this must be strong! Or perhaps I'm just going nuts myself.* She grabbed a handful of pretzels, thinking she'd better soak the vodka up fast.

As Kezia and Halinka wandered over to inspect the fairy-lit gazebo in the far corner, Patti was aware of a deep exhalation from Nancy. She hid it well, but the tension around her pretty jaw was obvious.

'No Dez?' Patti asked, and the tears on Nancy's lashes that day in the salon sprang to mind.

'No.' The only one not drinking, Nancy took a neat sip of her San Pellegrino. 'He's gone to London to see his mum.'

'And is… is everything OK?' Patti dropped her voice, although the others were on the other side of the garden now.

'Well…' Nancy looked at her very directly, as if weighing up the odds. 'Not really actually. The thing is, I think your mate Linda might have set me up.'

'*Linda?* What do you mean?' Patti felt her mouth literally drop open. 'With… with *that* video of you? No way!'

But actually, could she be sure?

Linda *had* been in the clubhouse just before the video played out, though admittedly, she'd also been so drunk she could barely stand.

Patti thought of Mrs Jessop's words about drunk men not lying.

'Why would she though?' And yet even as she said it, Patti knew the answer. 'You mean because of Neil being removed from the manager's role? But the thing is, babs, how would she have got hold of… you know, *it*, in the first place?'

'That,' Nancy said coolly, 'I couldn't tell you right now. But it doesn't mean it wasn't her.'

'Well, no, sure, but she'd still have to get her hands on it first.'

'It wouldn't be that hard if someone had sent it to her, would it?'

'Who would do that?' Patti wanted to ask if it could have been the faceless man in the video who had shared it, but was it her place to do so? Not really. 'And look, someone put Linda in an evil vlog post herself, before you, so…'

'That's true. Oh, I don't know.' Nancy's sigh was so heavy, Patti almost felt it reach her own heart. 'But it's easy to steal footage off the web these days unfortunately. I've researched it, believe me. And it's easy for things to fall into the wrong hands.'

'But *why*?' Patti felt like a child, naïve and not at all au fait with the rules of revenge porn – although it struck her suddenly that it was just another way of men controlling women. A bit like drowning supposed witches. And yet Nancy suspected another woman…

'I dunno. Yet.'

Nancy seemed different tonight, Patti realised. Like a grown-up for the first time. Super-clear and intelligent in a way Patti hadn't seen her before. She thought of the clever Brontë novel on the sofa, and she felt bad about how beautiful but dumb she'd imagined Nancy to be, with her daft comments about *Oliver Twist* in the salon last month. Except... perhaps that was what she was *meant* to think.

'But that's why I've asked you all here tonight.'

'Oh.' Patti processed this for a second. 'Because you think one of us knows something about it?'

'About what?' Meadow drifted back through the French doors. She stood, face up to the nascent moon, holding her hands out beside her as if to weigh the air. 'Oh yes, very... ancient, very sacred.'

Patti fully expected her to drop to her knees at any moment and start talking in Anglo-Saxon, or tongues, or some such.

'We're talking about the... about Nancy's video that got played in the clubhouse.'

Halinka and Kezia returned to the table now. 'That was bad.'

'Yeah, it was. And it's not that I think any of you know who did it – *necessarily*.' Nancy swept them all with her turquoise gaze, until Patti wanted to wriggle in her seat like a five-year-old. 'But I've noticed that most of the nasty vlog posts are about women.' She put the dog down on the ground, and he scuttered inside.

'Well, there was Neil,' Meadow said slowly.

'He don't count.' Kezia rolled her eyes. 'He's just stupid.'

'And Tony Burton,' Patti pointed out.

'He *definitely* don't count – such an old woman.' Kezia sniggered. 'I could beat him in an arm wrestle any day!'

'I didn't see your video, but I heard about it, and it's a travesty,' Meadow chimed in. 'So what *are* you saying, Nancy?'

'I don't know exactly.' Nancy gave a graceful shrug. 'But it made me wonder if it's a sexist thing – a thing against the women. Us mums.'

'This could be true,' Halinka said, very definitely. 'Yes, I think so.'

'Whoa.' Kezia breathed out loudly. 'I never thought of that. And Tony Burton *is* like a mum himself.'

'Can I just ask, then,' Patti said. 'The thing is, like, if you think it's being done specifically against the mums, why didn't you invite all of them? Like Hazel, and Liz Bauer, or Alex?'

'I did ask Liz, but she's in London for work. Maria had a family thing. And I didn't ask Hazel because… well, I'm pretty sure she was involved in outing Neil.' Nancy fiddled with the clasp of a silver bangle on one slim wrist.

'Hold up!' Patti raised a hand. 'My mate Hazel outed Neil?' First Linda, now Hazel. She felt her hackles rise a little.

'I reckon so. And Alex – how well do you know her? She's only just arrived in Tenderton.'

'What are you saying?' Patti hadn't realised until this minute that she'd really started to warm to Alex; to the haunted look in the other woman's eyes that made her think she needed a shoulder, a confidante, when the time was right.

Nancy had now named all three of Patti's closest friends.

'I just… I never trust strangers. Dez has taught me that.' Nancy's eyes were vivid in the lamplight. 'You don't if you come from where Dez does. Trust has to be earned.'

Patti wondered if Nancy's suspicion was also due to the fact that Dez kept being super friendly to Alex, but she decided not to flag that up now. And it was funny, because she'd felt a bit jealous initially of that attention herself, but she realised that had completely faded now.

'Plus, she'd only just got here when the vlog started. And nothing's been done about her on it, has it?'

'Oho!' Kezia looked both truculent and excited at the same time. 'That is true!'

'Nor me though,' Patti said – and then immediately regretted it.

Halinka turned narrowed eyes on her. 'Oh?'

'Is this a confession?' Nancy asked lightly.

'Good Lord, no!' Patti nearly choked on her drink. 'I'm just saying.' But she wasn't sure *what* she was saying really. 'What are you suggesting?' She tried to look enthused about searching for the truth, although in reality, she just felt confused and tipsy – and like she'd just made herself look guilty.

'The police don't seem interested; they're not going to do anything – and there's no surprise there. They told me it was stupid to share images of myself and left it at that. So' – Nancy snapped her bracelet back on – 'looks like it's up to me. And I'd love your help, girls.'

She turned her beautiful eyes on them all, and Patti felt the warmth of her smile.

'I'm proposing it's time we work out who's behind all this.' Nancy stood and padded over to the table. 'I've been making notes.'

'Who's behind the vlog, you mean?' Meadow asked slowly.

'Yep.' Nancy picked up a folder. 'It's definitely time to go all DCI Jane Tennison and do our own detective work.'

'DCI *who*? You mean, go like Sherlock Holmes, is it?' Kezia filled her and Halinka's glasses to the brim, then swung the bottle round wildly. 'Any more for any more?'

'No thanks.' Patti held her glass back. The vodka had gone straight to her head, and the pretzels hadn't touched the sides.

'I'm thinking more Lady Galadriel,' said Meadow dreamily.

Nancy frowned. 'Who?'

'The elven queen in *Lord of the Rings*. Keeps 'em all in line,' Kezia explained.

Meadow looked delighted – as delighted as she ever did anyway, which wasn't very. 'Yes, that's it. Queen of the Elves, Cate Blanchett. Gorgeous.'

'Well, yeah, I guess so.' Nancy looked impatient, and again Patti realised that there was far more going on behind that beautiful face than she'd assumed. 'I'm not a hundred per cent sure how we go about it, to be honest, but if you're putting on a Halloween do, we could start there. Ask questions, or set a trap or something. I've got a cousin who does surveillance stuff – I'm gonna get some tips off him.'

'Oh my,' Meadow breathed, and she suddenly looked girlish. 'Like the Secret Seven or something? Or Nancy Drew – very apt. I love that idea!'

'And Louie is a whizz with social media and the like, and his best mate's girlfriend's a hacker.'

'Louie's girlfriend?' Patti's toes curled in her high heels, and she hid her face behind her empty glass for a moment.

'No, Louie's single right now. His best mate's girlfriend.'

Patti felt a ridiculous surge of relief. 'Don't tell Liz, for God's sake. She'll have her arrested.'

'I was thinking I could pay her to dig around a bit. See if she can work out where the vlog is coming from. Given that the police don't seem interested. It's not a crime, apparently.'

'*Vive la révolution!*' Meadow stood suddenly and saluted, and the others grinned at her in some confusion.

'Let's have a toast, my lovers.' Kezia stood too, raising her glass of Prosecco, and they all lifted theirs in response, even Nancy with her fizzy water. 'Here's to detective work.'

'Hear hear!'

'*Sto lat!*' Halinka said. 'I am for anyone finding person who broke in flat and read private mail.'

'Up your bum. Not drinking, Nance?' Kezia turned her beady eye on the model. 'Not up the duff, are you, mate?'

'Oh God, no.' Nancy looked more than horrified. 'No, I don't drink really. Have to watch my weight.' She patted her tummy. 'Part of the job.'

'You poor cow.' Kezia sounded horrified. 'Must be well boring. And I don't think any of us should *have* to watch our weight.'

'You're right,' agreed Meadow eagerly. 'It's a completely male construct, isn't it? The idea of thin being beautiful.'

'I dunno about that,' Kezia snorted, 'but I do know it's bollocks. Women need meat on us; helps us grow babies and whatnot. It's how we're meant to be.'

'Doesn't sell bras and knickers though, does it?' Nancy said sadly. 'Cellulite and rolls of fat.' Her phone pinged and she reached for it automatically.

'More's the pity, 'cos we're *meant* to have 'em,' Kezia repeated stoutly. Meadow nodded along, and Patti recalled the footage of her shoving burgers into her mouth.

She felt sad and sorry that all the women she knew, from her mother to her daughter and all her friends in between, worried constantly about being the 'right size'. Funny, though, she didn't remember any of the older generation thinking that way; not her nanna, or her great-aunt Gwen. Perhaps they were just thinner naturally, used to war rations; less food, less sugar, more active probably. Though Gwen had definitely had what you might call a comfortable figure.

And thinking of Sam's ever-expanding belly, Patti *definitely* didn't know many men of her age who worried what they looked like.

Remembering Great-Aunt Gwen brought the body floating in the pool back into her head, and she glanced over at the hot tub.

Nancy, who'd been frowning at her phone and texting, caught her gaze.

'It's not working properly at the moment – the tub. Dodgy electrics. Next time, yeah?' She put the phone away and stood, indicating, Patti thought, that the evening was over. 'Bring a cossie and come over with your Ethan.'

'Nice,' said Patti, but she was sure she'd never get in that tub willingly.

'Fancy a boogie, Patti?' Kezia downed her drink and donned her jacket. 'We're gonna paint the town red now that we're out.'

'Yes, come.' Halinka retrieved a dark plum lipstick from her tiny bag and slicked thin lips with it. 'We go to Destiny club now, have cocktails.'

'Desire, I think the club's called now, babs,' Patti corrected her absently. The idea of a nightclub was anathema to Patti: throbbing music, hot bodies, sweaty men either too close or – more likely these days – ignoring her entirely. 'My bed's calling. I'm going to get a cab.'

'Louie'll give you a lift,' Nancy said as her brother materialised from nowhere. 'Won't you, Lou?' She gave him a look that seemed significant – and which Patti couldn't interpret.

'Course,' he said, grinning. He was wearing a thick grey hoodie and Nike track pants now, and for that, for some reason, Patti was grateful.

'Oh…' To her shame, she found herself stammering. 'That's so kind, but really, don't worry.'

'I'm not worried.' His half-smile didn't falter. 'Honest, it's no bother. I'm taking Vinnie out for his run, so I'm going your way.'

Patti left Nancy's with a promise to think of more ways to investigate the creator of the horrid vlog, and an agreement to meet soon to discuss how to put their Halloween plan into action.

'We'll have to involve the other parents,' Nancy said. 'This can't go on.'

Patti agreed on both counts. She was tired of living in the shadow of fear over her own secrets. 'Yeah, specially as it was Alex's idea to do something at Halloween,' she pointed out. 'And honestly, I think she's kosher, Nance.' She tried out the other woman's nickname, feeling that lick of warmth again.

But the idea of Alex had suddenly made her feel uncomfortable.

It had taken a few weeks, but Patti realised now that Alex wasn't aloof but shy and, she was fairly sure, very lonely. She rarely mentioned her late husband, but sometimes she looked like she hadn't slept, and Patti sensed she was still in the throes of deep grief. She also got the feeling that Alex's relations with her daughter Iris weren't good – and that was something Patti understood.

There were few things more devastating than your own daughter hating you, as Luna had for a while.

'Let's arrange a meeting at the club.' She slipped her coat on. 'Get everyone involved in the party. That way it'll be easier to work out who might be responsible for the vlog. And honestly, I don't think Linda would have wanted to hurt you.' She was too hurt herself, Patti didn't say, thinking sadly of her old friend, who kept rejecting all contact. 'She's just in a bit of a mess.'

'OK,' said Nancy lightly. 'Good idea about a meeting.'

Outside, as Patti waited for Louie, Meadow mounted her bike.

'Strange.' She nodded at the house. 'But when I went to the loo…' She trailed off.

'What?' Patti was curious.

'It just… it all looks so perfect and tidy.' Meadow strapped her helmet on. 'But upstairs, it's a complete state.'

'Really?'

'Like a tornado's been through it. And when I opened the kitchen cupboard to look for a water glass' – she put a sandalled foot on the pedal – 'everything just fell out, it was so full.'

'So?'

'So, untidy mind, untidy life.' Meadow pushed off. 'Not everything might be as perfect as the surface suggests, eh? Bye.'

'Ready?' Louie arrived with the big dog as Patti watched the other woman wobble down the drive.

And once again, following him to the BMW, she felt like a shy teenager, full of fear that she'd either bore him or make a fool of herself. Yet, deep down, she also felt a giddy excitement she hadn't experienced for years.

It was very strange. It was almost as if a spell came down as soon as Patti climbed in the car with Louie, wrapping her in its warm web; a spell that took her words with it, until she was almost soporific and speechless.

Inside the toasty car, the stereo played old dub reggae softly, and Patti felt herself begin to drift, half conscious, coasting on a layer of her own dreams.

Without her noticing, Louie had taken the woodland road, but she didn't feel scared this time. She just felt as if she was floating in amongst the dark trees, the big car's strong beam lighting the way.

She felt no concern at all until Louie's phone pinged and he slowed on a bend to check it. With a stab of fear, Patti saw they were near the place she'd almost hit the tree a few weeks ago when Louie suddenly pulled in.

'Everything OK?' She was puzzled as they came to a halt beneath a great oak.

He flicked the hazard lights on and checked his phone again. 'Can you hang on?' He was frowning. 'Won't be a sec.'

Before she could answer, he got out.

Bewildered, she sat listening to the dub, curious but not too worried – until she heard a whimper behind her.

The dog, Vinnie, was pawing at the rear window.

Instinctively, Patti clicked the central locking.

'All right, boyo,' she murmured to the big Alsatian, but if anything, his whining and panting increased, interspersed now with the odd sharp bark.

She pressed her face to the glass, but nothing much was visible in the dark, apart from the first row of trees lit up by the vehicle's beam. The blackness beyond was oppressive, and in the depths of her mind, that old ghost story wavered into life – the woman whose car broke down, whose husband went for help: the woman who waited terrified until something began to thump rhythmically on the roof, and the police got out a loudspeaker and said—

Patti, she told herself. *Stop right there, you daft* dwtty!

Then she thought: *If this was a film, I'd get out now and start to walk into the woods, looking for Louie…*

But it wasn't a film, and she *absolutely* didn't want to get out of the car. At all. He'd be back in a sec – he'd said he would be.

Though it *had* been a good few minutes since he'd left, hadn't it? She glanced at the clock, realising she had no clue how long he'd been gone.

Anxiety building, she leant over to check if he'd left the key in the ignition, but there was none – the car was too modern, it seemed.

Patti checked her knackered old phone. Nope, no bars. Dead zone, of course, like when she'd almost crashed her own car. God knows why Louie's was working; he probably had some supercharged expensive model.

The dog was still whining and pawing at the rear window, and Patti felt the tiny hairs on her arms and neck prickle. *Well if I do need to get out*, she thought, *I could take Vinnie with me for protection.*

'Couldn't I, Vinnie?' She looked at him in the mirror, but the dog was pacing the boot now, slamming his weight against the window every now and then, whining on and on until the noise began to grate unbearably on her overstretched nerves.

Where the *hell* was Louie?

Something else was flickering into her head; something about woods and the reason she avoided them; something she'd fought for over twenty years.

Tentatively, taking a deep breath, Patti put her hand on the lock.

22

Alex

After the call from Rich finally came, I couldn't bear to sit in the cottage any longer, but I also didn't want to upset the children.

It had brought up so many emotions, hearing his voice. I felt raw and suppurating suddenly, like someone had dug up all the feelings I'd tried to push down since the terrible day Fraser fell to his death.

More than anything, I was painfully aware that it wasn't the children's place to worry; I didn't want it to be. They'd had enough loss already in their short lives, and they were settling in well to Tenderton. I didn't want to rock a boat that was finally sailing on calmer seas.

As I sat in the dark living room, I found myself missing my parents really badly. I thought of my mother, and how she would have known what to do in her calm, stoical way. I thought of my laconic father, out in the fields on the farm, and I had a sudden desire to walk the hills like I used to do as a girl.

But it was already dark, and it wasn't the right time to go tramping into the wilderness – not that this part of Kent was anywhere near as wild as the landscape of my childhood.

And yet I desperately needed to get out of the tiny cottage for a bit, or the emotion might just start to overflow.

Iris had bolted down a sandwich after school and had gone to meet the rest of Ocean's band in the village hall anyway, and Harry was happily ensconced in his bedroom with his insect books and an episode or three of *Friends*. He didn't want to hang out with me tonight; he'd made it clear he was happy doing his own thing, which was becoming more common, and about which I had mixed feelings.

I couldn't walk off into the night – something that on occasion I'd felt seriously tempted to do since Fraser died, crazed with sorrow and guilt – so I did my next favourite thing.

Hazel's daughter Cynthia's new monthly vegan pop-up in the Black Cat is radical for Tenderton, Patti had joked in a text, followed by a ☺, *but def worth trying. She's an ace chef – and you can take your own booze!*

I checked again on Harry, now busy logging the woodlice he'd caught in his humane traps since last Monday.

Reassured that my geeky son was fine, I put my coat on, slid a bottle of beer into my pocket and went to eat a meal someone else had cooked.

The October evenings had turned cold and crisp as we neared the half-term holiday, and having sat in the unheated house for most of the day, I was chilled to the bone by the time I arrived at the Black Cat.

The village streets looked cosy – cottage chimneys with woodsmoke curling into the air like children's drawings; soft lights shining on the witch baubles in the curtained windows on Church Street – but there was something else in the air that felt almost alive, and I was relieved to reach the café. As I stepped inside, it felt like a warm, comforting hug, an amazing smell pervading the place.

Hazel waved, pointing at a small table near the window, the scent of garlic and Cajun spices making my mouth water before I'd even read the chalkboard menu.

A jolly group of women sat opposite, several empty bottles of wine on the table, all wearing tiaras and pink banners that declared them *Hens*, the drunkest wearing a printed T-shirt reading *2nd Time Lucky!*

In the far corner by the counter, Patti's daughter Luna was sharing a bottle of red wine and a big pot of chilli with a couple of girlfriends. She called over, 'Join us if you like?'

'Oh, thanks, but you're fine,' I called back, holding up the murder mystery I'd brought to read, as if it was a great reason not to mingle. They didn't want a middle-aged has-been like me barging in, and I didn't want to intrude on their night. Honestly, I was OK with a bit of me time, and a good book to boot.

Except I couldn't concentrate on Miss Marple. I kept reading the same paragraph over and over, replaying that phone call in my head, and what it meant for me.

Replaying my very real disappointment.

I suppose, deep down, I'd hoped Rich would offer help. Or *more* help, I should say. He'd been nothing but supportive since Fraser's terrible death. I couldn't fault him there.

But on the phone, he'd just said – very nicely, and as if he was truly sorry – that he couldn't see what else he could do other than tell the insurance people, as he had already, what had happened on their boys' trip: that Fraser had fallen, losing his balance when the landslide took them all by horrific surprise.

And honestly, I knew that Rich had done enough; that he had helped give me my best chance of getting the payout that would stop us starving in a ditch.

Because the unspoken fact was, as Rich and I both knew, the reality might have been far worse than he'd told them: that Fraser hadn't necessarily slipped at all. We both had a suspicion that he'd deliberately let himself fall, despite Rich's best efforts to keep hold of him. Given up – or worse, thrown himself over in what I could only imagine was abject desperation.

At the end of the call, I'd mentioned that the police had turned up at the cottage last week. Rich had sounded really concerned for me, and that had made me want to cry. So I couldn't bear to share what Jack Stanton had said about Rich himself.

'I'm so sorry, honey,' he murmured, and the tenderness in his voice was overwhelming. 'Did you tell them what you've been worried about?'

'God, no.' I was vehement about this. 'I didn't want to betray Fraser's memory like that.'

And lose the chance of getting the insurance money, a mean little voice said somewhere. *Suicides don't get payouts.*

'Probably for the best,' he agreed. 'You wouldn't want it to get messy. And I guess, too…' There was a long pause, during which he said none of the things I hoped he might, and I debated whether I *should* tell him about Jack Stanton. 'I guess if he was shown to have deliberately taken his life, his insurance really would be in question.'

'Sure.' It sounded so bald and blunt, put like that, and the words quashed my tears. 'How's Nova?' I asked.

'Oh, great, hon.' He sounded like he was lying. 'Kids love her!'

'I'm going to try and get it sorted to bring her over,' I said, suddenly realising that was the only thing to do. How *could* I have left Nova behind? 'If that's OK.'

'No sweat.'

'I'll get on it.' God only knew how much it would cost, but I suddenly felt an icy dread that I hadn't taken care of her properly in my grief. But then I'd barely been in my right mind when I boarded the plane…

There was another pause as I tried to assemble my thoughts.

'Well,' he began, as I simultaneously asked, 'How's Janine?'

'She's good, thanks, hon,' he replied brightly. 'Loving the new baby!'

The baby.

'Great.' I poked the grass savagely with my trainer toe.

'She's doing car pool right now. Troy's playing Little League this weekend for the county, and Mary-Lou's in a production of *Seven Brides*. Bit retro, if you ask me, but perhaps that's the point.'

'Oh.' I found myself wanting to scream at the ordinariness of their lives, the calm domesticity that I no longer had; that I missed. 'Sounds good,' I managed.

Though our lives hadn't really been like that by the end.

What I didn't say was, 'Leave her and them; come and see me.'

Of course I didn't, but I could have done.

'Is it my fault, Rich?' I said, very quietly, so he had to ask me to repeat myself. 'Did I push Fraser to do what he did?'

'What? No way, hon! He was a law unto himself, your good fella. It was just a terrible freak of nature.'

But I didn't believe him. Not on the day Fraser did it, and not now.

I'd been so fed up with Fraser and his bad moods, his ongoing depression, his avoidance of me; so angry that it had gone on for so long with him refusing to get help or explain things to me that in the end, I'd said something terrible. I'd told him in our last row that he might as well be dead, because he was acting as if he already was.

It was rash and impetuous and fuelled with fury.

But it was also something I'd have to live with for ever.

At the café table, sitting amongst the hubbub, I closed my eyes to stop the print on the page sliding around, the adventures in St Mary Mead the last thing on my mind.

'Woo-hoo, Alex!'

'Hey!' I was jerked back to reality by a jolly-looking Hazel, arriving at my table with a bowl of fat olives. She was running front of house for Cynthia, who was out the back cooking.

'On the house.' Hazel smiled, passing the shiny little globules over and brandishing a bottle opener. 'Hand it over.'

'Thanks! It smells amazing in here,' I said as she popped the lid of my beer.

'She's a talented chef, my Cyn. And it's really good to have the Manor House Airbnb coming in.' She indicated the middle-aged women in tiaras as she passed my beer back. 'It's been much busier than we thought. Join you for a sec?'

I nodded. 'Of course, please do.'

'Must say, I'm a bit put out about Nancy's, aren't you?' She sat, pushing her hair up in a gesture I'd already come to recognise as one of annoyance.

'Sorry.' I frowned. 'I'm not sure what you mean.'

'Didn't you know? Patti's been invited over to that enormous gaff for drinks.' Poor Hazel – she looked really indignant. '*And* I've just found out on the grapevine that Maria was invited too, *and* Meadow and Kezia!'

'Right.' I took a swig of beer. I really didn't mind, in the grand scheme of things. I knew I hadn't been very friendly since I arrived; overcautious was probably the right description, keeping myself to myself. And I'd never got round to contacting Nancy to offer my support, so there was no reason for her to invite me anyway.

'Is it to do with the football club?'

'I wouldn't know.' Hazel looked downright mournful. 'I swear, though, Dez has got his eye on a much bigger prize than the Tigers.'

'Like what?'

'His precious academy kicks off in December; big Christmas opening, I heard. He's got an empire in his sights, that man. Next stop, managership of a Premier League club.'

'Oh, I see.' Honestly, the whole football academy thing was still pretty much a mystery to me. Though I definitely *did* understand that farming the dreams of tens of thousands of British parents could prove extremely lucrative.

The door pinged and a duvet walked in.

'All right, Sheila? Your takeaway's ready. Joshy!' Hazel called her son, who appeared with a smile and a carrier bag. He was a nice boy, I thought, calm and gentle – and apparently, I was learning, with brilliant handling skills in goal now he was so often taking Ocean's place there.

Not all the team were pleasant, I'd already noted; many were nothing if not surly, or just downright competitive, and every bit as bitchy as girls could be.

'Thank you, Josh,' said Sheila. The little woman from the club shop, small and freckled, was terribly serious-looking, I thought as she avoided my smile, eyes on the floor. 'It smells nice. Thank you, Hazel.'

'You're welcome, love.'

The door pinged again, and a bearded young man in a duffel coat entered, nodding at Sheila as Luna waved eagerly.

Mike, from the clubhouse bar, I realised, as he grinned and joined Luna's table.

'Funny one, that Sheila,' Hazel murmured as we watched the duvet disappear into the dark. 'She's only about thirty, I think, but she looks forty-five, don't you reckon? And you'd never know it now, but she's got a mean left foot.'

'A what?'

'She used to play for the women's team, till they got run out of Tenderton. I'm not sure she's ever recovered from it.' Hazel's dark eyes danced with the thrill of the story. 'It was all handbags and football studs at dawn.'

'Run out? What do you mean?'

'Long story. Let's just say, not many round here seemed ready to move into the twenty-first century when it came to equality on the pitch.'

That wasn't entirely surprising, given that they kept a ducking stool on the village green, I thought.

'Hey!' Hazel said crossly. 'How did you get in?'

A black cat sauntered across the café floor as the door pinged again and a man I'd rather not ever see again strolled in.

'Jack.' Hazel nodded as she followed the cat. 'Have a seat and I'll check with Cyn if your order's ready. Shoo, you!' She chased the animal back to the door.

'Ta, mate.' Jack Stanton leant on the counter, barely looking up from his phone. 'I thought that was your lucky mascot.'

Hazel dumped the cat outside and shut the door firmly. 'Not ours, no. Won't be a sec, Alex.' She bustled off, and I flipped my book open again quickly so I didn't catch Jack Stanton's eye.

But it was too late; he'd seen me.

'Hi,' I said.

He raised a lazy eyebrow and went straight back to his phone.

I pretended really hard I was reading my book. It was truly gripping – a classic Agatha Christie from the cottage shelf – but I couldn't take in a single word, I was seething so hard.

'Mr Stanton,' another female voice said. 'Your order's ready.'

I glanced up to see Hazel's daughter, Cyn, behind the counter.

In her early twenties, she was gorgeous; the spit of her mother, her hair a combination of intricate braids and curls. I took a second look and realised, as she passed the steaming bag to Jack Stanton with the most charming smile, that it *hadn't* been Hazel I'd seen that day in the club car park.

No, it was *this* young woman I'd seen, wrapped in her mum's leopard-skin coat; it was Cynthia who'd looked as if she was thick as thieves with Dez.

And from the sound of what Hazel had just been saying about Dez – a man who was most definitely not one of her favourite people – she couldn't have any idea at all that her daughter was… what?

Dez's friend?

Or something rather more involved?

My email inbox pinged.

Glancing at my phone, an electric current skimmed across my skin.

It was from the offices of Fraser's company, Pacific Insurance, an email from Ernie, his old boss, telling me he'd signed off a final loyalty bonus for Fraser that he wanted me to have. He'd arrange transfer to an account if I sent the details; he hoped it would help us settle into our new home.

I could feel the heat round my collar as I read the email quickly, feeling like Jack Stanton must be reading the same thing at the same time.

Don't be stupid, Alex, I told myself. *Get a grip; you've nothing to hide.*

I looked up and out of the big glass window and felt a huge hollow in my heart. For a second, I'd thought I'd seen Nova, my beloved dog, pacing on the far pavement.

I must start the wheels turning to get her sent over.

Clutching my phone tighter, I sent a grateful reply to Ernie.

When I looked up again, Jack Stanton was watching me, an inscrutable look on his face, and the pavement opposite was empty.

23

Patti

In the tarry blackness of the woods, hand on the door, Patti could still see nothing but the first row of trees; beyond that, nothing but the night.

All was dark, apart from the weakening headlight the moths danced in, the moon no longer visible through the canopy of trees, mist starting to snake between the twisted trunks.

She knew that if she was watching herself on TV, she'd be shouting manically, 'Stay inside the car, for God's sake, you stupid woman!' Oh yes, Patti absolutely knew she shouldn't get out of the car.

But every second that ticked by without Louie appearing unnerved her more.

Where the hell had he gone? Worse, what if something awful had happened to him?

It's only the woods near where I live, she told herself strictly, and there was no reason to be scared of the dark. She hadn't been bothered as a girl, had she; she'd often walked home from the pub across the fields.

But she'd been sixteen, seventeen then, giddy and invincible with drink, plus fast on her feet. And that had been her home;

she'd known the paths and shortcuts and hedgerows like she'd inhaled them at birth.

And then perhaps she *had* grown frightened after that, after Nigel…

Fear mingled with the tendrils of mist curling through the trees, the anxiety climbing in her chest. This place wasn't really her home, however long she'd been here. And Meadow's words went round and round in her head, like dodgem cars, buffeted by alcohol.

The old house in the woods… the woman in the water.

But. She was a grown-up, and this *wasn't* a horror film.

Despite her misgivings, she opened the door and got out of the car. Using her phone torch, she edged ten very tentative feet around to the back, her idea being to let the dog out and take him with her for protection. Together they'd go and find Louie.

Except, fingers on the catch, she could hear something far off: far off, perhaps, but definitely getting nearer…

She froze.

It was coming from the woods, fast and loud, rustling through the undergrowth.

Her heart skipped beats so that even breathing felt difficult. As she rushed back to the passenger seat, her foot caught in a bramble. Panicking, she dropped her phone as the noise neared; feet snapping twigs as it came, pounding towards her…

In the back of the car, the dog was hurling himself against the window now. Her hands were shaking so much she couldn't retrieve the bloody phone from the ground, and she could barely see it anyway, as the torch had gone off—

A weight hit her, knocking her for six.

'*Oof!*' All the air left her as she went flying, sprawling forward onto her side. For a second, she couldn't think; fear or not, she just lay still, completely winded.

'Oh my God, Patti!'

It was Louie. Thank God, it was just him.

'Good Lord!' she said weakly, but he was already leaning down to haul her back up again by one arm, so roughly it hurt.

'Hurry up.' He was actually panting. 'I mean, sorry, but I can't... Just get in the car please.'

'Wait!' She turned, fumbling around for the phone. 'I dropped my...'

But she could hear something else now, something coming through the trees, and the dog was barking properly, barking and barking in the boot of the car.

'Get in the bloody car NOW!' Louie bundled her physically round to the passenger side, then sprinted back to his own door and almost fell into the driver's seat, slamming the door hard.

With a roar, they sped off into the dark, leaving Patti's phone behind them on the woodland floor.

And, although part of her really wanted to, she didn't dare look back.

Louie didn't take her straight home.

Largely, Patti suspected, because he'd forgotten she was even there.

But she didn't complain. She sensed his distress; it was palpable, in fact. So she just sat quietly as he took the turn before her cul-de-sac, the big car easily climbing the thin, twisting road up onto the hill.

Was that the only reason she didn't speak though – his distress? If she was honest with herself, not really.

Almost at the summit, Louie pulled into a turning by the gate to a farm and stopped the engine again.

'Sorry,' he muttered, still barely glancing at her as he pulled his own phone out and began to type something.

Patti didn't reply. She sat gazing out of the window, rubbing her elbow; bruised from where she'd fallen in the wood.

From here, the ancient burial mound on top of the hill was visible, the ten or so skeleton trees standing sentinel around it, the old stone circle from Druid days silhouetted against the night sky. She thought of Meadow's words about the old myths.

Funny to think that she lived in the shadow of a hill named for a gallant giant-slayer.

Above them, the moon was very large and bright in the sky and, out in the open now, Patti felt she could almost touch it. Her breathing slowed as she looked up at it. Was it a harvest moon? she wondered. Or maybe not – maybe it was the hunter's, changing with the month. Her great-aunt would have known; they'd always relied on the moon cycles for farming. Hunter's moon seemed more apt; Louie running through the trees as if he was being pursued.

She heard the whoosh of his text being sent. And she found she wanted to know what was going on – who or what he'd been running from – but at the same time, she really didn't.

'Was it the woman in the woods?' Patti turned to him. 'The witch?'

'Sorry?' He was uncomprehending. 'What do you mean?'

'Whoever you were running from?'

'Oh, I see.' He gave a shaky laugh. 'Yeah, something like that.'

'Aren't you going to tell me what's going on?' Patti felt a surge of something, a kind of fond irritation. 'I mean, what just happened?'

'I can't, Patti.' He looked at her, and his young face was scrawled with tension and fear. 'I'd love to, but I can't, not right now anyway.'

In the dim light, they gazed at one another. The stereo was still playing, very quietly now, and it was warm again, and his eyes were the same colour as his sister's, she noticed for the first time. Aquamarine, she thought absently; was that what the colour was called? Such a beautiful shade.

'It's kind of… it's too hard to explain,' he tried again helplessly.

She had the strongest inclination to put a hand on his poor anxious face, to just lay her hand on his cheek, but she knew she mustn't.

'It's all right, sugar,' she said gently, and her voice was the one she used for her kids, and yet she knew, implicitly, right down to her core, that she didn't feel the least bit maternal about Louie.

'Patti—' he began, but she cut across his words.

'I think…' She looked up at the pale moon and took a deep breath. She thought about her house, and the fact that Sam would either be watching *Top Gear* and eating cold beans from the tin, or snoring on the sofa yet again, his belly poking out from under his T-shirt, and Ethan would be locked in his room, Luna out and about, possibly with that tattooed new beau, and Patti would get in and no one would even notice.

No one would take the slightest bit of notice.

'Would you… could you take me home now please?'

More than anything, she wanted him to say no. *No, don't go home, Patti. Stay here with me…*

And she almost closed her eyes in the hope that he might suddenly feel compelled to kiss her, but she wasn't a silly soppy sort, and she didn't want to embarrass herself. She'd done enough of that since she'd first met him, or at least it seemed that way to her. And it was daft anyway.

'Please,' she said again, her voice louder now. 'If you don't mind dropping me back, I'd be very grateful.'

'Yeah, course.' Louie pushed his hand through his hair, as if he'd just woken up. 'If I…'

'If you what?' She didn't dare look at him again, at his nice hands and his broad shoulders that tapered down to a lean waist and—

'Nothing.' He started the engine again.

Patti looked out at the dark night, at the moon, at the road as he eased the car out of the turning, reversing it smoothly on top of that hill. She kept her eyes on the old burial mound that held who knew what secrets; and the stone circle that must have witnessed so many secret rites of passage.

As they left the mystical behind them, she clenched her fists against the sorrow descending; against all the answers she was still missing; answers that she longed for.

24

Alex

Mid October

After Jack Stanton had blanked me in the Black Cat, I'd hurried home under the huge moon, my palms tingling with irritation.

As I walked past the old manor house, all the lights were blazing, and I guessed that its inhabitants – the middle-aged hen party – would be out for some time; maybe they'd go clubbing in town after their meal.

Since they'd started letting it as an Airbnb, loud music and cackling were often heard late into the night, whilst its inhabitants sometimes indulged in daytime drinking sessions in the Witch's Head, a pub I'd not yet visited.

Blissfully though, back at Primrose Cottage, everything was quiet and calm.

Checking on Harry, I found him asleep over an episode of *Friends*, still chatting to itself. Turning the computer off, I pulled the duvet over him, removing the jam jar of beloved woodlice to the windowsill. God love him. Tomorrow I'd suggest he let them go.

Downstairs, I poured myself a glass of wine and slowly talked myself round to less agitated feelings about Jack Stanton's rudeness.

I had something to celebrate, didn't I? Fraser's belated bonus would be our salvation. Except it wasn't something happy, was it? It was just more sadness, more underlining of our loss. A loss that was taking its toll on our family.

As if she'd read my mind, Iris arrived home, slamming the front door behind her.

'Hey!' I said. 'Good night?' I patted the sofa beside me. 'Come and tell me about it.'

'It was crap,' she snapped.

My heart sank faster than a lift plummeting down its shaft. 'Why?'

I could sense her considering whether to bother to reply.

'It's the stupid bass player.' Iris kicked the bottom step with her hi-top toe. 'She wants to do a cover of a song I hate.'

'What song?'

'"Kooks".'

'Oh dear.' I knew exactly why Iris didn't want to cover it; her dad used to sing it to her when she was little, strumming it on his guitar as she grew older. 'You mean the Bowie song about his little kid?'

'Nah, Ma, I meant the John Lennon, *not*.' Iris rolled her eyes at my apparent stupidity. 'I said I don't want to do it. But they didn't listen, so I left.'

'Iris, I'm sorry.' I stood up to hug her. 'Maybe I could have a word?'

She pushed me away – hard. 'Don't you bloody dare!' My daughter glowered at me in disgust. 'You always make things a hundred times worse.'

'Oh come on! I've told you a million times not to exaggerate!' It was an old favourite of Fraser's, but I'd miscalculated badly.

'Why don't you just piss off,' I heard her mutter as she stomped up the stairs, making all the lights flicker. I didn't even bother telling her off; it was pointless.

I really must get the electrics checked, I thought wearily, slumping back on the sofa. More crucially, I really must get started on the commission for the gardening magazine I'd finally secured; it'd pay the peppercorn rent and the bills until Christmas.

But I had no energy left tonight – Iris's wrath had drained the last bit – so instead I just topped up my wine.

At least the phone call with Rich meant I knew that part of my life was really over. I could expect nothing from him apart from maybe a Christmas card. Whatever I had hoped for, which was all ridiculous anyway, I knew now I wouldn't get.

I was on my own with my children in Tenderton. And that meant one thing: making more of a concerted effort to fit in.

Midweek, Patti had popped round with spare shin pads for Harry, and standing on the doorstep, too busy to come in, she'd told me about the evening at Nancy's. Apparently, Nancy had suggested their own detective work to find out who was behind the horrible vlog.

'Do you want to get involved?' Patti was enthusiastic. 'You're very welcome – we really need to crack who's doing this. Ooh, and Alex, you should see Nancy and Dez's place.' Her eyes were as wide as a child's. 'It's proper lush!'

'Gosh.' I tried to look enthused. 'Well, I guess he *is* a rich footballer, so—'

'Oh, hello there.' Patti looked down. 'This your new friend?' The big black cat was winding round her shins – trying to get into the cottage apparently.

'No, not mine.' I barred its way. 'Next door's, I think.'

Shooing it away, I tried to appear interested in Nancy's mansion, but frankly, I wasn't.

Like everyone else, I lived nowadays with the constant niggle that I might be next on the nasty *Tales of Tenderton* vlog. So far though, I'd been cocooned by the fact that nothing had been written about my family yet, and I really didn't want to get involved with sleuthing.

I had more pressing things on my mind, like how I was going to get my work done on time to pay the water rates and the council tax.

On Saturday morning, over cups of tea in the clubhouse after training, everyone else agreed that Halloween was a good day to have a do at the club. It meant we had an excuse for a party, and we also had a theme to work around.

I was in a better mood: this morning had brought the letter I'd been waiting for all these months from America. The good news was that the claim on Fraser's life insurance *would* go through – *hallelujah!* – but the bad news was the payout might take up to a year.

Another year.

'Let's make it fancy dress,' I suggested to the other parents, feeling a little overwhelmed about speaking in front of so many strangers, welcoming as they might be. 'It could be a competition, maybe with prizes?' But they all leapt on the idea, and I felt shy but pleased that my suggestion had gone down well.

Someone else – one of the glamorous mums' coven, I thought – suggested they bring the ducking stool to the grounds as a gimmick: 'We could rent out rides on it!'

Fortunately, that was met with a suitable amount of horror, as was the idea of guessing the number of bones found in the Pool of Sorrow.

'That blinking pool,' Patti muttered, 'it'll be the death of someone else soon. If the vlog isn't first.'

As I went to collect Harry's muddy boots from the changing room, I passed the tuck shop.

'You want to be careful, my girl,' the white-haired old lady who ran the place was murmuring to that meek little Sheila. 'You don't want to let your sour grapes turn into bitter wine.' She spotted me. 'All right there, my dear? Anything I can get you? Nice Kit Kat, perhaps, or some Bourbons?'

'Bour*bon*, maybe,' I joked, but she just blinked her bright little eyes at me until I felt vaguely sordid for suggesting such a thing. 'Um, I think I'll have a Twix, thank you.'

I had no desire for a Twix, but in the laser beam of her blue gaze, I felt like I'd better buy something.

'I was just telling Sheila here not to get too despondent about the ladies' team.' The old lady plucked the chocolate bar off the shelf and popped it on the counter. 'That'll be fifty-four pence please.'

I found my purse. 'Do you miss it?'

'What?' Sheila looked vacant.

'The football?'

'No,' she said, but I had the feeling she was lying. 'Women aren't meant to play football.'

Mrs Jessop shook her head sadly.

'That's what Neil and that Dez both told me when I suggested starting the girls' under-16s team again.' From the look on the younger woman's face, I guessed she had found that devastating.

Mrs Jessop pushed the tip bowl forward incrementally as she sorted the leaflets by the till. 'Sheila was born to play, weren't you, my dear?'

'My daughter played a bit in the States,' I said. 'If you could start up again, she might be keen.'

But Sheila just shrugged and turned away.

'Seems a shame.' I dropped my change in the tip bowl, absently reading the motto on its bottom.

Revenge is a dish best served cold.

25

Patti

Sunday 18 October

Patti had hoped that Louie would turn up with Nancy to the meeting in the clubhouse on Saturday to discuss the Halloween do, but there was no sign of him.

She sat through the meeting as they drew up the poster to advertise the party, discussing events they could run in conjunction and how much money they might raise, but people were more tense than usual, suspicion about the vlog pointing its accusing finger at them all.

Tension or not, Patti's mind kept wandering.

Perhaps Louie had left Nancy's now and gone back to London. He hadn't helped Dez at training for the past couple of sessions. This Patti knew because, frankly, she'd looked, several times, lingering around the clubhouse pretending she was sorting kit.

To no avail. Louie wasn't here anymore.

Despite her disappointment, at least today's game against the Beauford Bees had been another good match, which was becoming more common for the Tigers. Still, despite a complex tactic of counter-pressing, along with some spectacular legwork from Maxi Bauer – including a sneaky midfield pivot that stunned his opposite man – and some super dives from Ocean in goal, it had ended in a draw.

There had been an extra buzz in the air, created, Patti suspected, by a rumour that an Arsenal scout was amongst the ever-growing crowd of spectators. Whether that was down to one of the opposition's dads turning up in a retro Thierry Henry tracksuit was still to be proved; but, certainly, none of the boys had been approached at the end of the game, so it seemed unlikely to be true.

But who knew so many locals without kids at the club were suddenly passionate about Sunday League football? No one had paid a blind bit of notice in the old days, Patti mused, perched on a camping chair on the sideline, too tired to stand throughout the game. She suspected this growing group of spectators had been enticed partly by the Tigers' new sponsor, courtesy of Dez: local brewery Kent Ales. But mainly, she imagined, the interest was down to the recent press about Nancy and Dez: people had come to see for themselves.

One of the tabloids had run a double-page spread about the academy, which was opening soon, alongside a few gorgeous shots of the family, the largest being one of a semi-naked Nancy, all peachy tones, on a lingerie shoot, which, given the horrible vlog, felt too close to the mark. Sadly for any lascivious spectators, Patti thought wryly, trying not to search the sideline for Louie, Nancy had attended today's match – the first one she'd been to since that awful afternoon – snugly wrapped in the world's longest fake fur (at least Patti hoped it was fake, as she had the rugs in Dewdrop Mansion).

For once, Sam had come to watch, and he took Ethan, Josh and a couple of the other boys for a burger afterwards.

'Go home and run a nice hot bath, love,' he told Patti in front of the other parents, which made Patti want to scream: *Don't believe the hype, guys, it's a once-in-a-lifetime occurrence.*

But she just smiled.

Her eldest brother Dai rang as she went to collect the filthy kit from the clubhouse. Patti let him have it with both barrels. 'Why did I marry such a lazy arse, Dai? Why didn't you warn me?'

And Dai, who ran a successful chain of hardware shops in Cardiff and spent every holiday in his Majorcan villa with his stay-at-home wife and their brood of kids, laughed gently. 'Because you're soft as putty, Patti Jones, but you're stubborn as hell. And because I seem to remember you swore you two were a pair matched in star-sign heaven.'

'Yes, well. I'm not a Jones anymore.' With her phone balanced beneath her chin, Patti shoved the muddy tops into the laundry bag, which felt like a metaphor for her life right now. 'You should have told me that astrology is rubbish.' She scooped up one more encrusted shirt and dragged the bag to the door. 'Or warned me not to marry a lazy Scorpio. I don't even think he's *tried* to get a new job since his business went under, despite what he's said. Ta, Mike.'

The barman, bringing in crates of lager, was holding the door for her. He had a nice smile, she thought absently; she could do worse for a son-in-law. Not that she wanted a son-in-law just yet.

'I don't want to say told-you-so,' her big brother sighed. 'But you didn't have to marry him at all, Patti.'

'I did have to, and you know it.' She stomped back for the second bag, passing little Sheila, who was just arriving. 'If he hadn't married me when I… *you know*' – she dropped her voice – 'I'd have been a single mum, out on my ear and up the swanny.'

At home, Patti peeled off her jumper and jeans, realising how grateful she was for a few minutes to herself. She was just about to run a bath when the doorbell rang.

Shoving her old kimono on, she answered it.

'This is getting serious now.' Hazel stumbled past her. '*Seriously* creepy.'

'What?'

'There's another bloody post on that hideous vlog.'

'Oh no.' Patti's heart skittered. 'Who is it this time?' she asked, at the same time as Hazel announced: 'It's only Liz bloody-perfect-life Bauer.'

'Liz? No!' Was it bad that Patti breathed a sigh of relief?

'It's awful.' Hazel passed her phone over. 'It's worse than Neil.'

'Worse, is it, sugar? How's that then?'

'Something to do with…' Hazel actually looked embarrassed. 'Sexual fetish.' She dropped her voice.

'Oh my God.' Patti was astounded. 'Are you sure?'

'Yeah, I'm sure. It's all there.' Her friend winced. 'Far too much of it, in fact. Someone's really got it in for us lot, but the thing is, Patti, I reckon I know who.'

'Really?' Patti had managed to get the post open now. It looked a bit different to the others, though she couldn't immediately pinpoint why.

Tales of Tenderton
So this one might be a bit of a shock to you…

The voice was so creepy. It sounded like a doll, put through some kind of machine, or an app. Who knew what was possible with technology these days?

> Who would have thought that holier-than-thou Liz Bauer, lawyer extraordinaire and mum of three, a woman who likes to draw attention constantly to her pro bono works for the greater good of the nation,

actually spends her leisure time in a Soho SEX
DUNGEON?

Liz, who earns a fortune representing the bad and the
ugly (including the horror who is racist EDN rep Terry
Fowler), has been visiting – according to sources – the
store Strap 'em Up in Berwick Street for some years
now, and has also been a member of the infamous fetish
club Torture Garden for a while too, hobnobbing – or
is it just knobbing – with who knows which illustrious/
sleazy members. Liz likes a threesome, it transpires.

Would Liz want you to know this?

I doubt it.

Take a look at this video footage of Liz entering
Strap 'em Up, and <u>these</u> photos of her Torture Garden
membership badge and shots of S&M gear…

'Oh God,' Patti breathed. 'That's really *really* not at all what
I'd have expected from Liz.'

'It's pretty disgusting.' Hazel looked cross.

'Not really disgusting, Haze, to be fair. More like, just a bit
weird. Still, each to their own, eh?' Patti hoped Hazel would go
now so she could have her bath. 'Shall we talk about it tomorrow?
I'm ever so tired—'

'And now I think I might know who's behind it all,' Hazel
repeated.

'Who?'

'That family that got booted out of the Tigers last year. The
Smiths!' She looked triumphant.

None the wiser, Patti shook her head.

'You do know. They live behind the leisure centre. They had
the fat boy, Paulie, who had to give up because he kept getting
"asthma".'

'Hazel!' Patti remembered what Ethan had said about dieting. 'He wasn't *fat*.'

'He *was* fat, love. If anyone's allowed to say it, it's me, given my struggles with Weight Watchers.' Hazel's humour was nothing if not caustic. 'And he had a proper nasty temper, that dad, plus the mum was a rabid churchgoer. They promised hell would rain down on us during his final game. You must remember – it was the most fun I had all season.'

'I must have missed that match.' Honestly, Patti felt so tired, she just didn't care about any of it right now. She was more concerned about the massive rates bill she'd just received for Beauty Bound, and also, she was just sad. That was what worried her most: her feelings for... well, her infinite *lack* of feelings for Sam.

'And what about your new best mate?'

'Who's that?' Patti was bewildered.

'Nancy.' Hazel took the phone back. 'Any news there?' She was definitely being snippy.

'She's not my new best mate, Haze, and she says they've drawn a blank with the enquiry. I don't think the police were very interested.'

'Well there's a surprise.' Hazel shook her head. 'I must say, I wasn't sure about that young copper who came round – didn't know her arse from her elbow.'

But then Hazel mistrusted all police, Patti knew; it was a family thing – and not without good cause.

She suddenly felt beyond exhausted. She just wanted to sink into the suds and forget about real life, nasty vlogs, S&M, drunken best mates and the lot.

Which reminded her, she *still* hadn't got hold of Linda.

Hazel turned towards the door, much to Patti's relief. 'I left Josh in charge. Better go before he burns the café down.'

*

Patti trudged upstairs to run the bath.

The last few vlog posts definitely seemed a bit different to the first ones. This one had had an avatar presenting it too, she realised, a cartoon-like little face, and that horrible electronic voice was stuck in her head now.

Passing Luna's room, Patti heard the old computer whirring. It was that decrepit, it was probably about to blow up, and it drove her mad thinking of all the electricity it must be using.

At Luna's desk, searching for the computer's off button, she glanced at the screen – and almost did a comedy recoil.

But it most certainly wasn't funny.

It was a far-right site – the EDN by the looks of it, Terry Fowler's face gurning out at her: the man who'd been mentioned in the first *Tales of Tenderton* vlog about Neil Forth and who'd just popped up alongside Liz Bauer.

What the hell was Luna doing on here?

The doorbell rang again, and Patti jumped guiltily. Hazel must have forgotten something.

'What did you forget?' she said as she pulled open the door.

'It's more what *you* forgot,' Louie said with a slow, shy smile.

'Oh,' Patti clutched her kimono tighter.

He extended his hand and opened it.

An earring she'd not even realised she'd lost; cheap and glinting under the hall light.

Wishing she had more clothes on, her hand went to her ear as she glanced upstairs, as if a dirty secret was hiding in Luna's room.

'Thanks so much. Um, come in, why don't you?' *Get a grip, Patti.*

'Thanks.' Louie stepped inside.

Next to her he seemed very tall, and she felt confused. 'I have to say, I hadn't even missed it.' She was gabbling. 'The earring. Funny.'

'I just… I wanted to say…' He was nervous too, she thought. 'About the other night. I'm sorry it was so… strange.'

Patti suddenly felt very light, as if she might float away.

'I did want to explain, but it's difficult because…' Louie trailed off, miserable. 'It's just… it's not really my place to.'

Shifting from foot to foot, his bright eyes catching the light, he looked so bashful and handsome, she felt completely floored. She could smell him again; like clean washing and something else she couldn't name.

Slowly she stretched her hand out, for what reason she didn't know. But, instead of backing off, he reached his own hand out to her. His skin was warm and dry against hers, and she felt like laughing as she gazed up at him, still feeling small and rather giddy and—

A key turned in the lock.

They pulled away from each other, her hand dropping back to her side quickly as Sam and Ethan came through the front door.

'Louie!' Ethan's eyes filled with delight.

'All right, mate!' Louie bumped fists with him, and she loved him just a little bit more in that moment as she grasped the kimono round her, feeling horribly exposed.

A little bit *more*?

'Louie, is it?' Sam offered a hand.

'Louie gave me a lift back from Nancy's the other night, and I dropped my earring in the car.' Patti held it up, her heart thumping as if she'd done something illegal, her voice sounding strangled even to her.

'Women, eh, mate?' Sam clapped Louie on the back. 'They'd forget their heads if they weren't attached to their pretty little necks!'

Did he really just say that?

In that moment, Patti felt cold, metallic rage, the intensity of which she wasn't sure she'd ever felt for her husband before.

'Fancy a beer?' Sam was still talking. 'You could tell me all about that fool who's taken over Millwall.'

'Ah, cheers.' Louie was backing out now. 'I would, but I've got to help Nancy with the kids. Dez is back in London again.' So polite – and already halfway out the door.

Patti didn't blame him.

Here she was, a forty-something mother/beautician/wife, wearing an ancient kimono and fluffy socks, and here was her sexist, overweight husband, grinning like an idiot, slightly tanked up and sounding like some kind of Neanderthal.

'I'll see you out.' Sam shepherded Louie to the front door, obviously wanting to chat man to man, and Ethan bundled upstairs. Patti was left standing dumbly, holding the earring Louie had just returned to her.

She turned it in her hand, the silver and plate gold glittering sadly in the dim lighting.

Someone as young and vibrant as Louie wasn't going to give a woman like her a second thought, she told herself furiously. He'd stepped out of the door without so much as glancing over his shoulder at her.

Who the hell was she kidding?

The blast of cold air that came back in with Sam made her shiver.

He caught her eye, and for a nasty moment she thought: *He knows how I feel.*

'What's for tea?' He rubbed his belly. 'I'm totally Lee Marvin. Takes it out of you, doesn't it, all that cheering for the boys.'

Before Patti could retort, the front door opened again and Luna stumbled in.

She looked slightly… skew-whiff, and Patti felt a fear she hadn't felt for a few years; not since Luna had gone so wildly off the rails.

'Evening all!' Her daughter saluted. 'Mike's come for a nightcap, if that's OK.'

'Are you drunk, sugar?' Patti asked, wishing vehemently now that she had more clothes on. Then, with a second lurch of fear, she remembered the site she'd just found on Luna's computer.

'Not drunk, no. Just a bit…' Her daughter rolled her eyes.

'What?' Patti shook her head.

'In lurve, eh?' Sam teased. 'With that nice Mike geezer?'

Good Lord, he was in a rare buoyant mood, Patti thought sourly.

'No!' But Luna giggled unconvincingly. 'We're just mates.' She turned back to the open door. 'Come in, Mike – don't be shy!'

'Come for a bevvy, have you?' Sam gave a suggestive wink, and Patti wished the earth would swallow her.

'Thank you.' Mike stepped inside, the cold emanating off his duffel coat. 'If I'm not in the way?'

'Course not. Sam, get Mike a drink, would you?' Patti plastered a smile on. 'I just need a quick word with Luna.'

'I've got the end of a bottle of Bushmills, if you fancy a small one?' Sam was saying as Patti pushed her daughter into the kitchen.

'Something you want to tell me?' She tried to keep her voice quiet, but she was too angry.

Luna frowned. 'Dunno what you mean, Mum.'

'I saw that crap on your computer.' Patti pointed at the ceiling.

'*What* crap?' Luna was getting defensive now.

'About the English Defence lot. What have you been up to? Either you've joined – which I don't believe for a minute – or you're the one behind that post about Neil.' Patti held her daughter's arms now and looked her firmly in the eye. 'Which is it, Luna?'

PART 3

The Halloween Do

26

Halloween Party: Saturday 31 October

Calling all Ghostly Ghouls and Creepy Creatures:
witches, wizards, werewolves and warlocks

Spook-tacular Halloween Disco… do the Monster Mash, the
Terrified Twist, the Skeleton Scuttle…

Fancy Dress competition: prizes galore. The scarier the better!

Raffle, Treasure Hunt

Trick or Treat – if you dare

Drink at Dracula's Bar: Bloody Mary, Poison Ivy, Lurch's Lager…

International DJ superstar Roy Roar will rock the beats at midnight;
old-school house music to mainline…

All profits and proceeds go to the upkeep of the club

From 6.30 p.m. till late @ Tenderton Tigers Football Club,
Woodland Road, Kent

BE THERE OR BEWARE!!!

27

Alex

31 October

I heard the argument long before I saw it; the loud female voices shouting. But initially I couldn't work out *who* it was.

The clubhouse had been transformed into a hive of activity. Outside, some of the boys were stacking wood, ready for a huge bonfire, whilst others were blowing up inflatable pumpkins and skulls to float on the murky surface of the Pool of Sorrow, which was marked by a hand-painted sign with a pointed finger, the other side of which read: *This way to the Underworld.*

Over on the edge of the Whispering Woods, Ocean was overseeing the construction of a fortune-telling hut, all billowing purple and white net, sprayed with 'cobwebs' for atmosphere.

The bad news was that there was a weather warning in place for freezing fog tonight.

But the incessant furious shouting pierced the hum of all this happy activity, until all around me people stopped what they were doing to listen.

Dropping my bags at the clubhouse door, full of Halloween decorations we'd spent the week making, I unclenched sore hands, taking in the sight of two women face to face in the middle of the bar.

Hazel and Liz Bauer – only a foot apart and spitting bile at one another.

'I've been waiting to ask you about this... You're the club secretary and it's wholly inappropriate. You make out you're all holier than thou,' Hazel was saying: no, *repeating*, over and over, 'but *look* what you've been up to yourself.'

'It's not what it seems,' Liz kept saying in her strident lawyer tones, but as I unpacked my decorations onto the table, she wasn't coming up with much of a defence.

'Being strung up in a dungeon?' Hazel was incredulous. 'It looked pretty obvious to me. And that's not the half of it, Liz! What about this?' She thrust a newspaper in the other woman's face.

'My private life is nothing to do with the club. And I went to the meeting to hear what they had to say.' Liz stepped back. 'It's part of my remit to represent anyone who deserves it.'

I gathered they weren't talking just about Liz's sexual fetish, which had been giggled and gasped over by the whole village by now.

'Oho!' Hazel planted her hands on her hips. 'And you think the EDN, the nastiest, most extreme racist bigots... you think *they* deserve representation?'

'That's not what I meant. I meant that everyone deserves a fair trial,' Liz finished lamely as Hazel's daughter Cynthia arrived, bearing a huge skull-and-bones cake.

'Amazing,' I admired it as Mrs Jessop bustled over.

'Put that there, dear.' Mrs Jessop pointed. 'Or Sheila, you take it.'

'All right, She?' Cynthia nodded at the smaller woman, who held her arms out for the cake board. 'Don't drop it, for Pete's sake. I was up half the night icing it.'

'It's beautiful, Cyn,' Sheila said, and the two women grinned at each other. It struck me that I'd never seen Sheila smile before. She looked completely different – years younger, and almost pretty.

'You're going to have to stand down,' Hazel told Liz.

'I'm not.' Liz crossed her arms. 'It was private, and it has nothing to do with the club.'

I wasn't sure how this was going to resolve itself. Should I step in?

'What's up, Mum?' Cynthia's eyes narrowed as, free of her sticky burden, she joined Hazel.

'Just asking Liz why she felt the need to have coffee with some racists, as reported in *The Times* yesterday.'

'I'm not racist!' Liz insisted. 'I've got lots of black and Asian friends.'

'How very modern of you,' Cynthia sneered. '*God,* I'm tired of white women like you coming with your "I'm no racist" thing when we all know exactly what you are. Either that or crying with guilt. White privilege abounding. I got one word for you, lady, and one word only—'

'But I'm married to a German,' Liz protested as I cringed inside.

The dads by the bar, putting up the Halloween bunting, started to laugh loudly.

'And we won the war, eh?' one said. '*Whistle while you work...*'

'*Ribbentrop's a twerp, Hitler's barmy...*' another sang, the others taking up the refrain. '*So's his army, whistle while you work...*'

'See.' Liz gestured frantically. 'That's what we have to put up with every day.'

'I'm sorry, truly, but you don't know the half of it, mate.' Cynthia rolled her eyes at the men. 'This is *everything* I tried to stop when I dished the dirt on Neil.'

Silence fell slowly in the clubhouse, everyone turning to stare at Cynthia, me included, the singing fading out as the fathers caught on to the women's argument.

'Hang on!' Hazel stared at her daughter. 'What are you on about?'

'Yes – what *are* you on about?' It was as though someone had just blown air into Liz Bauer, I thought; she'd grown inches. 'Are you disclosing?'

'OK, yeah!' Cynthia's dark eyes sparked with fire. 'Yeah, it was me. Hand up – I dug up all that old xenophobic crap Neil was involved with and shared it.'

'Cynthia!' Hazel was obviously confused. 'You're saying *you're* behind the vlog?'

'Not the whole vlog, Mum, no.' Too late, Cynthia looked as if she might regret what she'd just admitted. 'I just gave them the racist stuff.'

The room was as silent as a midnight grave as we all processed this.

'Just for that first post, about Neil. And I must say' – Cynthia took a tiny step nearer Liz – 'I don't think anything that stupid twat said was as bad as actually representing a white suprema-cist group. Or being trussed up in leather in some seedy sex dungeon.'

'No, I agree.' Maria Desmond joined Cynthia now. 'That's shocking. Just think of your kids. Of all our kids!'

Rampant hypocrisy right there, I thought, given what Maria had been up to herself with that Tory councillor.

But before anyone else could get involved or give an opinion, there was another loud shriek – from outside this time – and one of the boys came rushing in.

'There's a fight!'

Beside the big BBQ that had just been put up, two boys were locked onto each other like small stags, knocking into the unlit bonfire so the carefully stacked wood went flying.

I realised it was Hazel's son Josh and Thomas, Maxi's older brother, and they were being egged on by several of the other boys. To my relief though, Harry was yelling at them to stop.

'You *wanker*!' Josh was shouting, head down like a bull now, shoving it into the taller boy's chest, while Thomas was trying to gouge Josh's eyes out in retaliation. 'Your mum's a snob and a… a sex pest!'

'She's not!' The older boy was almost sobbing. 'She was just doing her job.'

'Boys!' As I rushed to separate them, Ethan Taylor sprinted from somewhere and piled in, also trying to pull them apart. At the same time, another boy arrived on a silver racer, dismounting as the bike was still moving. Declan O'Connell.

'Stop it!' he cried, pulling Thomas back just as a man came round the clubhouse corner and yanked Josh away by the scruff of his shirt.

'That's quite enough of that, eh, mate?'

Jack bloody Stanton: and by the way he looked at me over the writhing boys, I imagined he was here for a reason that had nothing to do with football.

28

Patti

Halloween: Moon in the house of Libra

Arriving at the clubhouse after a frantic morning at the salon, Patti had rarely felt less like partying.

Except for the fact that she might bump into Louie again, she really could do without the hassle of today, and she certainly wasn't sad when she heard she'd missed the argument between Liz Bauer and the two Calliste women.

However, she *did* arrive in time to witness her son bundling into a fight between two of his teammates.

Everyone had stopped to watch: some of the coven had been setting up barrels for bobbing apples, and right on the edge of the wood, Meadow and Ocean were finishing off her 'little cave', ready for fortune-telling.

It was the first time Meadow had deigned to come back to the club since the Neil furore. Ocean had asked if his band could play a set, and the committee had agreed gladly, so Meadow had relented.

'Good to support the youth,' they'd said. Though Patti thought it more likely they were just glad of free entertainment.

But the fight seemed *better* entertainment, given the number of people watching. Patti, rushing in to protect her son, was relieved to see Declan and Jack Stanton hauling the boys off each other.

Too late.

As Josh took a punch to the face, Ethan got in the way of another blow and went flying too.

While Patti sent Ethan to the bathroom to clean up, Hazel, in high dudgeon still about Liz Bauer and her motivations, shoved Josh into the Black Cat's van and drove him to A&E to check for concussion.

Just as she left, Riker Bauer arrived, ostensibly to help with the pig Kezia was supplying for the evening hog roast. On hearing what had happened, he promptly removed Thomas to his car, where he could be heard giving the boy a proper dressing-down. Soon afterwards, a muted Liz was seen hurrying to the car park, presumably to intervene.

'You all right, sugar?' Patti plopped her cupcake boxes onto a bar table with a thud. It felt like time for either a stiff drink or bed, except it was only 1 p.m.

'You missed the drama,' Nancy said comfortably. She was supervising children blowing up skull balloons, prompting great hilarity over the use of some bicycle pumps, whilst feeding Chloe neat little bits of rice cake with her other hand.

'Oh, I saw enough. Josh's going to have a proper shiner later, and Ethan's got a huge bruise on his shoulder. That Bauer kid's out of control. Good that Declan turned up, though I expect that's not the last of the drama.' Patti sighed. 'Hello, angel.'

'I'm not a angel,' Chloe informed Patti with considerable gravity. 'I'm a unicorn.'

'I can see that.' Patti smiled at the little girl, whose face was indeed painted as a glittery pink unicorn. Not very Halloween-like or scary from where Patti stood, but Chloe *was* only three, after all.

'Later I'm going to be a pumper.' The child crunched her last bit of rice cake and licked her fingers lavishly.

'A pumpkin, bubba, not a pumper.' The two women's eyes met over the child's head. 'I'm not bringing her, but she doesn't know that,' Nancy murmured. 'Yet.'

'Fair enough.' Patti could see the clubhouse mightn't be the ideal venue for a small child, given how high tensions were already running and what they planned to do later to find the culprit. 'Is Dez home?' He'd been splitting his time between London and Kent apparently, in the last throes of setting up the academy. Patti wanted desperately to ask about Louie, but she held back.

'Yeah, Dez was here for last night's training.' From Nancy's taut demeanour, Patti guessed the situation was still fraught. 'I've got the cameras, by the way,' Nancy murmured, neatly tying the end of a balloon one of the boys had passed over.

'Cameras?' Patti was baffled for a moment.

'My cousin brought them.' Nancy added the balloon to the bunch. 'Mike's onside too, and he's let him place them strategically.' She nodded at the beardy young barman, now hanging an orange and black banner behind the bar that read *TENDERTON TIGERS SPOOK-FEST 31st OCTOBER.*

Mike gave Patti a friendly thumbs-up and she waved.

'Good-oh,' she murmured to Nancy. She wasn't sure what the other woman was hoping to capture, but she didn't have the energy to argue. 'Is it legal, secret filming?'

'Even if it wasn't, I'd do it.' Nancy's pretty face closed, giving her a mutinous look. 'But Liz says it's OK, as long as we stick up disclaimers about being filmed for the club website.'

'Liz, eh? Is she onside too then?' Patti gazed out at the car park, where Alex was talking to Jack Stanton. What the heck was that about? 'I must say, I'm quite surprised she's shown her face today.'

'Yeah, well, she might be an S&M freak, but she's worth her weight in legal expertise. Have you heard about Cynthia Calliste?' Nancy took another balloon bearing the legend *DANGER* and added it to the bunch. 'She admitted she wrote that first post about Neil Forth.'

'Did she? Wow.' For the first time since finding the post on Luna's computer, Patti breathed a sigh of relief. She'd been terrified the culprit was far closer to home than she'd first suspected; terrified it was all her own daughter's doing.

To hear that Cynthia had admitted involvement was a balm for her anxiety.

If the cameras were to catch Luna doing something terrible at the disco – though Patti wasn't sure what – well, she didn't know how she'd cope: it had been a long, hard struggle to keep her daughter on track.

With Patti's current money worries, and Sam's lack of work, the worst thing in the world would be to lose her own clientele in the wake of a scandal.

Having unpacked the lurid cupcakes onto platters, Patti realised Ethan still hadn't come back.

You heard of those one-punch tragedies, didn't you?

She hurried to the men's bathroom and knocked.

Nothing. She pushed the door gently.

There was her son – crouched over a toilet in a cubicle he hadn't bothered to lock, throwing up.

'Oh God, Eth!' Patti rushed to stand over him. 'What's wrong?'

'What? Nothing.' He looked round guiltily.

'That's it, you're… I need to call an ambulance.' Fishing for her phone, she laid a hand on his forehead. 'Must be concussion.'

'No, Mum.' He pushed her off, wiping his mouth. 'I'm fine.'

'You're obviously not, baby. I'm getting the paramedics here now.'

'I *am* fine.' He flushed the loo. 'I just…'

'What?' She recognised his hangdog look. 'What is it?'

'I ate three doughnuts and a pork pie on the way up here, and now we've got the sponsored run and I want to do a good time.' His eyes were watery, whether with tears or sickness she didn't know.

'Hang on a sec.' Patti took him by the shoulders. 'You're saying you've been making yourself sick after you eat? Like – regularly?'

Ethan couldn't meet her eye, just nodded sadly – and her heart broke for him.

However tough it had been for her growing up on the wrong side of Cardiff in the eighties, somehow it seemed so much harder for the teenagers of today. Of course she'd encountered sexism – no equal pay, more glass ceilings, less pension and all the rest of it – but at least she wasn't contending with the ever-growing hydra head that was social media and constant photography. Today's kids lived under a barrage of perfectionism when the irony was, no one was perfect.

Perfection didn't exist. No one was perfect, and yet in Patti's mind, they all were.

As she left Ethan to clean up in the loo, Patti could hear voices further along the corridor.

'I don't want to play anymore.' It was Maxi Bauer, she realised, his father looming over him. 'I hate football. I'd rather do drama club like my cousins.'

'Don't be so stupid,' Riker was hissing. 'You *will* play. You might be scouted this season; that might be the only good thing that comes from that man taking over. If you get scouted, you can play for a proper club.'

'But I don't want to.' The boy was almost crying. 'I hate football. It's not my thing. It's Thomas's thing, and I don't want to do it anymore.'

'But you are a much better player than Thomas. We need you to represent the family. You need to be a man.'

'No, Papi.' Maxi looked both terrified and defiant. 'And I don't want to be a man!'

'How *dare* you!' Riker's jaw clenched, and Patti thought: *Oh God, he's going to hit him.*

'Riker!' a woman's voice called, just as Patti cried, 'Wait!'

Liz, vivid spots of colour in her white cheeks, was striding towards her husband and son, looking distraught.

'What the hell are you playing at?' she yelled. For a second, Patti thought she was talking to the poor frightened boy, but as she neared, Liz grabbed her son, hugging him fiercely to her.

'It's OK,' she said into his hair. 'We'll sort it out.'

'Let him go, Liz.' Riker's voice was cold, and he was icy with anger. 'He needs to learn that he must do what he's told.'

'Not like this,' Liz snapped. 'Just leave it, Riker.'

'Yoo-hoo!' A woman's voice cut through the tension. 'Where do we want this then, eh?'

It was Kezia, along with her husband Big Feen and their older sons, holding a whole hog aloft, courtesy of Abbot's Farm.

And Patti thought she'd never been quite so pleased to see a dead pig in her life – nor so determined to turn vegetarian.

29

Alex

Jack Stanton brought me a cup of tea from Mrs Jessop's tuck shop, and we sat at one of the old wooden picnic tables round the back of the clubhouse so no one else could hear our conversation.

For that, at least, I was grateful.

Jack offered me one of his chocolate digestives, from a packet of two he'd just bought. 'Have you heard from Richard Leonard, Mrs Ross?' he asked calmly. 'Your late husband's colleague?'

I took the biscuit. 'Richard?' I dunked it in my tea and then turned it upside down, biting off the soggy half.

'Why did you turn your biscuit that way round?' Curious, he cocked his head to one side, and I thought, *He reminds me of an actor – I just can't think which one.*

'Chocolate side down of course,' I said.

He grinned. 'That's just weird.'

'I'm not going to argue about that.' I shrugged, and our eyes met for maybe the first time, and I thought, *Those heavy-lidded eyes are really rather nice,* and then I wondered if that was a disloyal thought, disloyal to Fraser's memory, and finished off my biscuit.

He prodded: 'So, Richard?'

'Yes?' It was strange – almost as if I'd gone into a sort of other-worldly state…

'Have you spoken?'

'No.' Had I left a trail? My mind began to whir now.

'You're sure about that?'

I thought of old Westerns, and that book *True Grit* that I'd loved as a teenager; of cowboys on horseback, and sepia posters offering rewards for awful men who'd committed heinous crimes.

I ought to give him something. 'I did hear from Fraser's old boss, Ernie Aharon,' I said carefully. 'He ran the division that Fraser and Rich both worked for. Pacific Insurance.'

'Oh yeah?' Stanton took a swig of tea. I wouldn't have been surprised if he got out a hip flask and added rum. But instead, he produced a pack of nicotine gum, which he fiddled with for a moment.

I was almost warming to this man for the first time. More than warming, if I was honest. 'Yes, I had an email from Ernie last week. He paid Fraser's last bonus, which was a relief.'

'Is that right? The thing is…' He grinned, and I thought he looked a bit like a pirate. I thought I'd seen the glint of a gold tooth in the back of his mouth. 'I'm afraid we might be talking at cross purposes, Mrs Ross.'

And I looked at his sardonic face and I thought: *Oh! I've been lulled, like a ship on a calm sea*, and I hated myself for a moment. Then I thought, *I* really *don't like the feeling of where this is headed.*

When he'd said all the things he'd come to say, and I cursed myself for even thinking he might like me in *that* way, I left the club and went home, and I rang Rich. I couldn't even think what time it would be over on the West Coast, but I didn't care.

He didn't answer, but I left a message.

'What's going on, Rich? I thought Fraser's payout was all done now, all sorted, but the British police said' – I could hardly bear to say it – 'they said there's a problem at Pacific Insurance.'

Next, I rang Rich's office number. I didn't care anymore, because I had nothing to lose now, but of course it was Saturday.

Desperate, I went online, flicking through Facebook, but Rich seemed to have deleted his account. There was no trace of it, however hard I looked. On his wife Janine's page, however, was a recent post. A photo of Rich wearing a high-vis jacket and a yellow hard hat, waving from a huge crane overlooking a very blue ocean.

Beneath it, Janine boasted about him winning a recent deal in Canada: *Yay for my hero Richie! Viewing his new development… King of all he surveys!*

Was *that* why Rich had been so nice to me?

It made me feel sick, sick as a dog. How stupid to be reeled in. And then I thought of Jack Stanton again. What a fool.

30

Patti

The Whispering Woods looked very big and dark at night, Patti thought, parking Sam's old van outside the clubhouse.

Despite the red and green disco lights strobing and slashing the night sky, loud music throbbing already, the wood was an impenetrable silhouette behind it all, a black nothingness. She felt a great shudder of apprehension.

There was something about the lit bonfire, its gold and orange flames licking the dark grey sky, that only made it seem worse, something that brought back the crude drawings on the witches' exhibits in the churchyard: women alight, dying in fire, bound to a stake.

Tonight was meant to be about reparations – in part at least – but Patti couldn't help feeling the exact opposite might happen. God only knew what Nancy's quest would turn up.

After the boys' fight earlier, Patti had rushed home to collect the raffle prizes, thrown on her costume and then, on a whim, stopped at Linda's to beg her to come.

Given that Linda hadn't answered any of her calls over the past few weeks, it was no surprise that her greeting was less than effusive – although Patti was relieved to see she was at least sober.

'No way,' Linda replied bluntly. 'I'm hanging out with Angel tonight.'

But through the living-room window, Patti saw Linda's sister plaiting Angel's hair, and knew it was an excuse.

'I'd love it if you came, babs – I miss you up there,' she said, but Linda just shook her head sadly.

'I can't come, Pats. Neil will be so upset if I do.'

The first person Patti saw when she walked back in was Louie, standing at the bar.

She didn't want to name the emotion that flooded her as she crossed the dance floor, admiring ghosts, devils' horns and witches' hats. It took an age, but eventually, sweltering in her huge Dalmatian coat, borrowed from Luna, she was so genuinely desperate for a drink, she screwed up her courage.

'All right?' Louie grinned, dressed in a tight white T-shirt and black biker jacket, *T-Birds* scrawled on the back, cigarette behind one neat ear.

'Kenickie from *Grease*, right?' Honestly, it was ludicrous to feel this shy.

'Got it in one.' He looked down at her. 'Cruella de Vil, is it?'

He seemed very serious, and she felt… What *was* it she felt?

'I love that film, *101 Dalmatians*. And I like your hair, and your green eyes!'

Patti felt timid, bashful and fully seen. 'Thank you.'

Yes, *that* was it: she felt this guy actually *saw* her – not for being chief dishwasher, picker-upper, cook and now breadwinner too, but for herself.

'I missed you.' *Oh God!* She clapped a red-gloved hand over her mouth, hiding the shiny black nails her junior had done for her earlier; hiding her wedding ring. That had come out *completely* wrong.

'Did you?' He grinned again, and she thought, *Good Lord, please don't. Don't smile at me like that…*

'Sorry, I meant, you haven't been around, have you? I thought you'd… thought you might have left Tenderton for good.' Was she drunk? No, she wasn't; she hadn't even had one drink yet, for goodness' sake!

'I went to see the physio at Millwall. They were checking to see if I'm match fit yet.'

Over his head, Patti spotted Sam, whose back didn't look very sore now he was drinking with the other dads. He hadn't even noticed her outfit earlier, let alone commented on it – even when he'd had to zip up the back of her slinky red dress.

'And are you?' Her mouth was so dry, she could barely speak. 'Match fit?'

'Nah, not quite. Not far off though. Can I get you a drink?'

Patti hesitated, thinking, *This is ridiculous – he's young enough to be my son*, and she began to say no, and then thought, *Oh sod it. It's only a drink.* 'Yes please. A vodka and lime would be lovely,' she said, glancing at Mike, who'd caught Louie's offer.

'Your wish is my command.' Mike performed a semi-bow, dressed as Michael J. Fox in *Teen Wolf* – i.e. as a werewolf – which, with his hairy face, wasn't much different from his normal attire. 'Coming right up.'

Waiting, Patti began to sense Louie's own nerves. He was definitely jittery, drumming his fingers, constantly checking his phone, and once more, for the life of her, she couldn't think of anything to say.

'No Dez yet?' She was losing her mind; *that* was what she was doing.

'He went to collect Roy, but there's been some big pile-up on the motorway.'

Dez's brother, Roy Roar, was a big DJ on the New York and Amsterdam club scene, and Dez had promised he'd play tonight: a big pull for the younger crowd from the village, who'd bought tickets with alacrity.

Tenderton had never known such dizzy heights of fame.

'There you go.' Mike delivered the drinks with a wink that made Patti vaguely uncomfortable. But when Louie handed her the glass and their fingers touched briefly, she pulled back like it was an electric shock, everything else forgotten.

'Patti,' Louie's voice was low, and she thought, *He's never said my name before*.

'Mum.' Ethan was suddenly breathless at her side. 'Hunter says his mum needs you, in the loo.'

'OK.' Dragged back to now, Patti felt a mix of relief and irritation. 'Your sister needs me apparently.'

Louie forced a smile. 'Calm.'

I've imagined the whole thing anyway, she thought as she hurried away, face flaming with embarrassment.

'Where are *you* going?' she called after Ethan, now scooting out of the doors.

'On an adventure,' he shouted back over his shoulder.

It was only later that she thought, *Why didn't I stop him?*

In the ladies', Nancy was leaning over the sink, adjusting a false eyelash.

'Oh, don't you look good!' Patti was impressed. 'Very sexy!'

Dressed as a dead nurse, in a short white tunic, with dark smoky eyes and a huge hypodermic syringe sticking out of her neck, her red lips glossy as a plum, Nancy looked both amazing - and frantic.

'Cameras all up and running?' Patti asked, and then caught her eye in the mirror. Something was definitely wrong. 'Are you OK?'

'Have you seen it?' Nancy's voice was very quiet as she turned. 'I just… I can't believe it. He promised me he wouldn't.'

Patti shook her head in confusion. 'Seen *what?*'

'This.' Nancy shoved her phone towards her. 'I guess if you haven't, then no one has yet. I can't think what to do.'

'Oh, not another bloody vlog!' Patti's hands went clammy, as they did at every new post.

'No. It's worse than that – much worse.' Nancy swivelled her head to the right, to the left, as if to shake off the stress. 'I just don't know *why.*'

What could be worse than having your most intimate moments shared with your whole neighbourhood? Patti wondered, clicking on the link.

'Oh *bollocks!*' Immediately she saw what could be worse.

'Yeah, you could say that.' Nancy's face was a perfect blend of beauty and rage.

The *Mail*'s 'sidebar of shame' contained images of Nancy – and of what Patti now knew was called 'punishment porn', or 'image-based abuse'. It appeared the newspaper was sharing the story, not just with the neighbourhood, but with the whole world.

'It went up about an hour ago. I rang the beauty editor straight away; she's an old mate from the shows.' Nancy's eyes sparkled with unshed tears. 'She's mortified, and she said she'd see what she could find out about the source.' A tiny pause. 'And she's just rung me back.'

'Right,' Patti said slowly, feeling the charge in the air.

'It's worse than I even thought. It's worse, actually, than my worst nightmare.' Nancy looked at her. 'I just can't quite bear to admit it.'

*

Behind the decks, Tony Burton, dressed as Frankenstein's monster, was doing a pretty good job of massacring the music, but no one seemed to mind.

His mix of old disco classics and a lot of Rod Stewart had brought a throng of parents and girls onto the dance floor, whilst most of the boys were outside with glow sticks and lightsabers supplied by yet another of Dez's sponsors – Laser Tag on the London Road.

To Patti's great surprise, Linda – dressed as herself – was sitting at the bar with Kezia, who was clad as an evil angel with the most staggering cleavage. A row of shots was lined up in front of them.

'Linda! Good to see you, babs.' Patti faced down the mutterings of the coven, dressed as a variety of witches, from Harry Potter's Professor McGonagall to Glinda, the Good Witch of the North, and Elphaba from *Wicked*. 'I'm so pleased you changed your mind.'

'Davey wanted to see his mates.' Linda shrugged. 'So I brought him up.'

She was half-cut again, Patti thought sadly, though not nearly as drunk as she'd been last time she'd been here.

'I'm glad,' Patti said. 'But are those really a good idea?' She pointed at the shots.

'Yeah, a great idea. And I want a word with that Dez.'

'Oh?' Patti's heart sank. 'About?'

'Neil's lost so much custom since that vlog thing.' Linda necked a shot, banging the glass down with a wince. 'We need it back or the garage'll go under. Dez needs to say something to people.'

'Ah, I know what it's like to be shunned, my lover.' Kezia's broad face beneath its halo and glitter was all sympathy. 'It's crap.'

'But what can Dez do?' Patti didn't understand.

'He's got mates in high places, hasn't he?'

'Has he?'

'He must do.'

Over Linda's bedraggled bowl cut, Patti saw Nancy join her brother at the bar.

Fair heads together, they muttered to one another, and Patti thought of what Nancy had just told her in the toilets. She scanned the bar quickly.

'Where's Dez?' Hazel rushed up in a flowing vampire cloak. 'I can't bear much more of Tony's cheesy disco. And I need to talk to him about Cyn.' She gave Patti a meaningful look. 'He's got a little bit of explaining to do, that man. I think he might have misled my daughter.'

Everyone was waiting for Dez now, it seemed – except Patti herself.

Strange: she began to simultaneously almost pity him whilst dreading the idea of him walking in. The tension was so drum-tight, the whole club was ready to blow sky high.

31

Alex

As I was about to leave for the football club, tying the red-hooded cape I'd made myself in the week and loading my wicker basket with apples, my phone rang.

And when I saw it was an American number calling, I felt a surge of hope.

'Hello?' I answered quickly.

The woman on the other end was so hysterical, I couldn't make out what she was saying at first, but eventually I realised it was Janine, Rich's wife.

'What the fuck have you done to my marriage?' she was screaming, and when she stopped, in the background I could make out a child, also crying.

In the end, through her terrible distress, I managed to ascertain that Rich hadn't returned from his trip to Canada, and she suspected he wasn't coming back at all. His phone was dead and his email was bouncing back. She thought he'd left her.

'I haven't heard anything from him, I swear, not for...' I calculated: it wasn't that long ago, but he'd made no mention of any of this. He'd said things were good with Janine. 'He rang me about Fraser, that was all. How long has it been since he went away?' I asked, and she screamed a bit more, incoherently, and then I heard the deep bark of a dog.

Listening, I thought: *Is this the moment I admit I did sleep with him, but it was only once, and it was last year, when Fraser was still alive?*

Everything Janine was shouting down the line suggested she had a fairly good idea about that already, but it didn't seem the right time for admissions of guilt. And in the background, I'd heard Nova, I was sure, and I needed to get her out of there.

Honestly, it was strange, but I felt far less glad than I thought I would when I realised Rich might have left Janine.

That part of my life was behind me now.

Still, I knew I had to ring him again.

I called Bobbi about Nova, and then I found the pay-as-you-go phone I'd bought the other day, like the phones they used in *The Wire* and that stupid *Line of Duty* programme everyone went on about all the time. The burner phones that no one could trace.

I slipped the SIM in and left a message.

'They're onto you. And you didn't tell me – it's a far bigger fraud than I thought.'

I hung up and took the SIM out and threw it away. I wouldn't call him again.

At least, though, the insurance money had been agreed before all this came to light. Please God I would get it soon.

32

Patti

'Have you seen Davey?' Linda stumbled up to Patti, who was absently watching Luna and her girlfriends, dressed as Dastardly Tinker Bells, doing the 'Oops Upside Your Head' routine by the bar, all laughing hysterically. She'd caught herself wondering whether Louie fancied her daughter; she was a much more suitable age. But Luna really liked Mike, it was clear, and Louie looked more interested in checking his watch, she noted with relief, than checking out her daughter.

'Outside?' Patti replied absently, watching Luna shimmy close to Mike. 'Probably with Eth and that lot, running round the pitches.'

'He's so clever, Mum,' Luna had told Patti this morning. 'He's got a philosophy degree, and he says he'll help with my dissertation.'

Now Luna was giving Mike big eyes. Patti remembered what her daughter had said when she'd challenged her about the stuff on her computer.

'Everyone's got an absolute right to equality, Mum. It's just research, for my degree. I'm looking into bigotry and counter-movements like Black Lives Matter.' It was a coincidence, she swore, that the same info had made it onto the vlog all those weeks ago, but Patti wasn't sure what to believe. Luna and Cyn were friends, though they'd had a few fallings-out over the years, usually over boys, and Luna could be easily led. She wasn't the most confident of girls – unlike Cyn.

'Patti, can you help me?' A stressed-looking Liz Bauer, wearing a pair of red devil horns on a shiny black headband, appeared out of the crowd. 'Maxi's throwing up everywhere. I think he must have swiped some beer or something.'

'Oh God.' Patti hurried to the door with her. 'Where are the rest of them?'

'Not sure. They went running off into the woods.'

Patti felt her stomach lurch. 'The *woods*? Are you sure?'

It was at that precise moment that Dez arrived, striding in with his brother Roy and another man, whilst outside a furious Neil could be seen hurrying from his van, and all the things Patti had feared would come to pass – the tension that had brewed all season – erupted in one huge and horrible explosion.

33

Alex

When I got off the phone, I really wasn't in the mood for the Halloween party, but I knew I had to go.

I wanted to see Iris play her first public gig with the band, who had repaired the rupture by asking her to pick her favourite song. She had chosen Green Day's 'Wake Me Up When September Ends' – another anthem to her lost father, I feared. She was to sing that, instead of her original suggestion of Bowie's 'Kooks'.

I'd have one drink, listen to the band and then collect Harry and go, I decided – but when I arrived, *neither* of my children were there.

Iris, it seemed, had had a panic about the length of her skirt and rushed home on her skateboard to change back into her original Moaning Myrtle outfit.

But with all the commotion in the clubhouse, it took me longer to realise that Harry was properly missing.

34

Patti

The band, Ocean's Seven – though Patti was pretty sure there were only six of them – were setting up on the tiny stage as Dez strode through the bar, flanked by his two companions.

One was a short, thickset man who, facially, looked very like Dez, but older, lugging a big metal record box – his brother Roy Roar, no doubt. The other was a lithe young man of mixed heritage, clad in a red and white Sergio Tacchini tracksuit bearing the legend *Arsenal FC* in bold on the back.

Through the throng it was hard to see who reached Dez first, but Patti thought it was Louie, with Hazel hot on his heels. She circled him, shouting something about Dez corrupting her daughter.

But the person who made the biggest impression, striding through the crowd in black patent Louboutins with spiked heels, the throng parting before her like the Red Sea, was Nancy. In her tiny white dress, with her long racehorse legs, she looked impressive – and so did her punch.

Dez's nose spurted blood immediately as he roared in pain. 'What the actual *fuck*!' he yelled, almost louder than the music.

'*Oh!*' cried the crowd as one, and silence began to fall across the room, until all that was audible was Rod Stewart asking plaintively if anyone found him sexy.

'You know exactly what the fuck, Dez.' Nancy folded her arms calmly. 'How *could* you?'

Louie came to stand beside her, folding his arms too. They were a handsome pair, Patti thought absently, a pair who'd beaten the odds by climbing out of their own deprivation to dizzy heights.

It seemed that the tale Nancy had told Patti – of being discovered as a young teen in a shopping centre in South London by an internationally famous photographer – was not quite the truth. According to the *Mail*, she'd been discovered stripping in Soho by a drunken agency boss. Still, she'd turned her back on that past and climbed high, despite her latest antics.

They all stood mutely, watching the blood drip from Dez's nose as Rod warbled to the end of his song.

'So?' Nancy demanded coolly.

'Hey, hey, hey!' Dez's brother, the infamous Roy Roar, put his arms up as if about to referee a boxing match. 'No need for that shit now, Nance, is there?'

'There's every need, Roy. You don't know the half of it. And you.' She pointed at the man in the red tracksuit. 'Remind me who the hell you are?'

'Um, I'm Marvin,' he said uncomfortably, his voice a surprising falsetto, and Patti thought, *There's something going on here I don't understand...*

'Louie,' Nancy said, 'the boys are outside with Meadow, getting their palms read. Can you take them to the car? I'll be out in a sec.'

Thank God she'd left the little girl with the nanny, Patti thought.

'No probs.' Now Louie stepped up to Dez, very close, and whispered something in his ear that no one else could really hear, but that definitely included the phrase 'I'll kill you'. Then he cracked both sets of knuckles once and left.

Someone muttered at the back of the crowd, and someone else retorted, 'Yeah, all right, mate, who are you pushing?'

'You, mate, that's who!'

By the bar, to Patti's amazement, Dez was crying now, bent over double – in fact, sobbing – whilst Roy muttered to Nancy. His friend Marvin just stood, hands in tracksuit pockets, looking deeply awkward.

'Dez has something he wants to tell you all.' Nancy moved away from Roy. 'Don't you, Dez?'

'I think I know.' Meadow arrived now, ethereal in a shimmering white and gold dress, a long dark cloak over it, a silver tiara on top of her flowing locks. She held out her long hands to both of them, her bitten silver nails glittering under the disco lights. 'I sensed it in your house. And I want to say it's OK. Let me help bring you together now, to work this through.'

'Shut up, Meadow. Do you want me to tell them?' Arms folded, Nancy stared at her husband. 'Or will you?'

'Please, Nance.' His eyes were very dark in his handsome face. 'It'll ruin my career.'

High-pitched laughter cut across them: Linda, still sitting on a bar stool, laughing and laughing, pointing at Dez, hysterical with it. 'You thought you were so damn cool, didn't you – such a big man. But you're no better than us.'

Kezia put her arm round the other woman. 'Come on, my lover – let's get you out of here.' Like a child, Linda let herself be led towards the bar doors.

Meadow took Dez's hand, but Nancy shook her head. 'I'm fine thanks,' she said, her eyes glinting fire. 'Get a move on, Dez.'

And Patti looked at Meadow in the hooded cloak, and thought, *I've seen that figure somewhere before…*

At the back of the crowd, the tension was building. A sudden scuffle broke out. It took no time at all for it to quickly become a fight, spreading through the crowd like wildfire, as shove turned to punch after punch being thrown between the frustrated fathers – and a few of the mothers.

Kezia's husband, Big Feen, who'd been tending the hog roast, waded in, along with Neil Forth, pulling two men apart. And it was with a sense of wearied horror that Patti realised one was her husband Sam, the other being Riker Bauer. This row had been brewing for some time now; since Riker had refused to employ Sam a second time, turning down his application to work on the lake dredging.

'Good Lord!' Patti stood rooted to the spot as Neil Forth arrived beside her, sweating and out of breath.

'What's happened? Where's my wife?'

But when Dez saw Neil, he just sobbed harder.

'I'm sorry, mate,' he said, and now *everyone* was confused.

'For what?' Neil's pug-like face was a picture of bewilderment.

'Don't get me wrong, I still think you're a racist twat.' Dez wiped his eyes on his sleeve. 'But I should have just talked to the committee about it. I shouldn't have started that shit. I didn't know about your sick daughter either, how tough that must have been.'

'What shit?' Nancy shook her head at her husband.

'That stupid vlog,' Hazel sighed. 'It was Dez and my girl Cynthia who came up with the idea, isn't that right, Dez?'

'I just wanted the Tigers to have a chance,' he muttered.

'So you asked Cynthia to dig up anything she could find on Neil, and sadly, there was a *lot* of crap.'

'Oh,' Patti breathed, glad of yet more confirmation it hadn't been her own daughter…

She checked the room. A dishevelled-looking Luna was by the bar, gossamer wings askew. It reminded Patti of having to collect her from teenage parties when she'd been the one – invariably – to drink too much.

Her heart aching, Patti looked at her girl and thought: *That's enough now. I want to go home and take my children too.*

'Can I get some water here, mate?' Dez's friend Marvin asked Mike. 'Don't I know you from somewhere?'

'Don't think so.' Mike grinned through his bushy beard. 'Not unless you grew up on the Tenderton Estate too.'

'Nah, mate. The Pepys Estate in Deptford. Dez's neck of the woods.'

'We need to find the boys now and call this a night,' Patti announced to no one in particular, beckoning frantically to Luna. 'Dad's in a state too – let's go.'

'It's OK,' Meadow was saying to Dez. 'There's no shame in it. It's the twenty-first century.'

'In posting stuff about me online?' Neil said, confused.

'She doesn't mean that, I don't think, mate. And there's every shame in betraying your wife,' Nancy said, enunciating very clearly.

She must be an Aries, Patti thought, and realised she'd never asked her.

'I've already spoken to a lawyer,' Nancy continued, still eerily calm. 'I know it was you who deliberately swapped out the DVD of the advert and played it in here, in front of everyone. It was you who put it on the vlog. Worse still, I know it was you who rang the *Mail* with the story that's all over the paper today. Thank God they didn't print worse pictures than they did.'

'I'm s-sorry, Nance.' Dez looked at her and began to sob harder.

'You will be when I see you in court. Your bags are at the gate-house. Don't bother to knock.' Nancy turned on her three-inch spiked heels – and then turned back. 'Oh, and don't bring your boyfriend near the kids till I've had time to tell them the truth.'

And that, Patti thought dazedly, watching Nancy sashay through the crowd like she was on the catwalk, was an exit if she'd ever seen one.

35

Alex

After everything had calmed down a little and Nancy had left, followed by some other furious parents, Iris was disconsolate that the band wasn't going to play after all.

'There'll be another chance, I'm sure,' I tried to placate her, but honestly, I was more worried that we couldn't find Harry, either in or around the clubhouse.

Some of the other boys were outside, eating hunks of roast hog in burger buns, bobbing for apples or just throwing them at each other. But there was no sign of Harry or Ethan anywhere on the site.

'I'll check the other stalls, and round by the bonfire.' Iris sounded urgent, and I wasn't sure if it was because she was really concerned or because she was enjoying the drama.

'Harry,' I called, heading towards the woods with my torch. 'Harry!'

As I neared the trees, stumbling over the pockmarked field, something moved in the shadows.

An animal, skulking at the edge of the woods.

I froze. It was so big, I thought it was a deer; then, with fleeting horror, a bear. *Alex!* I laughed shakily, reminding myself I was in England now, not North America.

The animal's eyes were yellow slashes in the torch beam, and fear thumped through my chest.

'It's OK,' I crooned, wishing desperately that Nova was by my side as I inched nearer. The creature in the shadows looked remarkably wolf-like, and I thought, *Well, if it eats me, it will be apt at least*, dressed as I was in my silly Red Riding Hood costume. *And* my problems would be over.

But my need to find my son was greater than my fear.

'Harry!' I yelled more loudly, furious with myself for even contemplating the coward's route out – the route my husband had taken?

The creature turned and slunk into the fog that had threatened all day, the smell of damp pine and fear in the air. It was thickening fast now, adding to my anxiety, and visibility was terrible. I could barely see my own hand holding the torch, curls of dew making my skin clammy.

But at the trees' edge, steeling myself to go on, to go into the woods, I heard my name being shouted.

'Mum! They're here!' Iris was waving madly behind me on the field, where the fog had not yet descended, her stripy tights luminous in the dark. 'It's OK, they're safe!'

Inside Meadow's vacated fortune-telling cave, a few boys were merrily downing cans of beer, presumably stolen from the bar, as fast as possible.

Harry, thank the Lord, was one of them.

I left the other adults to clear up the mess, and took Iris and a drunken Harry home, driving super slowly through the fog.

Turning into Church Street, grateful for the lit-up manor house acting as a beacon at the end of the road, I was aware of almost nothing but my own exhaustion. I'd barely slept for days, and tonight's exploits had just about finished me off.

'Mum – watch out!' Iris yelled, grabbing my arm.

I swerved as the headlights caught another set of almond eyes through the fog.

Nova! I nearly shouted. Answering my prayers, come to protect us from harm – but it was only a slim fox, who regarded us coolly for a second before padding back into the fog.

Sorrow coursed through me; the memory of everything I'd lost.

Walking up the garden path, Iris in front with the keys, me holding Harry's arm as he staggered slightly, drunk for the first time in his life, I felt that prickle of unease again.

I was sure I'd left a light on, but the windows were all dark now. Perhaps the electricity had gone off? I remembered the frequent power cuts of my childhood in the hills; it wasn't unheard of.

Still, I was wary.

'Wait a sec, Iris sweetheart,' I instructed loudly, hoping that if anything *was* amiss, we'd announce ourselves. 'I'll go in first – put the lights on.'

As I unlocked the front door, something shot out past my feet, and I squealed, despite myself.

'How did he get in?' Iris gasped, watching the black cat disappear into the night, just as the fox had. All the creatures were walking tonight, it seemed: All Hallows' Eve, when the dead can't rest.

'I don't know, hon. He was probably inside earlier.'

But as soon as I went in, it was obvious from the mess, the pulled-out drawers, my bag upended, that someone else had been in the cottage.

We'd been burgled.

36

Patti

Patti kept going back to the pool to look for Ethan.

Round and round she went, sweeping the invisible surface with her phone torch, the pool that held God only knew what horrendous secrets – but she couldn't see anyone.

Fifteen minutes later, when he turned up back in the clubhouse with Josh, looking wild-eyed and unkempt, she could have happily killed him herself.

'Where were you?'

In the woods, he told her, with a couple of the other boys, looking for sticks to make swords with. The fog had come down and they couldn't find their way back.

'It was properly scary, but we found an old, ruined house, Mum,' he said, 'and it was sick! Declan said it's where the witch lives, and Thomas Bauer cried, he was so scared.'

Patti tried to contain her anger, but honestly, it had been such a difficult few days. She was frustrated that Louie had left without saying goodbye, and that if Nancy and Dez split – which seemed on the cards, given what had happened tonight – then Nancy would leave the club. And, therefore, Louie would too.

And that would be it; she'd never see him again – and the fact that she even cared made Patti despair.

And this was all on top of the fact she was *so* tired all the time, tired and sad; the fact that she'd started to loathe her husband, who'd been so stupidly drunk he'd come to blows with Riker. And worse, Ethan was possibly bulimic, and Luna would leave home soon, especially if she met a man she liked, and then Patti would lose her baby *and* her confidante.

All of those facts made her shout at her son more loudly than she had for a very long time. 'Do not ever go near that water, OK? Specially in the dark.'

'All right, Pats,' Sam slurred, and she wanted to punch him like Nancy had punched Dez, but she couldn't because she had no good reason to do so – other than that he was an idiot for fighting Riker.

'She didn't have a leg to stan' on, di' she, if she'd bin shaggin' around,' Sam said, as if he'd read Patti's mind. 'And she still went and punshed him…'

'I'd draw no conclusions.' Meadow wafted by with Ocean's guitar. 'There's more to it than we know. I felt it in their house, on the ley lines – I felt the auras that led to the cottage in the woods.'

'Cottaging in the woods?'

'That's not what I said.' Meadow shook her silver tiara sadly, and now Patti remembered Louie's tension that night he'd driven her home, leaving her to check something in the woods, running back to the car, Nancy's words just now about Dez's 'boyfriend'…

A few things began to take shape in the murk of it all.

'I've been trying to put the spirit to bed for some time,' Meadow said vaguely.

'I'll put some spirits to bed,' Patti muttered, thinking of the vodka she'd like to down now.

'Still.' Sam was querulous. 'I don' think violence is—'

'Shut UP, Sam. You're hardly in a position to lecture anyone about violence. Get in the van, you.' Patti shoved Ethan towards the doors in front of her.

It was freezing outside, the fog thickening fast as Mike carried her bags of Tupperware to the car park. He put them in the van, then patted Ethan on the head. 'Remember what I said, mate – be good for your mum.'

Ethan looked at him and nodded dumbly.

Inside the clubhouse, the music had started up again. Some people were still determined to party, it seemed.

'I'll make sure Luna gets home safe,' Mike assured Patti, and Patti, cold despite her big coat, tried not to feel jealous of her daughter's prospect of romance.

Riker Bauer stumbled out now, his Dracula fangs disappearing into his frothy fake Victorian beard.

'Have you seen Liz?' he asked, leaning down to the van window. Patti could see that Riker's eye was already swelling where Sam must have hit him and prayed her husband would keep quiet in the back.

''Fraid not,' she said shortly, remembering the man shouting at poor Maxi earlier, and she pulled away sharply.

The last thing she saw in the mirror was Riker stumbling round the car park whilst around him others packed up ready to leave.

On the village road, Patti put her foot down for a second in desperation, fighting her sadness, before the fog closed in again and forced her to slow down.

She couldn't have guessed her worst nightmare was only just starting.

37

Alex

Was it wrong that when I put the phone down from calling the police, I suddenly found myself hoping it would be Jack Stanton who attended about the break-in?

Wrong or not, it wasn't him who turned up an hour later. After I'd checked the children's rooms were untouched, I'd packed them off to bed, so it was just me and a yawning PC from the local town, one I thought I might have recognised from the clubhouse after Nancy's awful humiliation.

I thought of the sense of power in Nancy tonight, how deftly she'd handled the shame of the *Mail* having her story in front of the entire clubhouse, and I was in awe.

I needed some of that empowerment myself.

'What have they taken?' The PC scratched her ear disconsolately with her biro.

'Well, that's the weird thing. Nothing really.'

Not that there *was* much to take here anyway: I had nothing of value. No jewellery, no high-tech goods; just an old TV and a laptop – which was still here on the table.

It was on; I was pretty sure I'd left it switched off.

What the intruder *had* been through, in some forensic detail by the looks of things, was my few folders of paperwork, on the shelf in the living room.

'Is anything missing then?' the PC asked me, and I felt as if I was just an irritant. Which, given the time when she arrived, I probably was. 'How did they get in?'

'Through the kitchen door, I think.' The glass pane had been smashed, and so had the light in the hallway I'd definitely left on.

'How long were you out?'

'A few hours. My daughter was the last one here, about 7 p.m., but she said everything was fine then.'

'Perhaps she didn't lock the front door properly?'

'It was locked. Both doors were – but we leave the key in the back.'

'You shouldn't.' The policewoman took a few more details and then fingerprinted me with a small pad. 'For purposes of elimination,' she said. 'I can do the kids tomorrow if you prefer. Oh, and put something over that.' She pointed at the broken glass helpfully. 'I'll be in touch about forensic processing tomorrow.'

Upstairs, I checked on the children. Harry was snoring gently; Iris was reading an old skateboard magazine in bed.

'Sorry about your gig, baby,' I said.

She shrugged. 'There'll be another time.'

I moved across the room to hug her. 'So grown-up, Iris!'

To my surprise, she didn't recoil, and she smelt of all the things I associated her with. Hair mousse, and biscuits, and just Iris herself.

I didn't comment on the fact that she'd allowed it; I put it down to the stress.

But walking downstairs, I clutched the banister tighter as I thought about Iris having been home here alone when she came back to change. Thank God she hadn't interrupted whoever it was.

In the sitting room, I poured myself a bourbon, a habit I'd picked up in the States. Then I sat in the dark, my phone on my knee, thinking. I was strangely unperturbed, and not as scared as I'd thought I would be.

Thinking, and waiting for the next sign.

38

Patti

Sam and Ethan had both gone up to bed when Patti's phone pinged.

Despite her exhaustion after all the fisticuffs, she couldn't face shutting her eyes yet. She was slumped on the sofa, staring at a blank TV screen, wishing she could feel better about herself.

But she didn't. She felt old, and overweight, compared to the lost days of her youth. Over the hill.

Most of all, she felt a deep sadness, like the Pool of Sorrow she shouldn't have stared into, as Meadow had warned her, when Ocean first came to the Tigers – and again more recently at Nancy's house.

'There's a terrible sadness here, and it's linked to that cottage on the high street,' Meadow had said that first game she'd attended, pulling her old Afghan coat tighter round her, and Patti had taken little notice; still remembered thinking the woman was a bit odd.

When she heard the message come through, she hoped beyond hope it would be from someone who didn't have her number; someone she dearly wished *did* have her number, but of course it wasn't.

It was from Hazel.

I'm so sorry, Pats, the message said. *They've got you too now, haven't they? But I want you to know, it's not Cyn. She's been with me since we left. Hang in there, honey. I love ya* ☺

Patti had always known it was only a matter of time.

That this day had been coming, wheezing and panting like the creature that had chased her in her dreams since that distant night in the woods, hot breath on her heels; that had chased her for years now.

Around 1 a.m., Patti went upstairs, hoping Sam would be asleep; that he wouldn't know yet.

He was snoring gently, so she thought she'd got away with it, for now at least.

A few more hours of peace before the floodgates opened.

She'd just lie here beside him until the morning, and then she'd be the one to tell him; he'd hear it from her.

But, exhausted, she fell asleep too.

She was dreaming about huge dogs with lolling red tongues, slavering their way through a forest of dark misshapen trees that hid her worst nightmare, when Sam reached over her and put the light on.

Patti knew what he was doing, and why. She felt the weight shift on the bed, but she couldn't bear to open her eyes yet.

He was dressed, and from the fresh cold smell exuding from him, he must have been outside already.

'Pats.' He leant over her. 'Tell me it's not true.'

His face looked puffy in the half-light of dawn as she gave in, reluctantly, peering at him from beneath one wary eyelid. He'd been walking, she could tell; he always did when he was upset. She could see grass and mud on his trainers as she stared down at the floor.

In one chunky hand, he held his old phone. She didn't need to ask him what he was referring to.

39

Alex

Sunday 1 November

Sometime after dawn, I got up again to make coffee, unrefreshed after a restless night on the small sofa.

The knock on the front door was tentative; so quiet I thought I'd imagined it at first, but then I thought it must be the police, come back with some answers, perhaps.

I put the chain on and pulled the door open a crack.

'I'm so sorry to bother you, but I saw the light on.' Patti stood there, swaddled in her huge parka. It was the first time I'd ever seen her without make-up – except for a smudge of the sparkly green eyeshadow from last night's Cruella de Vil costume.

She looked small and exhausted.

'Come in.' I took the chain off and waited for her to pass me, half expecting that bloody cat to leap out of the hedge or appear between the tall domed flower heads I had no name for.

But both the street and our tiny garden were empty.

'Have you seen it?' Patti whispered as I shut the door behind her, and my heart nearly jumped out of my mouth.

'Have I seen *what*?'

'It's about me, not you, don't worry.' She passed me her phone, her pretty eyes big and sort of glazed. 'Sorry,' she said again.

'Patti, sit down.' I was worried she was about to collapse.

'Thank you.' She sat gingerly on the sofa. 'Honestly, I just wasn't sure where else to go.'

Tales of Tenderton

Who is the beautiful girl in these photos?

Yes, it's Luna Taylor.

Who is her mum? Yes, it's PATTI Taylor.

Who is her dad? You *think* it's Sam Taylor – and so does he.

But… maybe it's not. Maybe ?????

On Luna's birth certificate, you'll see that 'Father's name' is blank. And here is a blood donor form showing that Luna Taylor is blood type A. This chart explains how a child's blood group can be worked out using both its parents' types…

'I'm so sorry, Patti,' I said, passing the phone back. 'Really. Whoever's behind this is an evil bastard.'

Patti put her head in her hands. 'I just can't bear… I didn't want anyone to know… It's Luna's business, and I haven't told her yet. Or—' Her voice dropped. 'Or Sam.'

'But how did they find out?' I was confused.

'I'm not sure, but I think they hacked my email.' She was fighting tears. 'I had an idea already. Then Luna needed a blood transfusion a while back, and she wasn't a match to either of us – it meant she couldn't be his.'

'You don't need to say any more, Patti.' I hugged her awkwardly for a moment, but she was so tense, it was hard. 'Look, I've just put the kettle on. I'll make us some coffee and we can talk about what to do.'

As I stepped into the kitchen, I could feel the draught from the badly taped-up broken pane, covered with some cereal packet cardboard – all I'd had to hand at 1 a.m.

The black cat was on the windowsill outside, cleaning its face with an elegant paw, and it was strange, but I felt almost comforted by its presence.

I poured boiling water onto the coffee grounds and thought of how I'd waited the rest of the night for something that hadn't happened – yet.

Still, neither Patti nor I could know that her ignominy would be the last thing on everyone's minds in Tenderton today.

'I'm not a bad person,' she began to say, but at that exact moment, the first sirens started to wail.

40

Patti

It didn't take long for the news to get round the whole village.

There was so *much* news though, it was hard to know which was the most exciting item, or what to share first.

Patti needed to get out. She put her biggest sunglasses on, despite it being a cold morning, the fog still not fully lifted. She didn't care what people said now everyone knew; she walked down to buy some milk from the village stores.

Halinka was coming out clutching several packs of cigarettes, obviously on her way back from the casino.

'I hear bad news.' She looked grey-faced with exhaustion herself; she worked such long hours, longer even than Patti. 'I miss all drama.'

'Which bit of bad news, babs?' Patti asked wearily.

'About Dez and Nancy last night, and his bloody nose. About Dez liking men. About you and your Luna with no dad.' Halinka patted her with one bony hand, her fingernails a pearly pink, opalescent in the early-morning light. 'For this I am sorry. Good luck, Patti.'

'Thank you,' Patti said, meaning it.

As she skulked into the shop, the owner was chatting at the counter. Picking up a pint of milk, Patti hovered out of sight, thinking they were discussing her.

Until she heard the words 'dead body'.

Her heart clattered.

Luna.

Her daughter hadn't come home last night. Patti had just assumed she had stayed out with Mike, but...

'What dead body?' She rushed to the counter, the sirens earlier beginning to make a nasty kind of sense. 'Where?'

'Up at the football club.' Mrs Marshall, the shopkeeper, was vibrating with excitement as Patti fumbled for her phone. She'd switched it off when Sam had started sending abusive texts.

'The club? You're sure?'

'Positive.' Mrs Marshall was agog. 'Someone to do with the Tigers, John said, after that do last night. Was you there, Patti? Your boy plays, doesn't he?'

But Patti was running to the door, heart in her throat.

'Patti! Your milk, love.'

Patti literally sprinted through the woods to the club, dialling and dialling Luna on her new phone, which didn't work any better amongst the trees than her old one had, catching her jacket on a wire fence, tearing it as she pulled free.

She dialled again, sobbing with fear.

She didn't care any more about the stupid Screaming Woods or whatever they were called; she wasn't scared of the Hell Hounds, or the witches, or her own teenage memories or any of that nonsense; she just needed to know.

She fell, but she got up again and ran on, stumbling over roots and brambles, wondering how she had ever thought this place was scary. What was most terrifying was this burning love for her children, which would consume her alive if anything had happened to Luna...

*

An ashen-faced Tony Burton stood in front of the clubhouse, behind him an ambulance, a fire engine, two police cars. Crime-scene tape flickered lightly in the morning breeze, the tall trees strong and dark in the milky light.

'It's not…' Patti was sobbing now, barely able to breathe. 'Tell me it's not my girl!'

'No.' Tony held her arms. 'Don't be silly. It's not her. It's not Luna, love.'

'It's not… it's… Oh my God.' Fighting for breath, Patti sank to her knees. Tony dragged her upwards again. 'Who is it then?'

'It's Riker Bauer.' Tony's face was a picture of shock and awe.

'*Riker!*' she said wonderingly, and finally her heart began to slow. 'Oh, good Lord. Are you sure?'

'He's been dead a while, I think. It weren't a pretty sight, Patti. Not pretty at all.'

'How did he die?'

Tony shook his head. 'Drowned, by the looks of it. Fell in the lake last night and drowned. Pissed, I guess. Poor bloke.'

'Poor bloke,' Patti repeated stupidly, remembering Riker staggering round the car park after his fight with her husband. 'Oh, good Lord, yes.'

41

Alex

It was only later that day, after the sirens stopped wailing through the village, that I realised that there *were* things missing from the house.

But by then, it was too late to stop the inevitable.

42

Alex

America: a year ago

About five years after we'd arrived in America, Fraser had met Richard Leonard and Ernie Aharon playing tennis at the lawn club at Santa Barbara. A club that paradoxically was at the beach.

They all got on well, and Fraser, bored in his current job, was glad to accept a position at Pacific Insurance, working for Ernie in the environmental department. He did well, was promoted a few times and was taken under the fatherly Ernie's wing. Things were good for us – ostensibly, at least.

So when Ernie offered him the chance to come in on a private deal in international real estate, alongside his new best friend Rich, Fraser thought it was the chance he'd been waiting for.

'Insurance is boring,' he told me, and I could only agree, surprised he'd stuck at it for so long.

Fraser wasn't naturally a sticker; he bored easily. I always thought he'd have been more suited to working outdoors, tramping the hills with his hunting head on, but his dad had instilled some Puritan thing in him. Or just some messed-up ethic. It was hard to know which. He was forever competing with his big brother Wayne, who'd shot the biggest stag this side of Loch Ness as a teenager: Fraser had never lived up to that expectation.

'But I might make enough to retire early, princess,' he'd assured me.

Turned out there had been another reason entirely he'd stayed in the boring job.

When I found the woman's passport in his briefcase, about six months before Fraser's terrible death, I assumed what most wives would.

I thought he was having an affair: I thought he was leaving me for her.

And at first, in response to my shouting and crying, he let me believe that was near the truth: it was a flirtation with a colleague he'd met on a work trip.

It took a while to untangle some of the ends: to realise how deep Fraser had got himself into his mess.

Was I naïve, or had I just chosen not to look too hard?

Because when I *did* start to look, I didn't like what I found.

I only began to get near the truth after I overheard a muttered conversation between Fraser and Rich one night some weeks later, after a BBQ we'd hosted for Ernie and Rich's families. Fraser and I were meant to be patching things up – but it was more of an odds-and-sods patch-up than a beautiful quilt.

The two men were sitting on our back porch, nursing glasses of a very expensive cognac the boss had brought with him, while I'd gone inside to check on the kids and Rich's boy, Troy, staying over with Harry.

Ernie had left by then, ostensibly giving our neighbour Bobbi, 'a ride home' – to next door. Rich's wife Janine was riddled with morning, noon and night sickness, and hadn't come at all.

'You're going to have to pay it back, you know that, don't you?' Rich was saying urgently to Fraser as I pushed the screen door open. 'Like, every red cent, dude, or you'll be really fucked. I don't want that for you – and you don't want Ernie to find out.'

I looked at Fraser from the doorway. He caught my eye and shook his head very lightly, so I stepped back inside.

It was then that I realised something was really wrong.

The next Monday, Fraser flew to San Francisco for a meeting, and I rang Rich, with an excuse about choosing a birthday present for my husband.

'I'd love your input,' I lied. 'I always get it wrong, and it's his forty-fifth, after all.'

We met at a juice bar near the beach. My favourite beach.

It was dangerous. Iris and Harry were with friends for sleepovers. Was that a coincidence? I don't think so.

I was a free agent for the first time in years.

Janine was at her mother's for the week with her own children.

I drank green juice at first, but soon we moved on to the Heavenly Cabana on the beach and swapped juice for mojitos and Long Island iced tea.

One thing led to another.

Rich was so persuasive, and I was… what? Lonely? Bored? Betrayed? Rich explained that Fraser *had* been sleeping with this female colleague he'd met in Belize, but he was also in trouble at work. Embezzling company money out of desperation to bring us what he thought we needed.

I knew he had been distracted for months, and now I realised that he was in too deep – in all senses – and worst of all, not the man I thought I'd been married to all this time.

At first, I'd thought an affair was the worst thing he could do: but it turned out that robbing his own company was worse. At least it explained so much of his stress and depression.

Drunk, lonely and confused, I'd slept with Rich that evening – and when Fraser found out, it just made him even more desperate.

So desperate that, in the end, I was certain he'd taken his own life.

43

Alex

Sunday 1 November

I had trusted Rich until a few days ago; I'd thought Fraser was the bad guy in this equation.

It had taken me this long to realise how naïve I'd been. Blind.

Fraser was far too trusting himself; he always had been. Too impressed by the big boys, too desperate to be one of the gang, from the moment we'd met in the Highlands and I'd seen him round the posh rich youths from the public schools and the top universities who came up to Scotland to hunt.

Deep down, I'd known he wasn't really secure in himself. He wanted to be richer. Better. A banker like his big stag-killing brother.

Misled by charming, funny Rich – and oh God, Rich had even delivered the eulogy at Fraser's funeral; that sad, horrible little ceremony in the too-neat chapel, with only photographs of my beloved husband. No body to bury because no one, not the fire service or Mountain Rescue, could reach him in the deadly ravine.

The terrible raw grief of the kids; Fraser's mother so pinch-faced and furious with me, as if I'd killed her son with my bare hands.

And now Rich had disappeared.

*

Around 3 p.m., I dropped the children at the bus stop on the village outskirts, with twenty pounds each for treats and tickets for the new Marvel film. 'Call me when you're nearly home' – I blew them both a kiss – 'and I'll come and meet you.'

Then I went back to the cottage.

Frantically I rifled through the paperwork that littered the floor, rifled over and over again.

Think, Alex, think: what's missing?

I looked up at the manor house, lights blazing, and had a sudden thought.

I picked up my phone and sent a text.

Then this time, I *did* call the man I'd been thinking of.

44

Patti

By the time Patti returned home from the clubhouse, having learnt that Riker Bauer was dead, Sam had packed a bag and left for his sister's in Rochester. To Patti's enduring surprise, it had to be said: he'd actually showed some gumption for once.

Luna was home by then, horribly hung-over.

'Luna, sugar.' Patti tried to hold her daughter's hand. 'I'm so sorry. I need to explain.'

'Get lost, Mum.' Luna refused to even look at her. She rushed out, up to her bedroom, Patti hot on her heels.

'Stop! Wait—'

'Fuck off, you bitch!' Luna turned and screamed in her face. 'You've ruined my whole life.' She slammed the door, locking it immediately.

'Luna.' Patti rattled the doorknob, but now Luna put her stereo on loudly.

She'd leave her for a bit, to calm down. *Except she's not going to calm down, is she, Patti, you silly fool? Not when you've done what you've done…*

Luna might be furious – she undoubtedly was, Patti thought, switching on the kettle – but at least Patti knew where she was. Safe – and alive.

The football game had been cancelled – for obvious reasons. They'd forfeit it, but anyway, who the hell was going to run the team now? And, given all the scandal currently leaking through the village, the WhatsApp group had gone remarkably quiet.

Patti looked at the armchair Sam usually sat in, and she couldn't say she was sorry he had gone.

For now, or for good?

Things had been bad for a long time. Not even bad, maybe, just… nothing.

She kept thinking about the Bauer boys, and whether she ought to ring Liz, but they'd never been close, and honestly, she didn't know what she'd say right now. She'd send flowers tomorrow, when she was a bit more together.

Nancy had sent Patti a text though, and that had touched her.

I'm so sorry, it read. *I can't imagine what you're going through with Luna, but I can imagine the pain.*

For some reason, this made Patti cry.

Ethan came downstairs and ate some Weetabix, white-faced and hollow-eyed. Patti tried to talk to him. There were so many things that needed saying, but he was surprisingly angry – or perhaps, all things considered, it *wasn't* surprising.

'I'm going to see Josh,' he muttered, pocketing his phone, and she gave him a fiver and tried to cuddle him, but he pushed her away.

'Come back for your tea, baby, OK?'

Like his sister, he slammed the door behind him.

Patti went back up to try to talk to Luna, knocking politely. 'We need to talk, sugar – please let me in.'

But Luna just shouted, 'GO AWAY!'

So eventually she did.

Dozing on the sofa, Patti thought absently, *What a shame, I was just getting to know Nancy, and now she'll be leaving.*

But what she really meant was: *And Louie will go too.*

It was dark when Patti woke, and she was lost and bewildered.

She'd been dreaming of Riker Bauer in a coffin, with his fangs and his mutton chops and his cloak, banging on the lid to get out – and then she realised that someone *was* actually banging, but it was on her front door.

'Mum!' Luna came down the stairs in her tracksuit, eyes like a panda. 'For Christ's sake, get it together. They've been knocking for ages!'

It was Liz Bauer. 'Is Maxi here?'

'Maxi?' Patti repeated stupidly, still dazed.

'Yes, Maxi!'

'No, I don't think so. Luna?' Patti tried to focus, but she was so groggy, she was struggling.

'There's no one upstairs.' Luna shrugged. 'I'm sorry about Riker, Liz. Really awful for you.'

'Yes, good Lord.' Patti hauled herself up, awake now as if someone had chucked cold water over her. 'I'm so, so sorry, Liz. If there's—'

'It's not about Riker right now,' Liz snapped, her face deathly pale: as white as snow. 'I'm just worried about where Maxi has gone. He's been missing all afternoon, and he's not answering his bloody phone.'

It was 5.30 p.m., Patti realised dazedly, looking at her dad's old carriage clock on the mantelpiece.

'I'll check with Eth.'

Patti rang Hazel, who was just shutting up the café.

'Hang on a sec, can you… Yes, love, that one's gluten free and dairy free. Yes, lemon drizzle. Sorry, Pats.' Hazel came back to the phone. 'Busy day. Have you heard about Riker?'

Patti tried not to look at Liz's petrified face.

'Can you get Ethan for me, Haze? I need to ask him something.'

'I haven't seen Ethan all day, love. Hang on, let me check with Josh.'

It didn't take them long to realise that Ethan was missing too.

45

Alex

As I walked towards the manor house, I heard my phone pinging and pulled it out, but it was only the Tigers' WhatsApp group.

Up a couple of steep stone steps to the thick wooden front door, painted that old-world sage green.

It was shut – but when I tried the handle, it wasn't locked.

I pushed the door open and walked into the hallway.

It smelt antique. Musty. Like mothballs and... something else.

Music was playing somewhere, and for a moment, I couldn't think what it was, but I knew it was familiar.

The hallway was dark, and someone had lit a thick church candle and left it on a shining mahogany chest under the shuttered window, where it flickered in a draught.

Slowly I walked towards where I thought the music was coming from.

I took a deep breath and pushed open the door. A large, dark room, the main living room I assumed, with the heavy wooden shutters also bolted, a single Victorian table lamp the only light, spilling onto a small marble-topped table.

In the doorway, as I hesitated, my phone rang.

Harry. I had to answer it.

'Hal? You OK, sweetheart? Are you at the pictures?'

'Mum?' His voice was cracked and very distant, like he was in outer space. 'I'm lost, Mum – and I'm scared—'

The line went dead.

46

Patti

She'd always known it would end in the woods.

From the moment her mother's terrible then-boyfriend Nigel drove her the wrong way down the track from their small council house, on the pretext of giving her a lift to town, Patti's life had changed course entirely.

Yet for all the horror, Luna was the result, and for that she was beyond grateful.

Sam hadn't guessed the baby wasn't his; she'd always prayed – harder than anything in the world – that Luna *was* Sam's, in fact. There was an outside chance – she'd had to provide that opportunity to pull off her duplicity – but of course the signs became clearer as Luna grew up.

And finally, when Luna had an operation on her leg aged sixteen after she'd fallen badly, very drunk, and needed a quick transfusion, the doctors had checked Patti's blood type against her daughter's.

'You can't give blood, I'm afraid; you're not a match, Mrs Taylor. What about her dad?'

Sam was away on a job in Birmingham, but Patti already knew his blood type. She knew he wasn't a match either.

But with Sam at her side for all of Luna's life so far, Patti hadn't needed to stare into the abyss of her sin and guilt and trauma.

Not that it was a sin to be raped by your mother's boyfriend.

And now she was headed back into the woods to save her second child, the happy little boy whose beginning had been so much more simple, so much less fraught than his big sister's.

If she couldn't find him, she didn't know what she'd do.

Luna had been a May baby. They were the happiest of the lot, May babies, apparently. Born too small and too early, still she was a fighter, and it was from the midwife who delivered her that Patti had acquired her love of astrology.

'She'll be fine, pet.' The homely woman had hugged Patti before whisking the baby off to an incubator. 'She was born under a full moon, in the house of the bullish Taurean. She won't be going anywhere, this lunar child.'

Some people turned to religion in times of need, but for Patti, it was the stars that held her on course.

So what were the stars telling her now about her Ethan?

Patti stopped for a second as she ran to Liz's big Volvo and looked up at the skies. Gazing at the constellation of Orion – the hunter's belt – she prayed to him with every cell and fibre: *Help me find my son.*

Liz had tracked Maxi's iPhone to the middle of the bloody woods, and Patti thanked God for technology.

But as Liz drove, with Patti next to her texting Sam the grid reference, her own phone rang.

'I'm on my way, love, but have you heard? The bloody vlog again.' It was Hazel, sounding breathless. 'It's gone live – and I don't like the sound of what it's saying, Pats. I don't like it at all.'

Tales of Tenderton
THE ULTIMATE HORROR! These poor kids in the Tenderton Tigers. All they want to do is play football, and yet they are used by their parents as pawns in a capitalist game, a game that's been taken over by the pricks who run the British Football Association, UEFA, the IFA.

The Tiger parents are so busy with their own dirty little secrets, like all these sad little British villages that are dying on their arses, no money pumped in – full of sordid scandals, rivalries and pathetic ambitions – that none of them give a shit about any of their kids really.

Watch these idiot parents use their boys (forget the girls – Tenderton's stuck in the Dark Ages) to try to achieve their own dreams. To climb out of poverty, or life's monotony, pushing these kids till they have no self-worth off the pitch.

The doll-like voice of the last few posts changed now: it sounded like a rasping baby's.

And the saddest thing is, these parents don't even notice what's happening with their kids – what their struggles *really* are; whether they are sad, or mad, or addicted, abused by aggressive managers or paedophile coaches, exercising too much, or not eating.

Parents like the Taylors. Sam Taylor, layabout extraordinaire, and his lying wife Patti. I mean, look at her with her tacky little beauty salon, peddling dreams to women who ought to know better, who ought to just leave themselves alone, thin, fat, however God intended them to be.

But worst of all are men like Dez Fullerton, married to whores like Nancy. A man who's been through the system himself but who still keeps fucking people up.

The voice was changing again, and everyone who heard it stopped in their tracks with a shiver. The fury in it was something to witness.

Dez Fullerton didn't give a shit that he damaged other players in his fight to climb out of his own deprivation. He fucked our lives up good and proper – and he didn't care. He was so desperate to take over the silly little Tenderton Tigers, he chose to destroy another man's life by posting his shame online, deserved or not.

'Whose voice *is* that?' Patti looked at Liz, terror in her craw. 'I'm sure I recognise it. Do you?'

Could it be – Louie? Patti felt sweat break out beneath her arms, on her top lip. Oh God, what had she done…

'I've got a horrible feeling about this.' Liz's face was rigid as a mask, and she clutched the steering wheel as if she was holding on for dear life. 'I think… I'm guessing it might be something to do with Riker. Sheila rang me from the club…'

'What do you mean?' Patti whispered. 'With his death, you mean? What are you saying, Liz? I thought it was an accident.'

Liz didn't answer immediately; she just put her foot down. 'Let's find the boys, and then we can see.'

And so now I'm going to take my retribution.

I'll look after these poor boys FOR EVER, instead of their useless parents, who only use them to try to make their own lives better.

Goodbye, all. It's been a blast watching you squirm and weep.

47

Alex

'Harry?' I cried, but he wasn't there – the line had gone dead.

Fumbling with my phone, I tried to call Iris, but it just rang out.

And now I heard footsteps on the old floorboards, and another song came on the stereo, a song I'd heard recently.

Suddenly, I knew, even before I heard the voice.

'Fancy seeing you here.' He was in the shadows still, and I froze. 'So you finally rumbled me. Took a while though!'

And despite all my suspicions and all of my imaginings over the past twenty-four hours, my entrails turned to ice, even before I saw his face.

He stepped forward into the solitary pool of light.

'I don't believe it,' I whispered. 'I can't believe it's true.'

48

Patti

As they parked at the edge of the now pitch-black woods, by the path nearest the map reference Liz had plotted from Maxi's Find My Friends, an old red car pulled up that Patti didn't recognise. A woman in jeans, followed by a tall, well-built boy.

'Meadow!' Patti's jaw almost dropped. Meadow looked completely different in a fleece and boots.

'Needs must, mate, if we're going to get to work quickly.' Meadow tugged on a yellow cagoule, lit her lantern and put an arm round Patti. 'So let's find these boys of yours.' She nodded at Liz. 'I'm so sorry about Riker, Liz. His soul will soon be at rest though.'

'Thank you.' Liz inclined her head as a big car came round the corner too fast, almost skidding as it pulled up. The silver X6.

'Hunter's missing too.' Nancy flew out of the passenger seat, blonde hair tumbling around her face, Louie behind the wheel. 'He took his bike and disappeared a couple of hours ago. I thought he'd just gone to let off steam round the estate, after everything that happened. But when I rang him, he kept hanging up, and now…' She was fumbling with her phone to show them. 'Now he's texted me that he's not coming back. I've called the police again.'

Louie got out of the car with Logan. Patti looked at him over the boy's head, and tears sprang to her eyes. Whether it was because she was pleased to see him, to know it wasn't him behind this terrible vitriol and the kidnap of their boys – a fear she hadn't even acknowledged until now – or because she was so terrified about her own son, it didn't seem to matter.

'Patti.' His voice was quiet. 'I brought you a torch.' He handed her one, and another to his nephew, who looked as if he was about to cry.

'Come on, big man.' Louie took the boy's hand. 'Let's find your brother, shall we?'

They set out on the path, Patti and Nancy just behind Liz Bauer, who strode ahead like a woman possessed, Meadow behind.

Others were arriving now. There was Declan on his bike, with his parents, who carried a flaming torch; Kyran and Mikhail brought up in a car by Halinka. Josh had cycled with his big sister Cynthia, Hazel following in her old banger, bringing Luna too.

Luna caught up with Patti, slipping her hand into hers. 'Dad's on his way from Rochester. He won't be long.'

Patti's heart flip-flopped. 'I need to explain, Luna.' She gripped her daughter's hand tighter. 'I'm so sorry—'

'Mum. Later.' Luna's face was set in the dim light. 'Let's just find Eth and the others first.'

As the torchlight and the flickering flame showed the group they'd reached the second row of trees, another engine whined behind them with that bee-sting noise fast cars made – Dez, accompanied by the man in the tracksuit.

And Patti thought she couldn't care less if she never saw him again, because with his arrival in Tenderton had come all the pain and sorrow of this past season.

Gazing up through the canopy of the trees, just before it closed over them as they entered the denser part of the woods, she pinpointed Orion's Belt again in the vast sky, and silently she made a promise to the great hunter that, if he just let the boys be safe, she'd give up astrology for ever and dedicate her life to motherhood.

49

Alex

I have never, before or since, felt more shocked than I did in that moment.

'I've missed you, princess.'

My dead husband stood in front of me, in a pool of lamplight like a spotlight on a stage, in a setting that, in other circumstances, might have been perceived as romantic.

'You're the cleverest woman I've ever met. I should have known you'd work it out.'

But there's *nothing* romantic about knowing the man you've spent half a lifetime with, the father of your beloved kids, is a liar and a cheat. Far worse than that – that he's allowed you to think he was actually dead for almost a year. A man I'd thought I'd buried; a man I'd thought I'd killed.

'I *didn't* work it out,' I said slowly. 'I thought you were Rich.' I swallowed hard, trying to recalibrate. 'So – it was *you* who broke into the cottage last night, wasn't it?' I was stuttering in shock; face so tense it felt like my jaw might lock permanently. 'I thought it was Rich, but it was *you*.'

'It wasn't very hard to get in,' Fraser said, pointing at the old armchairs. 'Sit down, princess. You look tired. You ought to be more careful, given that you're caring for our kids.'

I bit back the curses I wanted to rain on him; I didn't dare provoke him.

'Our kids, Fraser.' I held my phone out. 'I think Harry might be in trouble. I need to call him back.'

'What?' For a moment, Fraser looked unsure, and I said quickly, 'He just called me, and he sounded scared.'

'Pull the other one.' He grinned again, his top lip curling back. *My God, he must be mad*, I thought.

And in that moment, I knew not only that I could never forgive him for what he'd put us through, but that if Harry was in trouble, if something happened and I couldn't reach him because of this charade, I'd kill Fraser myself with my bare hands.

'Let me just call him,' I pleaded, still holding out my phone. 'Look, you can watch me dial.'

'Give me that,' Fraser snarled. He snatched the phone from me, unbalancing me so I fell hard against an old horsehair chair, hitting my head on the arm. 'You fucking liar, you're going to ring the police.'

'Christ, Fraser!' Frantically I pulled myself up from the floor. 'What the hell's happened to you?'

'Nothing *happened* to me.' His smile was horrible. 'I'd just had enough of playing happy families. I just wanted out. I had done for years.'

My head throbbing, I realised suddenly that the music, on a loop now, was from our wedding day. Our actual wedding day!

'It was a bit worse than I let on,' my late husband said, and I looked at him and thought: *When did he go mad?*

But *I* must have been the mad one, because I'd married him; I'd been with him all those years, and I'd had no inkling he was capable of this level of deception.

'I thought you were dead.' I sat on the floor where I'd fallen. 'We had a funeral for you. We've been mourning you. Iris has been beside herself.' Vaguely I registered tears were running down my face, but I'd never felt less like crying. I wanted to kill him – but he was dead already. 'You *bastard*!'

'I am sorry, princess,' he said, but his smile was still horrible.

I looked at him, and in that moment, I hated him more than I knew was humanly possible.

'You don't need to make it difficult now, Al.'

'What do you want?' My voice caught in my throat.

'I want my old life back.' Some of the pretence dropped suddenly, and he looked old and haggard in the half-light. 'But I think I've fucked it up.'

My phone was pinging in his hand.

'Fraser,' I whispered desperately, 'is it Harry?'

'Alex!' He held a hand to his head as if it hurt him, and I thought, *He's not right – he's definitely not right.* 'It just got out of hand. And for all my sins, I wanted to see the kids one last time.'

'You're joking, right?' My anger was spilling out. 'You want to see the children who've believed for nearly a whole bloody year that you're dead?'

He glanced at my phone screen, which was vibrating now. 'Harry's with someone called Ethan, this says. In the woods.'

'In the *woods*?' My stomach lurched. 'Are you sure?'

'He'll be fine, but I've lost everything,' Fraser was whining now. 'I messed up and now I need some money to start a new life.'

'But you've *got* money!' I stammered with actual fury, pulling myself to my feet. 'The property fraud.'

'Yeah, well,' he snarled. 'It got complicated. Assets frozen, as it were.'

'And Rich?'

'Lover boy is in Venezuela, the lucky bastard. No extradition there. He was sensible, and I… I didn't plan it so well.' His smile was more a grimace, his top lip still folded back. 'Look, Al, if you just give me the life insurance money, I'll go, and you'll not have to see me again.'

'I don't have it, Fraser – you must know that.'

'You do.' But again I felt his confidence dip. 'I saw the paperwork. Just write me a cheque now, in the name I give you, and I'll disappear again. I won't bother you again, I swear.'

'I have the promise of a payout, for us to live on,' I said very slowly and deliberately, 'but I don't have it yet, and I won't for ages.' I put my hand out. 'And if I did have it, I wouldn't let you have it anyway. Now give me my phone so I can ring Harry back.'

I should have said I'd give him the money, of course. But I was too angry.

So I didn't see it coming – and wasn't that the story of the last few years. It was then that Fraser sprang at me, and truly, he was a man possessed.

50

Patti

The party tramped quietly through the trees, one behind the other, the fear palpable in the cold air.

At least the fog had cleared, but the night noises of the woods were crowding in: the querulous chatter of a scuffling badger, the sharp bark of a fox, and overhead, an owl's piercing screech. Something rustled past their feet, pattering over Patti's trainer, and behind her, someone muffled a scream.

Every one of them was trying desperately to keep quiet, to walk straight, to not cry out in terror at the situation. Holding herself together frantically, Patti could have sworn she felt the hot breath of the Hell Hounds on the back of her fingers. She shoved her free hand in her pocket as another noise began: a siren, whining through the night.

For a moment, she felt relief – until she realised it wasn't the sound of a police car or an ambulance, but rather the type a loudhailer made.

'Stop right there!' an amplified voice said. 'Everyone go back.'

They stood petrified in the freezing dark; no one sure what to do.

'Go back all of you. All except the mothers of these boys.'

They didn't even have to think about it, not for a second.

The three mothers walked on alone.

'What have you done to them?' Patti's voice came out like an old creaking door. 'What's up with them?'

The three boys were huddled on the ground around a fire – like sleeping babies. No, not three. Four. Because Harry Ross was there too.

Babes in the wood, Patti thought absently, and she wanted to run to Ethan, scoop him up, despite him being the same size as her. But something about the man between her and the boys stopped her.

'Stay there.'

Liz let out a huge sigh, sinking down on the spot where she'd been standing.

'Please!' Nancy implored – but she didn't move; just stood stock-still, as if she'd turned to stone.

Patti took a few steps forward, inching towards the campfire.

'They're sleeping, not dead,' the man said, and he looked up and grinned, his teeth ghostly white in his hideous skull mask. 'Took you a while, hey?'

'But why? What have they done to you?'

Dez burst into the clearing.

'I said, *stay back*!' The man in the mask stood up now, his body language all furious menace, and Patti saw with horror that he was holding a huge rock. And she also saw the tattoo on the back of his hand. 'I said just the mothers.'

'Mate!' Dez held his hands above his head as if he was at gunpoint. 'Just give my son back, OK, and we'll say no more about any of this. Just give me Hunter.'

'*All* our sons, thanks, Dez,' growled Patti. Good Lord, the man was an arse: to think she'd once fancied him. 'And he told you not to come here.'

'Please, please don't hurt them!' Nancy begged, holding her hands out to the man. 'They've done nothing wrong.'

'No, I know. I have no intention of hurting them.' He shook his head as if confused. 'It's you lot I want to save them from. You nasty poisonous lot.'

Patti took another step forward. 'Mike?'

He froze.

'Mike? From the bar?' She peered at him. 'Is it... it *is* you, isn't it? And it's *you* who's been writing all the poison, after Cyn and Dez started on Neil.'

'Rumbled! Very good, Patti!' The young man pulled the stupid mask off, his grin demonic. 'Top marks. Whew, it was hot in there.'

'Mike,' said Nancy wonderingly, but Liz Bauer just sat where she'd landed on the ground, gently rocking herself from side to side.

'I took over, yes – without their say-so, of course – at Riker's behest.' He shrugged.

'*Riker?*'

Even now, Liz didn't react, her eyes fixed intently on Maxi's comatose form. She looked like she'd shattered mentally into a million pieces.

'Yeah. He offered to pay me, but I was happy to record what you lot did anyway. We'd been chatting in the bar for a while about the cesspit the club had become. That's all I did – I just put it out there into the world, so everyone else would know how dangerous and corrupt you are.'

'Why would *Riker* want to vlog about us?' Nancy asked.

'He wanted to take over the club. He was pissed off when Dez got the spot.'

'My mate thought he recognised you.' Dez's voice was fraught with stress. 'He thought he knew you from the club.'

'What club's that then?'

'Arsenal. He's a team physio there.'

'I never played for Arsenal.' Mike shook his head slowly. 'But my big brother did.'

'Oh, right.' Dez looked almost enthused. 'What's his name?'

'Good God, Dez, you don't even recognise me? You were the one who ruined his career.'

'I did what?'

'My big brother, Alfie Abey. You destroyed his life.'

'No way.' Dez sucked his teeth. 'I never ruined no one's career.'

'That's a double negative, I think you'll find, you tosser, and you definitely did.'

Ethan stirred a little, moaning in his sleep. The boys looked like they'd been drugged, Patti thought.

'How?' she asked, keeping one eye on her son. 'What did Dez do?'

'Fouled Alfie. Badly. High-tackled him in the quarter-finals of the Champions League two and a half years ago. Double compound fracture to his right shin. Took them ten minutes to get him off the pitch and clean the blood off the grass. They thought they might have to amputate. He never walked again properly, let alone played a game. You ruined the whole fucking thing for him, and you got to walk away scot free.'

'Oh,' muttered Dez. 'Right. Sorry.'

'I can show you the footage if you like. Remind you.'

'No, no,' said Dez. 'Alfie Abey, yeah, I remember him now. Great bloke.'

'You've got no idea, have you? Not a clue.'

'No, I do. It was bad, that injury – I am sorry. Was just a timing mistake.'

'High tackle, studs up? Don't think so. It looks pretty deliberate on the footage. You were lucky to get away with it.'

'Know what, you do look just like him,' Dez blustered. 'Top geezer, Alfie. What can I do to help him out, d'you reckon? Nice little job at the academy?'

'Oh yeah, that would be great.' Mike's tone was curiously flat.

'Nice one.' Dez took a step towards Hunter, still motionless on the ground. 'I'll get your number. So we can call it quits, yeah?'

Mike went on as if Dez hadn't spoken. 'It *would* be great, if he was actually alive.'

'What?' Nancy whispered. 'Your brother's… he's *dead*?'

''Fraid so.' Grief transformed the young man's features. 'Killed himself last year, threw himself off Waterloo Bridge.' It was almost conversational, the way he said it – if he hadn't looked so devastated. 'Couldn't pay his mortgage, started drinking and gambling. Wife left him for another player, took his daughter. He lost everything. Every penny he'd ever made. No one wanted anything to do with him. Football's an evil sport.'

'You can say that again,' Liz muttered absently, as if she'd just come round.

Patti had almost reached Ethan now.

'Press barely bothered to report it,' Mike added.

'So look, Mike. How's this going to end?' Nancy moved forward now. 'Because I know you don't want to hurt the boys. You're just grieving and angry – with us, maybe, with Dez, us foolish parents, I get that. But I don't think you're angry with these wee lads.'

'No.' Mike looked bereft. 'You're right. They're great kids. I wanted to help them.'

'And Alfie wouldn't want you to hurt them in his name, would he?' Patti said. For a second, she thought she'd gone too far, but

Mike looked at her across the crackling fire, and though it was dark out here, she could read the expression on his face.

It was the perfect picture of hopelessness.

All the anger and the fury, the spite and the vitriol, it hadn't helped him after all.

Revenge, as Mrs Jessop's bowl said, was a dish best served cold.

There was a huge gust of wind through the woods now, and everyone in the clearing looked up to see something white soar through the branches of the trees above them.

'I'm sorry,' Mike muttered. 'I haven't been able to see straight since Alfie died.' He started to cry. 'I really… I just miss him. And my parents aren't the same – they're…' He couldn't talk for weeping now.

'It's OK, Mike.' Patti put her hand on his arm as he bent his head and sobbed, and she thought: *What is it about this bloody game that affects grown men like this? Makes them puppets to ambition, or as flies to wanton boys.* That was a quote she remembered from her English A level. The only thing she remembered from that terrible time, just before she dropped out of school.

'I just wanted to protect them from you lot.'

'I know, sugar.'

Luna came through the trees now and went to Mike. As she put an arm around him, rolling her eyes over his head at Patti, Nancy ran to the boys and shook them frantically one by one. 'Wake up!' she hissed urgently.

And then Louie was there, picking up Ethan, whilst Dez took Hunter. Liz, still staring blankly, went to Maxi, and Ocean and Kyran, Declan and Mikhail helped to half carry, half drag him and Harry Ross out of the clearing.

Meadow stood there, hands extended into the air. 'I can feel the white witch's energy,' she murmured. 'She protected them, you know. The woman they killed in the pool – she is here.'

The owl hooted, and the crescent moon was obscured by clouds as the trees shook overhead.

'Really?' said Patti, her teeth chattering with terror and relief; and she thought how very cold it was in this clearing, and how much she wanted to get out of the wood before that huge dog she was sure she'd just glimpsed through the dark trees returned.

51

Alex

I didn't see where the first blow came from, but I recognised the shriek of fury.

Then a figure came charging back across the room, this time with some kind of stoneware in her hands.

My daughter Iris – and for a second, I shrank back…

And then she brought it down hard on her father's head.

I'd never thought she'd pick my side, but apparently she had.

'*Oof!*' Fraser rolled over and lay still, and I looked at him from where I had fallen seconds before and prayed harder than I ever had: *Do not let my daughter have killed her dead father and have to now pay that price too…*

And then, thank God, he opened his eyes. Thank God.

Lying on his back, Fraser must have looked up and seen her face. Seen his daughter standing above him, jug raised again high above her head.

He went to get up.

'Don't you dare!' she cried, and she was crying, the tears streaming down her face. 'How could you, Dad? How could you?'

'Iris, princess,' he started to say, and he was trying to get up, but she pushed him down with her hi-topped foot.

'Stay there, Dad!' And as she said his name, she cried harder. 'I knew you had been in the house. I didn't know how I knew at first, but when I went to bed last night, I knew you'd been in my room. And then I found this, this afternoon.' She uncurled her hand. Another button, not the grey one I'd found on the doorstep weeks ago, but a gold-plated stag, from his old hunting jacket. 'It was by my bed.'

'I want to explain,' he began, but I could see the fight had gone out of him as I pulled myself up, dizzy and nauseous, my neck smarting where his hands had been.

'I don't want to hear it,' Iris sobbed.

It was then that I heard a car pull up outside, its blue light flickering round the white walls of the old room; and on the stereo, Green Day broke into 'Wake Me Up When September Ends', another song from our wedding.

The song that Iris was going to dedicate to her father's memory at the gig last night.

If I had not called Jack Stanton before I went to the manor house and left a message. If I hadn't felt such a strong sense of danger.

If I had not messaged Iris to say I loved her, and to give her my brother Gray's number, just in case, and to tell her to go to Patti or Hazel if I didn't come back.

If Iris, worried, had not gone home after Harry said he wanted to meet Mike and his mates at the club; if she hadn't tracked me on Find My Friends.

If I had not left the front door of the manor house ajar.

If Iris had not arrived the moment after I went down so hard on the old stone floor that I nearly blacked out, my own husband's hands around my neck.

I might have died.

I was already half dead inside though.

I had half died when my husband fell to his death; a death I realised later Rich had helped him fake, had even let himself be beaten for, to make it look like they had both fallen, then paid off a cop to keep his mouth shut that he hadn't actually seen the body in the ravine.

In the end, how vehemently I wished Fraser hadn't come back.

I wished he'd stayed dead after all.

The ensuing damage was so much worse than what had gone before.

PART 4

Afterwards

52

Patti

November: Scorpio (passion v. jealousy)

Patti was deeply relieved to leave the month of Scorpio behind.

It was her least favourite of the signs at the best of times. All that supposed passion, but they were usually just overemotional buggers, with a dollop of spite about the worst.

Although Patti was aware, as she opened up the salon for the special charity day for the local hospice, that she was biased largely because Sam was one.

Mrs Jessop, who was a benign Piscean, suggested to Sheila that it was time she took over as Tigers team manager.

'Don't mind if I do,' said the small woman with the mean left foot. 'And we'll start a girls' team again next season.'

And that was fine with everyone who decided to stay on the team.

Some of them wanted to leave immediately – including Davey Forth, whose mum had signed up for rehab now, and Maxi Bauer, who was taking up drama instead of football – but they all agreed to play the last game, against the Kingley Knights.

Hunter would be leaving soon too; Nancy planned to sell up. She was buying a big house in Chislehurst, to be near her parents.

Her modelling career was going from strength to strength. She'd stopped doing lingerie and dieting and started doing more body-positive work. She'd filled out a bit, and it suited her.

Best of all, she'd become a sex and equality school advocate, talking to both teen girls and boys about rape culture and image-based abuse.

Dez had done a huge piece for *Attitude* magazine about being the first openly bisexual Premiership footballer in the twenty-first century, and he was setting up an Alfie Abey scholarship at the Fullerton Academy too, he was pleased to announce. He was heralded a hero for his courage – though much online abuse immediately followed.

'Football fans aren't the most modern of people,' sighed Tony Burton.

But behind closed doors, Nancy was still furious that her soon-to-be ex-husband had played her sex tape to everyone in the club.

Over G&Ts in her hot tub, she explained to a few select mums that he'd hoped it would take the onus off him.

'I found out he was meeting men in the woods.' She turned the bubbles on. 'I think he thought that if he proved I was sleeping around' – she looked at them all with those beautiful eyes – 'it would distract from what he was up to. He'd long lost interest in me, anyway.'

'And were you?' Kezia asked bluntly, toasting the stars with her drink. 'Sleeping around?'

'Only with one guy, and I was stupid to.' Nancy sighed. 'It was Dez who stole the footage, not my guy who sold it. But it backfired on him in the end.'

Although given Dez's new status as a queer icon, no one else was really sure it had.

Personally, Patti was just relieved she'd stopped seeing the body in the water, since Riker had been found dead.

She had her own very real fears about whether Sam had been involved: she knew he'd hated the man; she knew he'd been outside at dawn the morning the truth about Luna had come out on the vlog. Could he have pushed Riker in the pool?

Nor had Luna fully forgiven her yet: the whole thing was too much for her to process. She'd applied to go away in January for an Erasmus year, to study in Madrid. Patti could only pray her daughter would come to understand why she'd lied, but it was tough. She hadn't yet revealed the full truth of Luna's conception; she wasn't sure Luna ought to hear it. Enough damage had been done.

Louie had gone back to Millwall, though, apparently, he was considering other careers. But the money and the lifestyle were deeply tempting, if he got picked for the full squad – Patti could see that.

She still thought about him daily, now she was alone with her children and her thoughts. But in the long run, it was good, she supposed, that Louie wasn't here. One less distraction from rebuilding her life.

She was glad that Alex was staying in Tenderton, for now at least; she needed friends after what she'd been through with that terrible crook of a husband, who'd tried to kill her when she'd discovered the truth about him.

The trial was set for next summer; it would be in America. Patti hadn't asked Alex yet if she planned to attend, though she was going to offer to accompany her if she did. She rather fancied a trip to Universal Studios.

Harry, Ethan and Josh were thick as thieves, and Declan often joined them to ride their BMXs on the rumps, or to teach them how to ride his family's ponies bareback.

Ocean and Iris's band had had its first gig, and it had gone down so well they got some more bookings. She didn't play the Green Day song, or the Bowie one.

Meadow drove them around, only she'd invested in an electric car now. More fitting, she said, for someone with her green credentials. She'd sometimes stop at McDonald's on the way back for a cheeky Filet-O-Fish.

The parish council decided to sell the ducking stool to a museum; a more appropriate home, it was agreed by a committee in Tenderton.

53

Alex

December

I met him in the Witch's Head for a drink, one wintry Friday night.

He'd ordered a good bottle of red wine and a cheeseboard of rubbery Cheddar and Brie, but I really craved bourbon on the rocks. Old habits, as they say.

He returned to the bar, standing beneath an old broomstick to order.

'How are you?' he asked as he sat down again. I didn't ask him if he could see the dog in the corner, my dog Nova, because I knew she wasn't really there, although I had sent for her now.

'Oh, you know.' There weren't really words for what I wanted to say. My children had been beyond devastated to discover that their dad had been alive the whole time they'd believed him dead. A good thing, of course, in one sense, but that he'd been happy to deceive them wasn't. Nor was the fact that he was standing trial next year and facing a prison sentence.

I hadn't told them he'd tried to kill me, but Iris had seen enough.

'I'm not sure I'd be here without you.' I swished my bourbon round its glass, the amber liquid catching the candlelight prettily.

'Ah, I reckon you would. You're pretty tough, as is your daughter. It's her you owe, I reckon.'

I thought of my darling Iris, who had been so furious with me for so long. She was a little less furious now, and at least the lights in the cottage had stopped flickering. That mutant teenage energy, the poltergeist wrath of the hormonal girl, was subsiding.

Meadow had turned up one evening to show me a book she'd been working on for some time.

'Your cottage was originally Angelica's Cottage, named for a powerful plant.' She'd sketched it on the page. 'It still grows in your garden and has manifold healing properties. A so-called witch, the last woman to be drowned in the Pool of Sorrow, lived here and used it.'

'Here!' I almost gasped. 'Are you sure?'

'Yes. Hester Reading, her name was, midwife and herbalist.' Meadow bowed her head sadly. It seemed poor Hester had paid the ultimate price for daring to help women like us.

The house had only been renamed in the early twentieth century – 'Primrose Cottage' was deemed a little more quaint.

That weekend, we built Hester a shrine of shells and flowers in the garden, near the angelica plants, to mark her courage.

I set down the jug that Iris had found outside the cottage that terrible night: an old stone jug containing ancient hair and a felt heart – a crude witch bottle that she'd grabbed and taken with her to the Manor House, in need of some kind of protection, or weapon; that had saved me when she'd brought it down on her father's head.

The black cat watched from the fence.

'I know I owe Iris – she doesn't let me forget it.' I grinned at Jack Stanton. 'And I'm not so sure about the tough bit.'

We gazed at one another. He had a mouth that curled up at one edge, and I thought, *God I want to kiss it. Must be the bourbon.*

'We can't.' He caught my eye with a grin. 'You're vulnerable.'

'Oh.' I looked down for a second. 'I thought I was tough.'

'Well,' he said, and I felt the warmth of his knee against mine, 'I won't tell if you don't. And it's no longer my case, so…'

Iris was at Ocean's, at band practice; Harry was with Ethan for the night.

So Jack Stanton came home with me, and when I closed the curtains, the black cat padded off into the dark.

After all, I thought, turning away, *everyone else broke the rules. Why shouldn't I?*

54

Patti

Venus in Sagittarius

The morning of the game dawned frosty and clear. The Kingley Knights' pitch was frozen, so it was agreed that it would be played at Tenderton.

By half-time, Sheila's first stab at managing the Tigers looked like it was going to end badly. At least two of the dads were muttering they could have told anyone who asked that a woman just couldn't manage a football team. The mothers ignored them.

The few attempts on goal had gone wide, including star striker Hunter's shot from the D, which led to so much groaning from the parents on the sideline that his uncle Louie snapped at them to be quiet.

Patti had never seen Louie so tense, and she wasn't sure why – largely because she'd decided to steer clear of him today.

He'd waved cheerily as he arrived with little Logan, and she'd hunkered down into her parka and managed a wave back, hating the fact that she was so pleased to see him; hating the fact that she felt too self-conscious to go and say hello.

Alex and Iris arrived, wrapped in scarves and hats, but Patti needed to be on her own right now, and she knew Alex understood that sort of thing. 'I'll see you later,' she mouthed.

As the boys finished their oranges, Sheila gathered them around her.

'So look, I know you've had a hard time recently, and there's been a lot of upset, but I'm here to say I know you can do it.'

'But they're proper nasty.' Ethan was sporting a massive bruise where an opposition player had studded him. 'Look at my ankle.'

'That ginger nut won't let go of my shirt.' Hunter tipped water over his head in a manner he'd learnt from his dad.

'And I swear that lanky number 10 called me the N word.' Kyran was fuming. 'If he does it again, I'm going to smack him.'

'I'm sorry, mate. I'll make the ref aware.' Sheila put her arm round the boy's shoulder. 'But you show him with your feet rather than your fists, yeah?'

''K,' he muttered, unconvinced.

'The ref's a tosser.' Declan grimaced. 'He's well biased.'

'You've just got to get the goals in, boys. Forget about the referee and don't drop down to their level. Be proud – lift your heads and your hearts.'

Patti, collecting the orange rinds, heard this last and was so moved she almost wept. It had been a long autumn.

'Let's make this last game together one to remember.' Sheila stood with her hands on her hips. 'Who are we?'

Ethan and Harry muttered, 'Tigers.'

'Come on, boys. You owe it to yourselves – and you need to mean it!' Her face was flushed with enthusiasm, her voice stronger than Patti had ever heard it. 'Let's say it loud: who are we?'

This time at least the response was unanimous. 'Tigers!'

Sheila punched the air as they ran off, then growled loudly, with matching claw hands – much to the Knights' hilarity.

'Grrr,' they mocked, mimicking her. 'Dead Tigers.'

'Jeez,' muttered Ocean, shuffling back to the goal. 'That Sheila's more embarrassing than my mum.'

*

Unfortunately, the Knights' own team talk had been equally rousing.

Within the first five minutes back, they'd scored, despite Ocean's best effort to stop the ball that whistled over his head into the top left-hand corner of the goal.

As the Knights' striker placed the ball on the centre spot, he smirked at his opposite number, Hunter. 'You play just like your gay dad, you pussy.'

Patti had to hand it to Hunter – it was a punch every bit as good as his mother's a month ago, and it put the other boy straight on his backside.

The Tigers cheered loudly – until Hunter was shown a red card, which meant they were immediately down to ten men.

'Shame your shooting's not as accurate as your punching,' said the spotty winger as Hunter left the pitch, still fuming.

If Louie hadn't dragged his nephew back, a fight would have broken out.

'Mate,' Patti heard Louie murmur to the boy, 'I know it's tough at the moment, but just walk away. It's not worth it.'

'Nah. It *was* worth it,' Hunter muttered and stomped off to the clubhouse with his brother.

With the Tigers a man down, their performance mirrored their despondency, and as the Knights continued to put on the pressure, they struggled to compose themselves.

It was only Ocean's cat-like skills – amazing for such a well-built lad – that kept the ball out of the back of the net. Iris's presence was definitely an aid, thought Patti, watching the two of them grin at one another, and once again she sneaked a look at Louie, standing with his hands thrust deep in his winter jacket.

The second time the Knightley defender called Kyran the N word, everyone heard it –apart from the ref. Kyran looked at his dad, Trevor, who gave him a huge thumbs-up, and before Sheila could alert the referee, Kyran had put a genius tackle in to win the ball and was off and running. The goal was a neat rocket from twenty yards away, so fast the Knightley goalie barely saw it pass him.

The Tigers yelled in joy.

It was 1–1 and they were back in the game.

With two minutes to go, the Knights' striker was headed towards the goal when a sneaky boot from their midfielder took Declan out, and both the linesman and the referee missed the dirty tackle – again.

It meant a big gap suddenly opened in the Tigers' defence. Worse still, the striker's shot was on target.

Holding her breath, along with all the other praying Tigers parents, Patti watched the ball soar, but to everyone's vast relief, Ocean palmed it over the crossbar.

The ref pointed for a corner, and the lanky Knights' striker ambled to take his place as the rest of his team crowded into the box, jubilant already.

The striker crossed the ball, but it went over his team's heads. Ocean jumped high and caught it neatly, rolling it out instantly to Josh on the wing.

To the roar of the Tigers' supporters, Josh legged it up the pitch, with the Knights in hot pursuit. At the edge of the box, he leant back to shoot, just as the Knights' right back slid in to take his legs from beneath him.

Josh went flying sideways, lying stunned and motionless.

Within seconds, Sheila and Hazel were on the pitch, and the ref blew for a penalty.

'How long, ref?' Declan asked as Josh groaned and sat up, rubbing his head.

'Thirty seconds.'

'I'll take it,' Tony Burton Jnr offered, but the other boys looked unsure.

'Josh or Hunter always take the penalties,' Ethan said tremulously, but Josh was being helped off the pitch now.

'You take it, Ethan,' Sheila said coolly. 'You've got a strong kick.'

'Ethan's wet,' Mikhail muttered.

'He's not,' said Davey Forth. 'He's calm.'

Ethan placed the ball and walked backward, and Patti found she was actually praying again.

He glanced up at the right corner and took a deep breath. With seconds to go before the final whistle, he took his run-up and kicked the ball with all his might into the left corner.

The goalie had gone the wrong way.

'*Goal!*' the yell went up.

'That's the way to fucking well do it!' screeched Meadow, much to everyone's hilarity.

'They think it's all over,' said Tony Burton Snr. 'Woo-hoo!'

The Tigers went mad, the other boys jumping on top of Ethan as the referee blew three times.

'It is now!' cried Hazel with a massive whoop, grabbing Josh in joy, and Patti couldn't help herself: she burst into tears.

Everyone went for one last drink in the clubhouse, but Patti's heart wasn't really in it.

Sam had arrived in time to see Ethan score, and he took him to stay the night in his new flat on the other side of the dual carriageway, along with Davey Forth for company.

Neil hadn't come back to the club yet; no one was sure if he ever would, but Linda was there, drinking lemonade, sober for the first time in a while and looking much better for it.

Alex offered Patti a lift home, but Patti said she was fine, she wanted to walk, and she'd see her for coffee tomorrow.

Alex hugged her. 'Thank you for everything.'

Patti didn't really know what she was thanking her for, but she enjoyed the closeness for a second. She considered Alex a proper friend now.

She debated taking the woodland path home, and then decided against it. It wasn't time yet to walk into the darkness.

Pulling her pink bobble hat on, she began the long trek down to the main road. The sky looked positively forbidding now, the blue all gone and the air heavy with the threat of something.

Patti felt sad and cold and tired still, but relieved too, and proud of her son today. Now she just had a load of bridges to build with Luna.

A big car slowed beside her.

'Give you a lift?' Louie was smiling shyly down at her.

'Oh, ta, sugar, but you're all right,' she mumbled, hands in her pockets, her nose freezing.

'Patti! It's going to snow,' he said. 'Get in the car please!'

So she did. 'Where are the boys?'

'Dez sneaked in to pick them up. Didn't you notice that elaborate disguise?'

Patti had vaguely wondered who the tall man in the deerstalker and Ray-Bans was.

'It's his weekend.'

'Oh, dear,' she said. Her marriage wasn't the only one that hadn't survived the season. 'We're doing that too. Sharing.'

'So you've split from…' Louie kept his eyes on the road. 'Sorry, I forgot your husband's name.'

'From Sam? Yeah. It's been a long time coming, to be honest.'

He indicated left. He had such nice fingers, she thought absently, long and thin. He'd turned off onto the woodland road before she could even think about it.

'Where…' she began, and then she stopped.

She didn't care, to be honest – she would go anywhere with Louie right now. The longer she sat in this car with him, the better.

It meant fending off the real world a while longer.

'Nance is in London,' Louie said quietly as he pulled into the driveway of the big white house, a *For Sale* sign at the end of the front lawn.

'OK.' Patti hesitated for a moment.

They looked at one another. She didn't argue; she just followed him inside.

Snow had started to fall, very gently, speckling the back garden, which was almost dark now.

It felt warm and strangely safe as Louie turned the stereo on. Al Green. 'For the Good Times'; she remembered it from her teens.

'I love this song,' she whispered, and she realised she was crying again. 'Sorry,' she sobbed, 'I don't know why I keep doing this.'

'I bet I do.' His smile was so sweet, and his aquamarine eyes so clear. He held his hand out to her.

'I can't… I shouldn't. Louie, I'm too—'

'Shh!' He leant forward and put his finger on her lips so she couldn't finish the sentence. 'You're beautiful, Patti.'

But it was obvious that he was nervous too, and somehow that made it easier as he put his arms around her.

She laid her head against his chest, and it was so warm, and she could hear his heart beating. He smelt of clean laundry and sweat as he had done before, and for once, Patti stopped fighting and let herself go with it.

As he held her, they moved slowly around the room, not really dancing, but just there, together, and Al Green kept singing about sad things, and her tears kept coming.

Outside, the snow had begun to fall harder. The garden was covered, all white now, everything hidden by night and snow.

When Louie leant down to kiss her, she didn't feel like Patti, mother of two, soon-to-be divorcee, disappointed and tired. She didn't feel like someone who'd become older than she'd realised before she even knew it.

And Louie didn't seem like such a youngster anymore; he just felt like her equal in this moment.

There was a big dog out there, sitting patiently in the corner of the garden; Patti could see it out of the corner of her eye. But Louie had said all the dogs were with Nancy in London, including Vinnie. And when he took her hand and led her to the stairs, it was gone.

Patti didn't know what was going to happen – in the next day, in the next week, in the future – but after he led her upstairs, after he shut the bedroom door and she laid her head on his pillow, it didn't matter anymore.

'What star sign are you?' she whispered, and she thought his hand was shaking slightly on hers.

He grinned. 'Does it matter?'

'No, not really,' she answered quietly, 'but tell me anyway.' She smiled and felt her eyes crinkle. 'As long as you're not a Scorpio.'

'I'm a Sagittarius.' He was still grinning as he kissed her again. 'Birthday's the nineteenth of December.'

Patti didn't ask him how old he'd be.

She felt about eighteen again, and it was so nice. And wasn't that all right, for now at least?

It was. It had to be.

EPILOGUE

When the police studied the CCTV of the body in the lake, they declared it inconclusive. The only figure visible was too faint to identify, although they weren't absolutely sure it wasn't a woman in a hood.

But Mrs Jessop and Sheila had an idea of the truth; they'd seen on the other camera in the shop how Riker Bauer might have ended up in that lake.

They wiped the footage, and then they made a call.

After Mrs Jessop indicated it was possible she knew what had actually happened to Riker Bauer on Halloween night, there was only one thing to do.

Liz Bauer was aware of that really.

Since Riker had died, she'd seen the boys start to relax a little.

Well, Thomas and Maxi had at least; little Frederick was still a whirling dervish at the best of times, often to be found hurting insects if he got half a chance. She'd have to keep an extra eye on him.

But Liz? She'd stopped having to pretend to be something she wasn't; no more threesomes; she'd hung up her leather gear for the last time.

Now it was all about Maxi and Thomas.

She'd thought Riker would kill Maxi that night, so angry had he been. She'd sat in the car with them, begging him to leave the boy alone, pulling his arm down as he tried to reach his son over and again. And it wasn't the first time it had happened – she'd had to step in to save her middle son more than once. Every time he missed a goal, she had to protect him from Riker's wrath.

Later, when she was trying to find the kids to leave the party, Riker had been horribly drunk and belligerent. Following his skirmish with Sam Taylor, he'd found Thomas drinking cider with some other boys and had collared both his elder sons; taken them down to the lake to show them who was boss.

Holding the pair of them by the scruff of the neck, as he had done weekly pretty much since they'd been born, Riker had tried to push first Thomas's and then Maxi's face into the water, to teach them a lesson.

But he'd reckoned without their fury at being treated like animals for so long.

There had been a struggle to get away, to pull themselves out of their father's cruel iron grip, and in the dark, on the muddy slope, Riker had slipped and lost his balance.

In the freezing fog, the boys couldn't reach him, although they tried. To their enduring credit, they both tried.

Maxi went running to find Liz, who rushed back with him, her only thought to save her husband – in order to save her sons.

But there was no way she could reach Riker, already floating motionless out into the foggy darkness, face down. She knew it was too late.

Outside the clubhouse, down by the Pool of Sorrow, Liz listened to Mrs Jessop, and then she explained her plan to turn herself in.

'Do you think that's necessary, my dear?' The old lady patted her hand kindly. 'I imagine it was self-defence.'

Liz looked into the old lady's worldly blue eyes and nodded slowly. She zipped up her neat jacket and wrapped her scarf tight, then went into town to sign Maxi up for drama club.

And Mrs Jessop?

Satisfied that the right decision had been made, she returned to the little shop to restock the dark chocolate and the nut bars. They were far more popular these days than the old-style snacks. Who could say why?

Truth be told, Mrs Jessop recognised that, like so many things that had gone before in all her years here, fashions would keep changing: sometimes for the better, sometimes not.

She imagined Sheila would do well in her new post.

Undoubtedly things would change again both at the club, and in the village of Tenderton, and Mrs Jessop would not forget anything she'd seen over the past few decades. She would keep her secrets close, until the day she left this earth, or the day she might need to relinquish them for someone's greater good: whichever came first.

With a contented sigh, she emptied the chocolate box and pulled the shutter down for the night.

A LETTER FROM CLAIRE

I want to say a huge thank you for choosing to read *The Parents*. If you did enjoy the book, and want to keep up to date with all my latest releases, please just sign up at the following link. Your email address will never be shared and you can unsubscribe at any time.

www.bookouture.com/claire-seeber

Partly inspired by years of shivering on the sidelines of various athletics and football meets for my children, I was never unlucky enough to know anyone as horrible as a few of the characters in *The Parents*, though that's not to say there wasn't drama. There were definitely some pushy parents – the dads, in particular! I think the positives for the children usually outweighed the negatives, though – but *The Parents* is about what happens when things go awry, and ambitions and dreams are horribly broken.

I really hope you loved *The Parents*, and if you did, I'd be so grateful if you could write a review. I'd love to hear what you think, and it makes such a difference helping new readers to discover one of my books for the first time. Also, I love hearing from my readers, I'm always so grateful – you can get in touch on my Facebook page, Instagram, Twitter or my website. Thanks so much.

Warmest wishes,
Claire

        ClaireSeeberAuthor

        @Claireseeberauthor

        www.claireseeber.com

        @ClaireSeeber

ACKNOWLEDGEMENTS

Thank you so much to my agent Eli Keren. You make such a big difference to the process, and you make me laugh too: perfect!

Thank you to my new editor, Sonny Marr, for both hitting the ground running and stepping into the breach (can you do both simultaneously?!) with such enthusiasm. Thanks to Cara Chimirri, who always cheerled and cut with a smile, and to Laura Kincaid's eagle eye, again.

Thank you to Noelle Holten for taking the time to explain and suggest; to Kim Nash, Natasha Harding, Laura Deacon, Ruth Tross and all at Bookouture who help us make our books what they are. A very hearty thank you to the great bloggers who help promote the books – and to all the readers who take time to write a good review; it's really invaluable.

Thank you to dearest Jude Treasure for being the eagle eye on the first draft, as well as being a brilliant friend who gave up her bed for me when I badly needed a break. You are the original parent!

Thanks to Sarah Pearce for giving the boys' team your time – along with all the Kidbrooke Knight coaches and managers; to both Sarah and my friend Niki Born for the football know-how, suggestions and advice.

Thanks to Neil Lancaster for some police procedural help; to dear Rowan Coleman and Kat Diamond and the Think Tank for insightful plot details/suggestions when I got stuck.

To Colin Scott for stalwart support.

To my son Raffi for being the original football inspiration – I've actually enjoyed all my years of to-ing and fro-ing from the games. It's been a bit of parenting pleasure (along with your brother's guitar playing) to watch you outrun the defence, or plant a ball firmly in the back of the net. I am very proud of you.

To Verl for introducing me to Sunday League (not through choice really!) and for going through the final match with me whilst I raced against the clock!

If I've forgotten anyone, I'm sorry; it's because it's been such a challenging year. Thank you one and all who support me. I'm truly grateful.

Made in the USA
Las Vegas, NV
10 June 2022